SON OF THE LAKE

ALBERT JOYNSON

MRS D'S PUBLISHING HOUSE

PART ONE
THE KISS

I sighed as I trudged down the streets of Starkton. Olivier had insisted I would find my first charge here, although on the subject of how I might do that she had remained frustratingly vague. "You'll know it when you see it," probably sounded like great advice to someone trying to appear wise and mysterious, but as a recipient of said advice, I can say it was all but useless. So far, all I knew, from what I could see, was that there was an M&S across the street and its sign said it didn't just have a meal deal, it had an M&S meal deal. What that meant, I wasn't at all sure of.

What I was not prepared for was Starkton's pigeon problem, and I struggled to find a town bench that hadn't been liberally decorated by said pigeons. I needed to sit, laden down as I was, with one, mostly perfunctory sandwich, an iced tea, a can of kombucha, an orange juice, two small lattes and a bottle of water. Unfortunately, the meal deal doesn't make allowances for when you find yourself drawn to five different drink choices at once. This is why they say don't shop thirsty, whoever *they* are.

"Shouldn't you be in school, young man?" asked an older woman, glaring at me with an intensity to match Olivier's. I didn't reply. In fact, I felt myself shrinking into the bench until whoever this woman was got bored and went on her way, tutting and shaking her head as she went. I couldn't be too bitter though; she had given me an idea. If the only way to find a charge is to know them when you see them, then the best plan would surely be to go somewhere where I'll see plenty of people. So why not the local school? Parents, teachers, students… if I kept an eye out, I could probably see a thousand people all in one place.

It was worth a try, and the only decent idea I'd had all day. So off I went, to the school grounds, or rather, to a tree, perched on a branch opposite the school grounds. Turns out schools have all sorts of gates and fences and such to keep strange people out. Two meal deal lattes later, the school doors opened and whilst the coffee had kept me awake, I was no less tired. Instead, I was tired and jumpy, and maybe a bit twitchy. I was also desperate for the loo.

There I was, in my tree, watching boys and girls and the odd teacher stream out of the school gates. Whatever it was that I was supposed to know when I saw it, I wasn't know-ing, and presumably wasn't seeing. Until a horn blew, and a rush ran up my spine like electricity. I jumped, branches and leaves and wind rushing around me, and before I knew it, I was on the ground. White pain flooded my senses and for a moment that was all there was.

"You okay?"

And there he was, dark hair flopping in front of his

4

amber eyes, offering an outstretched hand, which I took. I didn't reply; I'd found myself struck dumb.

"That looked like a hard fall," he said, his voice kind and deep. He smiled as I took his hand, and without pause, he lifted me to my feet. "You want to be careful, climbing trees like that. There might not always be someone here to catch you when you fall."

"Yeah, silly me," I mumbled, lost as I was in his deep, warm eyes. Who is he?

"I'm Michael. Anyway, don't think I've seen you round here before."

"I'm Adrian," I breathed, as I found myself knowing things, as I saw them.

CHAPTER

TWO

"I'm Adrian," said the boy as he pushed his white-blond hair out of his face, and I almost dropped my jaw; his eyes twinkled sapphire in the sunlight. For a second, I couldn't think of anything to say, and by the time I'd gathered myself he'd smiled at me, turned on his heel and was wandering down the street.

"Who was that?" asked Jess, meandering up behind me. Jess was probably my best friend at school, although there wasn't much competition.

"Adrian... he said his name was. I don't know other than that, I don't think I've ever seen him before."

"Me neither. Weird, thought I knew everyone our age around here. He must be new," said Jess, stepping into my eyeline as Adrian shrank evermore into the distance. Her shirt was untucked and her tie was tied as short as it could possibly be, as usual. I tried to look past her without seeming obvious. I couldn't put a finger on why, but I didn't quite want to stop looking at Adrian yet. Unfortunately, by the time I'd got Jess out of my way, he'd vanished.

"Do you think that hair of his was natural?"

"What?" I asked, only half listening.

"Well, it did look very blond indeed."

"What? Yes, he's blond, sorry what were you saying?" I asked, begrudgingly looking back at Jess. Jess returned my look with her patent mischievous grin.

"He's proper caught your eye, hasn't he?"

I rolled my eyes.

"I'm just curious. You don't see new people often," I said to myself as much as Jess.

"You see new people every day, but most of them aren't pretty blond boys in need of rescue after they've fallen out of a tree."

"So, you think he's pretty?" I deflected, feebly.

"If you're into that sort of thing," Jess crooned, her voice drenched in smugness.

"And how would you know what I'm into? I don't even know what I'm into," I huffed.

"True enough. You are tragically single."

"You're single too!"

"Am I?"

"Are you?" I asked, wheeling around on her.

"I don't know, maybe. Watch this space," said Jess, a grin spreading across her face.

"Why are you being so vague and mysterious?"

"Don't try and change the subject, you're crushing on that blondie." Jess simultaneously teased me and expertly changed the subject.

"I am not, I barely even spoke to him," I said, with a pout.

"Because you got tongue tied," said Jess, sticking her tongue out.

"Well, he doesn't go to school here, so we'll probably never see him again." I shrugged.

"Probably not," Jess agreed.

"Haven't you got after-school detention you're supposed to be at now?" I asked, changing the subject before I sweated through my sweater as well as my shirt.

"I'm double-booked, so I'm just gonna tell 'em both I was with the other one." Jess shrugged.

"You know teachers can talk to each other, right? They'll find out."

"What are they gonna do, give me detention?" Jess asked, giving me a wink before she set off. I followed her but something pulled me at me, and without thinking I looked back over my shoulder and for a moment everything in me wanted to see him there, but he was still vanished. I sighed and strode off after Jess.

THREE

I wonder, should I have said something to him before I left? Probably. Too late now anyway, time to finally report back some good news for Olivier. I meandered down the street until I was sure I was out of sight, and then cut across into someone's front garden that had a particularly big tree in it. I took a quick glance over my shoulder to make sure no one was looking and stepped into it. Stepping out the other side, I was home, trees in every direction, green as far as the eye could see. The little spiderwebbed path ran throughout the forest, leading who knows where. Everywhere, I suppose. The dense canopy above had the initially pleasant effect of casting a permanent dappled shadow and tinting everything a perpetual shade of green.

"Hey Adrian, good luck with the mission. We know you're the nymph for the job!" called a couple of passing sylphs, waving their long spindly arms as they went.

That was the trouble with being an agent of the Excalibur system; everyone knew what you were up to and had an opinion about whether you were the one who should be up to it. It's a lot of pressure being sent out to find charges who might become champions, who might become tomorrow's heroes of the fay forest. I try not to think about it too much, especially not to think about the people that said I only got the job because Merlin liked me.

"I'll do my best," I called, waving back before putting my head down to hide the cringe curling my lips, and started walking as fast as I could without arousing suspicion.

Before I knew it, I was outside Olivier's cottage. That's how things are in the fay world; if you're not careful, you end up where you're going much faster than you intended. *Don't forget to stop and smell the roses,* Merlin's voice echoed in my mind.

"Come in," came Olivier's voice before I even had a chance to knock. I hate it when she does that. I sighed and pushed open the door. Even when I had good news, she had a way of making me feel like I was coming in for a telling off.

"So, how did it go? Any luck?" she asked, peering over her papers, her thick glasses doing nothing to diffuse the intensity of her gaze. Olivier shared my white, blond hair but sported the characteristic squat features of a gnome, and somehow it suited her.

"I've found him, I think I have anyway. It was just like you said, I knew it when I saw it, or rather, knew him. Michael is his name."

"Good show, Adrian. So, tell me all you know about him." She had a way of sounding hungry as she asked questions, like she might starve without more information.

"He goes to Starkton high school, he's got floppy dark

hair, warm ember eyes, a nice strong jaw line, good smile, his voice is deep—"

"Ahem, everything useful, we're not writing him a dating profile," she said, and sneered, dragging me ruthlessly out of my daydream.

"Oh. Well, just the Starkton high school bit then, I suppose, that and his name."

"Well, you know what that means then Adrian."

CHAPTER
FOUR

"Hey, are you free first period?" I hissed across the desks to Jess as registration filled up before everyone filed out to their various classes and study halls. My first period on a Monday was always free. I had half a mind not to come in for it, but if you missed registration, they called home and it wasn't worth getting in my mum's bad books over a boring hour of school.

"No, I said I'd help some of the guys rehearse for their theatre studies coursework. You could come too if you like," Jess hissed back as Mr Brown started the register. I offered a bored shrug in response; it wasn't like I had anything better to do.

"Michael Tombs!"

"Here sir," I groaned, planting my head on my desk as I began to worry about what embarrassing part they'd try to cast me in for their rehearsal.

"Right class, now that's out of the way, we've got a new

form member joining us today, so everyone, make sure Adrian feels welcome."

My head shot off the desk, and there he was, standing next to Mr Brown; the boy from the tree. I'd been looking for him outside of school for days, but he hadn't shown up again. Until now. Suddenly, I had a squirming, sickly feeling in my stomach.

"Why don't you go take a seat next to Michael, Adrian? Michael, you're free first period, I believe. So is Adrian, and you should give him a tour."

I swallowed as my mouth went dry. I couldn't even put a finger on why, and before I had a chance to think about it some more, he was there. Or rather, here, pulling up the seat next to me.

"It's you, my hero!" I could feel myself sweating through my shirt.

"Your what?" I croaked.

"From the other day, it was you, right? Who helped me when I fell out of that tree like an idiot?"

"Oh right, yeah, that was me!" I said, trying not to pay attention to my clammy palms. I scratched the back of my head awkwardly and then realised I might be flashing him a pit stain, and dropped my arm.

"So, what's a boy gotta do to get a tour around here?" he asked, smiling at me from ear to ear. He had a pretty smile; it seemed sincere, and he had teeth so white you'd think he was off the telly.

"Oh right, yeah, errm, well, after me!" I said after an awkwardly long pause. I'd been paying so much attention to his teeth I almost forgot I was supposed to be taking part in a conversation. As I led him out of form, I found myself opening doors for him without even thinking. Somehow it just felt right.

"So where to first?" he asked brightly.

"Well, in a second the corridors are gonna be full of the lower school. They don't have free periods, so first things first... let's go to the lawn and you can have the actual tour when class starts up."

"The lawn? What's that then Mr Tour Guide?"

"Well, Mr Guidee, this big brown vaguely prison-like building is the second building. The old school is a littler building around the back, and before it was a school it was this big grand house. So it had its own garden, which we call the lawn. They even have blossom trees there which are in bloom now, I think."

"How romantic." He smiled, and I found myself almost choking on air.

"Haha, errm yeah, good one. Anyway, it's just through here," I said, holding open yet another door for him for some reason.

"Oh wow, it really is romantic." His hair shone as he stepped out into the spring morning sunlight. I don't think I'd ever really seen anyone look like Adrian did when the light hit him. He skipped out onto the lawn and sat himself down under a blossom tree and there it was again, my stomach fluttering.

CHAPTER
FIVE

I t really was beautiful on the lawn. The forest was great and all, but it was always, at its heart, shrouded by its endless canopy, cast in half light. With it came the weight of expectation and responsibility. It was nice to watch clouds roll by lying on the grass, feeling the sun prickling my skin. Which is exactly what I was doing when the bell rang. Michael hadn't joined me in my sunbathing — he was standing over me like a kind of a guard, which was a little bit odd, but sort of endearing too. He almost seemed protective, and he couldn't seem to stop himself opening doors for me.

"Five, four, three, two… one," Michael said, and right on cue, out poured a wave of children, filing into the old school building. The rumble of hundreds of little feet and scraping chair legs thundered in the air for about a minute, and then there was silence.

"Come on then, tour time," he said, offering me a hand, which I took but then hesitated.

"Just five more minutes?" I pleaded, not yet ready to

leave the morning sunlight behind me. He looked like he was mulling it over for a second, and then shrugged.

"Why not," he said and with that, he flopped down next to me in the grass. It must have been thirty seconds before I realised I was still holding his hand.

"Oh, sorry," I said as I let it go, the slightest tinge of regret nagging at me as I did. Whatever connection I had to Michael must have been stronger than I realised.

"Hey, no worries."

"So, what school did you come from then?" he asked after a minute or so of comfortable silence.

"Oh erm, you wouldn't know it, I just moved to town," I lied through my teeth, suddenly aware of the tension in my jaw.

"Why did ya move?"

"Errm…" I fished for a lie, realising I probably should have thought about some of this stuff before I enrolled.

"Bullying!" I blurted out, probably louder than I needed to, and definitely more enthusiastically than I should have.

"Oh, that's so shit. I got a bit of that when I came out, but it wasn't too bad. I suppose it didn't hurt that I was on the football team, and that Jack and Alex in the year above had been out for years. And a couple."

"Oh, that's pretty cool… do you have a boyfriend then?" I asked, trying to distract from my bullying lie, which I was already feeling awful about.

"Nah, kinda tricky when there's only three out gay guys out in the whole school and two of them are together. So, what were you bullied for anyway?" he asked, propping his chin in the palm of his hand as he looked down at me. His hair fell around his eyes in ribbons and my mouth got very dry all of a sudden.

"Erm, same as you," I lied again. I'm an awful person.

"Oh wow! The gay population of the school just went up thirty-three percent! That's awesome, and hey, good news is most people here are pretty cool with the gay thing. Then again, if anyone does give you any trouble, just come to me and I'll sort it out for you." He gave my shoulder a little squeeze and my heart jumped into my throat. I was sure I could feel my cheeks burning. Perhaps it was just the sun.

"Thank you, I feel much safer now." At least that wasn't a lie.

"Hey, don't mention it. What are tour guides for?" He laughed and, he had a nice laugh, a little rolling chuckle.

"So what about you, any boyfriends on the scene?" Michael asked after a little lull. I'd let my eyes fall out of focus, admiring the dappled pink light shining through the blossom.

"No, nothing like that," I said, turning to him as I blinked my eyes back into focus, only to find his warm amber globes looking back at me. For a second I was sure I saw a tinge of pink colour his cheeks before he looked away.

"Well, errm, I'm sure the right guy will come along," Michael said, clearing his throat and sitting up. For some reason he'd fixed his gaze on the school building opposite.

"I hope so," I said, clutching for what a normal teenage gay boy in high school was supposed to say as I tried to discreetly wipe my now sweating palms on the grass.

"Any brothers or sisters? Didn't move here on your own I hope?" asked Michael, still staring at the school building.

"I didn't grow up alone, but I am now," I said, trying to

find a way to answer his questions without lying to him again.

"That's weird. None of your brothers and sisters came with you?" Michael asked, looking back at me, obviously confused by my vagueness.

"Cousins, they didn't move with me, but we did grow up together," I corrected, praying for plausibility. Olivier always said the best way to lie was to mix in as much truth as possible and we *were* all raised together. A fay child is a rare thing. There might be only ten or twenty to a generation, so when we're born the entire forest comes together to help raise us.

"Oh gotcha. Yeah, I've got loads of cousins, but I didn't really grow up with them. Mum was the youngest of seven, so they're all older than me. It was just me and Dan growing up. He's off at uni now though. So just cousins for you then, no brothers and sisters?"

"I have a sister. She's at uni too," I said, hoping that was the most believable option possible.

"Wow, we've got a lot in common," Michael said and chuckled, smiling again.

"I guess so," I said, silently unclenching a little. Somehow, I felt like I'd gotten away with something.

"You were lucky, growing up around all those cousins. It must have been great being raised around so many kids your age. I bet you never got bored, or lonely."

"You'd be surprised," I said. It slipped out before I had a chance to think, honesty getting the better of me for once.

"How d'you mean?" Michael asked, fixing me again with his amber eyes. Something in his face had changed now. It'd softened.

"I just mean… well, you know, you can feel lonely even in a crowd." As I spoke, a little relief came over me. This wasn't something I could talk about in the fay forest. Not coming from the family I came from.

"I think I know what you mean," said Michael.

"You do?" I asked, looking back at him, my breath faltering as our eyes locked again.

"Yeah…" He looked as though he was going to say more, but his breath faltered, and he turned his head back to the school. My stomach flipped as I resisted the urge to take his hand in mine, to hold it, to squeeze it, to let him know I was there. I'm not sure how long we sat there, with something unspoken lingering between us, but eventually Michael sniffed, cleared his throat and got to his feet.

"Tour time," he said, offering me a hand up, which I took and squeezed, just gently.

"Good day at school Michael?" Mum asked as she tumbled through the hallway into the kitchen. She was shedding hats, coats, bags and scarves as she went. In the time it took her to get from the door to the kitchen, she'd almost halved in size. Mum worked in an office, but from the amount of stuff she took with her, you'd think she was going on a four-day trek.

"Fine," I responded, not looking up from the staring contest I was losing with my English homework. Why I took this subject, I don't know.

"Oh, come on, Mikey, spill the beans, dish the dirt, give me the hot goss, work was so boring," moaned Mum, flopping down next to me in her chair. She relaxed into it so quickly it was as if she'd got no bones at all. I sighed and put away my English homework. It wasn't like I was getting anywhere with it anyway and when Mum got the bit between her teeth there was no stopping her.

"Well, we had a new kid in form who sits next to me now. He's called Adrian."

"Oh perfect. What's he like then?" she asked, perching her chin in her hands.

"He's nice, kind of funny, he's little, and I must have a whole head on him. Longish white-blond hair, amazing eyes, they're blue like when people say water is crystal clear but mean blue and…" I trailed off noticing Mum was now grinning from ear to ear.

"Oh, shut up Mum!"

"What? I'm not saying anything. Come on, keep going, this is the best goss I've heard all day."

"Fine… well, what else? Oh yeah, he said he's moved here from out of town because he was being bullied at his old school."

"Oh, Mikey that's terrible. What was it over? Kids can be so cruel these days." She sagged a little. She didn't talk about it much, but I think Mum was bullied a lot in her time at school.

"I know. It was over him coming out as gay, and he's so sweet too. It pisses me off just thinking about it, actually." My fists clenched instinctively as my heart started to pound in my ears.

"Language. But you're right, that is awful. You two will have to stick together. Maybe you should introduce him to those nice boys. What were they called? Albie and Jake?"

"Alex and Jack."

"Yes, those two, they seem nice."

"Have you ever even met them, Mum?"

"I don't need to, the amount you talked about Jack that one summer."

"Muuum!" I moaned.

"Sorry! Sorry, bad mum, very embarrassing, now keep going. This is good stuff."

"There's not really much else to tell. I told him that most people were cool when I came out, and about Alex and Jack, and that was about it, I think."

"Well, sounds like you've got a new friend there then. Cuppa' tea?" she asked, climbing out of her chair.

"Yes please. I guess I did sort of promise that if anyone bullied him, I'd beat them up."

"That's nice dear," said Mum as she popped the kettle on. She is a bit unconventional, my Mum.

SEVEN

Music vibrated through the forest as I stepped out of a particularly large oak I'd found around the side of the school. The choirs of my people have all kinds of songs we sing for all sorts of different reasons, and they are all beautiful, but there is one song we all dread to hear. The song of the lost. It had been months since it'd last filled the forest air. A tear rolled down my cheek as it dawned on me what I was listening to.

Life and death work a bit differently for us. Fay can live for hundreds of years, some even longer. Plus, with us all growing up together, everybody tends to know everybody. So an untimely death can shake the whole forest.

I let myself wallow for a minute or so before setting off for Olivier's. She'd know exactly what happened and to who.

"Adrian my boy, hold your horses, where are you off to in such a hurry? Remember, what do I always say? Don't forget to stop and smell the roses." I knew who it was before I even turned around.

"Merlin, thank goodness it's you," I said, turning on the spot and giving a small respectful nod. Merlin smiled and placed a hand on my shoulder. At the moment, he was about six feet two with salt and pepper hair, wearing a long-draped cloak over some ceremonial leather armour, but he never really looked one way for too long. The only thing you could rely on were his eyes. All his age glistened in his white-grey eyes.

"Your mother wouldn't be too pleased to see you out in public without your Stone of the Naiad in pride of place," Merlin remarked, taking me in with his appraising gaze and giving me a wink.

"Well, at least I'm consistently disappointing then," I said, chuckling. My hand instinctively finding the smooth cool stone in my breast pocket and rubbing it for a moment.

"Pish posh, you're part of the Excalibur system. I'm sure she couldn't be prouder. Now, your mother aside, where were you off to in such a hurry?" Merlin asked, giving me a knowing look.

"I was just on my way to Olivier's to… you know… find out what happened." I blinked as the momentary distraction Merlin had provided abated, and tears threatened to spill again.

"You sweet, sensitive soul, take a seat," he said, jamming his pinkie inside his ear, then stabbing it into the forest floor. Within seconds, a chair-sized toadstool popped out of the earth, and he plopped me down on it with a friendly shoulder squeeze. All the finger in ear stuff was totally un-necessary, of course, but then Merlin always did have a flair for the dramatic or goofy.

"So, what happened?"

"Nasty bit of business, Adrian. I'll give you one guess," said Merlin, sweeping his cloak up under himself before plopping down cross-legged on the ground opposite me.

"Another incursion by mirelings?" I asked. He nodded, and I shivered.

"Why are they pushing into our territory so much?" I asked as I stood, nervous energy no longer permitting me to sit. Everyone in the fay forest knew about the mirelings, ancient enemies of the fay that live in the dark swamps outside our borders. Until recently, they'd just been a scary story and a place to stay away from, but things were changing. They were pushing into our lands, growing bolder, causing casualties.

"If only I knew, dear boy, alas, I've not got to the bottom of that mystery yet, but I will. In the meantime, this means the work you're doing is all the more important. We're depending on you to find us our new champions."

I gulped and tried to ignore the squirming in my stomach as Merlin placed an encouraging but firm hand on my shoulder.

"So, what happened with the incursion?" I asked, hoping for a distraction.

"Well, the blighters seem to have formed an alliance with a particularly nasty rebel element. I was out on my weekly excursion to the lake with Cynthia and Evelyn when they struck. Two dryads, a water nymph and perhaps a dozen goblins. Between the three of us we managed to see them off, even captured one of the dryads, although the water nymph did get away." Merlin paused as his eyes grew misty, the lines of age returning to his face as most of his hair gradually greyed.

"What? What happened?" I asked, urgency taking hold of me as terrible thoughts started popping into my head.

"It was Cynthia you see." My stomach dropped, Merlin's words hanging in the air. He'd paused. He knew Cynthia and I were close.

"She was nicked by a goblin arrow. She seemed fine at first, but it looks like the blighters are poisoning their weapons now, and she was gone before we knew what had happened." Merlin sighed and let his face fall into his hands. Suddenly a cold feeling overtook me. I sagged back onto my toadstool and my head dropped as the world span around me.

"As you can imagine, Olivier's taken some time to herself."

Cynthia was Olivier's first ever charge, and she'd been a member of Merlin's guard for as long as I'd known her. She was nice, and always seemed to have spare apples somewhere about her person.

"She'd... she'd been like a big sister to me," I whispered, watching tears tumble through the air, splashing against the mossy floor of the forest. Merlin took my hand, and I struggled to my feet, as together we joined our voices to the chorus of the lost.

EIGHT

I made my way to the lawn, telling myself that it was just nice to see the cherry blossoms, but if I'm being honest I think I was hoping I'd see Adrian. We weren't in any of the same classes on Monday and the only class I didn't have on Monday was English. It was our last hope of sharing a subject. Which was a bit of a problem, as it was becoming increasingly hard to concentrate on anything other than Adrian recently.

Turning the corner onto the lawn, I spotted something unusual. Edward, captain of the rugby team, and a couple of the other lads from the team all gathered around one of the bigger blossom trees. I think the last time I remember seeing these guys on the lawn was when I was in year seven.

"Aye up, lads, what's going on?" I called over to them. One of them jumped out of his skin, which told me they were up to something, although Ed managed to keep their cool. As they turned to face me, they left a crack in their conspiratorial semi-circle and there was Adrian, huddled up against the tree with his knees pulled up to his chest.

"Hey, Adrian, you okay man?" I asked, pushing the others out of the way.

"He's not saying anything, just been sitting there crying," said the one that jumped.

"It's weird mate, I know he's the new kid, but it can't be that bad on day two," said Ed.

"Shut up Ed!" I barked without thinking, my body already tensing up.

"Whatever. Have fun with the new kid," said Ed, walking away, flanked by his teammates.

"Bye!" I almost growled, struggling to keep aggression out of my voice, before turning back to Adrian. The sight of him screwed up so tight, his knees pulled to his chest, quickly softened whatever had been bubbling up in me as I sat myself down opposite him in the grass.

"Did Ed say anything? I can tell him to back off if he did."

Adrian shook his head, his eyes sparkling with tears. He was sort of heart-breaking to look at. Everything in me was telling me to hug him, but I settled for just putting my hand on his knee. For a while he didn't say anything, he just sniffled. I should have been getting to class, but I had absolutely no intention of leaving Adrian like this.

Eventually he took a deep, shaky breath and whispered, "My... erm, my sister... died."

I didn't think as my arms wrapped around him, pulling him into me, his little body rocking softly in my arms. He didn't resist at all. In fact, he clung to me as he gently sobbed into my chest. A lump formed in my throat as I held him. Something inside me couldn't cope with seeing him like this. I needed to help him, to fix it, if I could.

"You shouldn't be in school today, Adrian, you need time

to grieve. Come on, let's go. Let me take you home." He shook his head and looked up at me with twinkling teary eyes.

"We can't go to my home," he whispered, his breath catching.

My heart ached for him, he looked so vulnerable. I guess he couldn't face being around any reminders right now.

"Let's go to mine then." He nodded, and for a second looked like he might crack a smile.

"Won't we get in trouble for skipping school?" he asked as the threat of a smile vanished again.

"Who cares?" I said with a wink, ruffling his hair. He gave a little giggle, and it took everything in me not to smother him with more hugs.

"Okay then," he said after a moment, wiping his eyes on his sleeve. He still had tear streaks down his cheeks, but at least he wasn't crying anymore.

"Up we get," I said, getting up and pulling him to his feet by the hand. He really was such a lightweight little thing.

"Thank you," he whispered as we made our way down the path.

"Don't mention it. You know, if you ever need anything, you can always come to me."

"You really mean that, don't you," he said, finally cracking a half smile, which sent my stomach fluttering.

"I really—" I paused mid-sentence, as a flurry of petals tumbled down through the air around us.

"Beautiful," Adrian whispered, wide eyed as the storm of cherry blossoms whirled through the air, catching us in a world of pink. I wasn't looking at the blossom. I couldn't tear my eyes off him, turning in the centre of it.

CHAPTER

NINE

I'd barely been able to stop crying since I'd heard the news about Cynthia. I was like a leaky tap. I don't know what had possessed me to go back to Starkton today. It was a bit mad in retrospect, but I think I was just trying to run away from all the mourners. Michael had been amazing, though. His hand kept drifting towards mine as he led me down the street, then balling up into a fist and drifting away again.

"What was she like, your sister I mean? Or… sorry, that's so stupid of me. You don't have to talk about that right now if you don't want to." He had this worried look on his face, like he was afraid he'd break me. His eyes were so warm, it made the guilt over lying to him sting all the keener, but I didn't know what else to do, and Cynthia really was like a sister to me.

"She was kind and funny and brave, and she always had apples," I sniffled as another pea-sized tear rolled down my cheek. Michael gave my shoulder a squeeze. I wish he'd hug me again. People didn't touch me like that in the fay forest. It made me feel warm inside.

"What was her name?"

"Cynthia, my big sis." Her face flashed in my head and for a second, I thought I was going to be sick. Like all this was too much grief to fit inside me and it was going to spill out, and then my legs went all wobbly.

"Adrian, hey Adrian, are you okay?" asked Michael, panic written across his face. I nodded.

"Sorry, I just felt a bit funny," I said, only now realising that Michael was holding me by the waist, steadying me.

"Hey that's okay, take your time," he said, and then he did it again, pulling me into one of his hugs. His warm, strong, gentle hugs. I buried my face in his chest and sighed. It was like magic, and my chest started to loosen almost immediately. No-one had ever told me that when you find your charge, it would be like this, otherwise I'd have gone looking sooner. All too soon he let me go and then knelt in front of me.

"Climb on," he said, looking over his shoulder with a smile on his face.

"Really?"

"Your piggyback awaits!"

So, I did and with that we set off.

"Aren't I too heavy?" I asked, although I had noticed the boys our age in school seemed bigger than us water nymphs back in the forest.

"Honestly, you're like crazy lightweight, and it's only a couple minutes now, anyway. Can't have you collapsing into the road, can we?"

"I guess not," I said, resting my head on his shoulder and

closing my eyes. I yawned. Five more minutes and I think I'd have been asleep.

"Here we are, home sweet home," he said brightly, plopping me back on my feet after what turned out to be a regrettably short walk. His house wasn't huge, part of a row of terraces, but the front garden was fun. Not perfectly ordered or anything, it was full of wildflowers and those little statues the gnomes back home find offensive. I think they are more accurate than they'd like to admit. You might not spot it at first because of how busy everything was, but in the corner there was a little bench with a plaque that read David on it.

"Mum's a bit mental when it comes to garden decorations — she loves gnomes," said Michael from the doorway.

"I like it. Nature isn't meant to be all clean lines and borders," I said, following him into the house.

"Mum's gonna love you then. Cup of tea?" he asked, kicking his shoes off as he disappeared out of the hallway. The house was a little chaotic; the whole of the entrance hall wall was plastered with pictures. Lots of Michael, some with another boy who looked similar but a little older and thinner. I guessed the brother he'd mentioned. There was some of a smiley, slightly portly lady with a wild mop of brown hair. Along with the odd few of an older man, handsome, with dark hair and a strong jaw. Walking into the next room, which turned out to be the kitchen, the chaos continued. Coats and hats and scarves were hung in a great mound on the back of the door, and a large family of shoes formed a sort of assault course across the floor.

"Sorry about the mess, me and Mum live in a sort of organised chaos. It used to drive Dan mad, but he's moved out for uni. You did want tea, right?" Michael asked, setting up two large mugs by the kettle.

"Oh, yes please," I said, perching myself on the kitchen counter, to not seem like I was hovering around Michael, taking notes on his tea making technique. Human tea had always somewhat evaded the fay.

"Milk, sugar?"

"Erm, sure two?" I guessed.

"This tea is amazing!" said Adrian.

He was sat cross-legged in Mum's squashy armchair holding our massive mug in his hands like it was a bowl as he gulped down what must have been his fifth cup. Adrian really seemed to like drinks. I had to admit, he looked adorable. The size of the mugs only made him look smaller. He'd stopped crying now, which was nice. We'd tried to play some video games, but he'd never heard of them before, which seemed insane to me. Anyway, we settled for watching movies. He'd also not heard of those. We started on *The Wizard of Oz*, Mum's favourite. Mostly because he liked the box, now we were onto Lord of the Rings, which had successfully distracted him.

"Best review I think I've ever gotten. Do you want anything to eat? Some biscuits to dunk in it?" My stomach was beginning to protest as well. A man cannot live on tea alone.

"Dunk?" he asked, looking away from the TV to give me such a confused look you'd think I was speaking Greek.

"You've never dunked biscuits in tea?" He shook his head.

"Really?" I asked, struggling to wrap my head around what he was saying. It somehow didn't quite seem possible.

"Am I missing out?" Adrian asked, looking genuinely perplexed.

"First video games, then the movies, and now dunking. You've not lived! Right, you stay here, keep watching, there's a good bit coming, I'll be back in a tic." I headed to the kitchen to get him some chocolate digestives, wondering what else Adrian might not have heard of. Or how someone could go seventeen years in England without dipping a biscuit in some tea. Then I heard the front door go.

"MICHEAL DAVID TOMBS!" I flinched, and a second later, Mum was barrelling into the kitchen looking as red as a tomato.

"Hey Mum." My voice came out smaller than normal.

"Don't you hey Mum me mister!" she barked, glaring up at me.

"What the hell do you think you're doing skipping school? Skipping mock exams, no less."

"We weren't really skipping Mum, it's just—"

"It's my fault." There was Adrian in the living room doorway, looking like he was about to cry again.

"Please don't be mad at him. He was just looking after me. I'm Adrian." He crossed the room and offered his hand to shake, and I could see the tears welling up in his eyes.

"And why do you need looking after, dear?" All the tension was melting out of Mum's face as she looked at him.

"His sister died yesterday," I whispered. Without a second's hesitation she grabbed Adrian and pulled him into a tight hug.

"There, there, dear." She stroked his head as Adrian started to sob again.

"For heaven's sake Michael, get the poor boy some biscuits," she hissed.

TEN

Adrian ended up staying over, spending the night in Dan's old room. Mum had asked Adrian what his mum's number was so she could let her know where he was, but it turned out both Adrian's parents were out of town. Visiting all those cousins he'd mentioned. Mum was fuming and insisted that he shouldn't be alone, so we basically ended up kidnapping him.

He didn't seem to mind much.

Knock Knock

Mum didn't wait for my reply before poking her head round the door.

"Michael, I've gotta dash off for work, but I've called the school and said you're taking a sick day, and I've left some money on the table. Take Adrian to a movie or something. Thursday is your half day anyway, right?" Again, she didn't wait for a reply before disappearing back round the door. It didn't seem like a good idea to remind her that today was Wednesday, anyway.

As I passed, I knocked on Dan's door and called,

"Get dressed, we're going to the movies," before making my way downstairs to wait for

Adrian and eat Mum's crusts. He appeared on the stairs a few minutes later, looking a bit dishevelled.

"Adrian, we can't go to the cinema with you in your school uniform! You'll look like you're skipping school."

"But we are," said Adrian, looking confused.

"We don't want them to know that though, silly. Hang on." I chucked him my hoodie and jogged upstairs. I grabbed another hoodie and started rooting around in the back of my wardrobe. Somewhere in there was a pair of black skinny jeans Mum refused to throw away. In her words, "an arm and a leg", but they didn't ever really fit me, even before my growth spurt.

"Found em!" I jogged back down, and there was Adrian, stripped down to his pants and socks, pulling on my hoodie. He was thin, but not bony. He sort of looked like he'd be drawn that way, like he was just meant to be slight, like big muscles wouldn't have suited him. His skin was smooth and pale, and what little body hair he had was so blond it was almost invisible. It made him look kind of shiny. I realised I was staring and turned away.

"Here," I said, dropping the jeans from the stairs.

The cinema was just a ten-minute walk into town and me and Adrian kept our hoods up the whole time so we didn't get recognised. We might have looked like we were in some sort of gang, were it not for the fact that Adrian's sleeves dangled about a foot past his wrist in my hoodie, which came to just above his knee. It was completely adorable.

"What kind of movie do you wanna see?" I asked. Adrian

didn't respond at first. He seemed transfixed by the slushie machines.

"Whatever you fancy."

"Well, you liked Lord of the Rings. Let's see what you think of a superhero movie."

"Sure, do you want snacks?" he asked, now looking at the snack bar, and my stomach rumbled. I think it must be every teenage boy's fantasy to just eat the whole snack bar at the cinema, but you'd have to take out a mortgage with the price of cinema food.

"I've only got enough for the tickets, Adrian, sorry," I mumbled, trying not to seem as embarrassed as I was.

"My treat," said Adrian, who was already ladening himself up with Maltesers, Minstrels, a popcorn bucket, chocolate raisins, and those sherbet flying saucer things. I didn't even know they still did those. He looked a bit ridiculous as he dumped it all on the counter.

"You sure about this Adrian?"

"Why not?" he asked, beaming.

"And two of those things please, as big as you can make them!" he said, pointing to the slushie machine with wonder in his eyes. My eyes nearly popped out of my head when they rang up the bill, and then again when Adrian casually paid with a fifty-pound note like it was normal. I don't think I'd ever seen one before in real life.

"Here you go," he said, dumping his hoard in my lap as we got to our seats.

"Don't you want any?"

"Nah, I've got this," he said, holding his slushie out as if he was showing off a winning lottery ticket.

"So why did you get… so much?" I asked, looking at my glorious pile of plastic wrapped sugar.

"I had to make sure I got your favourite, so I thought I'd just get everything," he said. It was a good job the cinema was dark, so he couldn't see the blush that was burning its way across my cheeks.

"But Adrian, this is too much."

"You're worth it," he said, beaming from ear to ear.

"And besides, you can pay me back in piggy backs if you like."

"Oh, so that's what this is all about?" I said, and chuckled. He giggled, and the woman behind shushed us.

ELEVEN

I'd been avoiding the fay world for a little while; Michael's house was like a happy, messy little cocoon where you didn't have to worry about charges, or Merlin, or uprisings, or rebellions. Those two are basically the same, but they're so worrisome they're worth mentioning twice. You just drank gallons of tea and listened to Linda, his mum, talk about her plans for garden gnome expansion. I'd let myself stay one more night before deciding I had to leave, and even then Lin took some convincing. I'd have stayed longer, but every time I had to lie about my parents being out of town or Cynthia having died in a car crash at uni, I felt sick to my stomach. Not to mention I hadn't seen Olivier since… it happened, and I was starting to feel like a very bad friend.

"Come in!" she shouted from inside the cottage as I fidgeted at her door, trying to work out what I was going to say. I braced myself as I pushed the door open, expecting mess, strewn tissues, and tear streaks, but Olivier looked the same as always. Impatient.

"Well, where have you been?" she barked.

"I've been… getting to know my charge and giving you some space, like Merlin suggested."

"Bah! I don't need space, I need to work. Not everyone's as emotional as you, you know," she said it, as if most fay wouldn't literally cry over a fallen tree. It was true that Olivier hadn't always been the most emotional, but around here she was definitely the exception, not the rule.

"Nonsense! Anyway, enough of that. What have you got to report? Have you started to investigate what kind of gifts he might have?" she asked, her gaze drilling through her thick spectacles.

"I… err… well… not... I mean… he gave me a piggyback the other day." Olivier rolled her eyes.

"You need to start testing him so we can know what we're dealing with, and most importantly, so we know you've got the right guy, Adrian. These are the basics!"

"Well, it is my first time," I mumbled.

"What?" she growled.

"Don't worry about it. I mean… how would you suggest I go about testing him?" I asked, hoping she wouldn't refer me to some draconian text Merlin had written three hundred years ago or something. She rolled her eyes again; it was a wonder she didn't strain herself.

"Get him out in nature, see how he interacts with the world… you know this really is beginner level stuff, Adrian," she said as she frowned over her spectacles.

"I know, I know, I'll get right on it. Oh, and before I forget, I'll need some more human money."

"What are you spending it all on?" she asked, looking sceptical.

"Erm… mission essentials," I lied.

"Right…" She was getting more sceptical by the second, so I turned to leave before she could inquire further, but something in my pocket poked me, and I stopped.

"Yes?" she asked, as I paused in the doorway.

"I just… picked it up on the way over," I said, offering Olivier an apple. She froze for a moment, sniffed, and took it.

"Thanks Adrian," she whispered. It was hard to make out through the glasses, but I could have sworn for a moment she got a little watery.

"Don't mention it." I was getting a little watery, too.

TWELVE

I was waiting for Michael to come out of the school gates on Friday for almost an hour. I had a free period last thing, but he was stuck in P. E. Whilst I was waiting, I'd ended up drinking all my orange juice and going back to the canteen for another carton. One thing I have to give humanity credit for is a broad and excellent selection of drinks choices. I'd been trying to replenish myself all day after last night's escapades. So far, the only drink I'd not enjoyed was coconut water, which I frankly can't see the point of.

My stomach fluttered as I saw him leave the school gates, still in his P. E kit. It suited him. His legs were a little muddy, but you could see how broad his shoulders were in the t-shirt.

"Were you waiting for me?" he asked, smiling. I loved his smile.

"Maybeee," I replied, trying not to blush. I was sure it wasn't normal for a charge to make you blush this much.

"Cool. So what's in the bag?" he asked, looking down at

the little plastic shopping bag I'd been failing to hide behind my back.

"It's a surprise." I grinned, and he grinned back.

"For me?"

"Who else? But you've got to follow me to get it."

"Well then, lead on!"

"What are you up to?" he asked, as we reached the edge of Starkton forest. It was a surprisingly large wooded area that the town was built on the edge of. It was also the reason a lot of fay ended up drawn there. The borders between our world and the still world, which is what most fay insist on calling the human world, are thinnest in forests.

"Well, you showed me what you like to do, with the movies and those video game things, so I thought I'd show you what I do for fun," I said, as I started trekking into the woods.

"Oh cool, so you're a hiker?" he asked. I laughed and shook my head.

"You know, it's still crazy to me that you've never played a video game."

"I don't understand how you control the little man with a little stick," I replied, panting slightly as we turned off the path towards an unfortunately steep hill. Michael chuckled and ruffled my hair. My cheeks burned, and my stomach flipped. I love it when he does that, but I wanted more. I wanted him to wrap his arms around me, like he did that day on the lawn.

"You're mad you are, you know?"

"Am I? I've always thought of myself as a ra-AHHH!"

As I took another step, the earth beneath my foot crumbled away and I lost my balance and tumbled over backwards. I braced myself for a thud that didn't come. Instead, Michael's powerful arms scooped under me.

"You okay?" he asked, peering down at me, before putting me back on my feet. I nodded and thickly struggled for words. I didn't really want him to put me back on my feet if I'm being honest.

"I still owe you a piggyback."

"No! I'll be too heavy and it's slippery," I protested.

"Don't be daft, you're not heavy at all, and my shoes have spikes on them, look," he said, and showed me his spiked football boot and grinned before kneeling with his back to me.

"Climb aboard!"

I sighed and relented; truth be told, I wasn't sure I particularly wanted to win that argument anyway.

"You sure I'm not too heavy?" I asked, already resting my head on his shoulder. He smelled nice.

"Don't you worry about a thing," he replied, steadily making his way up the hill. He moved so surely, grabbing hold of tree branches where he could. He'd barely broken a sweat by the time we got to the top of the hill. This was probably exactly the sort of thing Olivier was talking about.

"So where to now?"

"Do you see that little archway of trees?" I said and pointed.

"Yep, that's so cool. I don't think I've ever seen this place before," he said, reaching the tree arch, which formed a kind of canopy tunnel.

"The surprise is through the tunnel, but I'm just gonna do this," I said, covering his eyes as he set off down the path.

"Hey, I can't see."

"That's the point. It's a surprise."

"But what if I drop you?"

"I trust you."

"Good."

"Okay, you can stop now. We're here." I let my hands drop from his eyes, revealing a small crystal blue lake. It was about one hundred feet across, thickly bordered with trees which dispersed dappled green light over the water.

"Oh my god! This is amazing," said Michael, gently setting me down beside him.

"Do you like it?" I asked, enjoying his smile.

"It's incredible. How did you find it?" He looked back at me with awe in his eyes. My heart skipped a beat.

"Just luck I guess." Truth be told, I'd made it. It'd taken me all night, with the help of a particularly productive dryad named Cord, who had been born the same year as me. He dug out the ground and grew all the trees over it whilst I'd drawn water in from miles around to fill it.

It'd been exhausting and bribing Cord to come help had been expensive, but it was all worth it for the look on Michael's face.

"So, what's in the bag?" he asked, after staring at the lake for a little while.

"Oh yeah, I almost forgot!" I opened the bag and handed him a pair of orange swim shorts with palm trees on them I'd found in a local surfer shop, which was a bit odd given we were nowhere near the sea.

"You're mad! We can't swim in there, it must be freezing!" he said with a chuckle.

"Are you scared?" I asked, grinning as I started to

unbutton my top and kicked off my trousers to reveal a pair of bubbly blue shorts.

"I'm gonna regret this, aren't I?" he said, grabbing the shorts and disappearing behind a tree. He reemerged wearing them a minute or so later.

"What do you think?" he asked, grinning.

"Looking good," I replied, trying not to stare at his chest, or arms, or stomach or shoulders. In the end I couldn't find a safe place to look, turned on the spot, and dove into the lake.

He dived beautifully, although I couldn't quite believe he'd dived at all. This was a lake in Starkton in spring, not the Mediterranean ocean in August. I rushed to the waterside to see if he was okay and there he was, under the water. His hair glistened, and he moved so gracefully, I'd never seen anyone swim like that before. It was like he was at one with it. He surfaced in the middle of the lake and slicked his hair back. For a second, I was lost for words, so I just stood there staring at him like an idiotic lamppost person.

"Are you coming in?"

"Aren't you freezing?"

"Try it and see... I dare you!"

I sighed, balled my fists, took a deep breath and jumped, bracing myself for it to be freezing, but it wasn't, it was just pleasantly cool. I swam over to Adrian, much less gracefully than he swam.

"How's this possible? It should be so cold in here," I said, panting slightly as I trod water. In the centre it was just a foot or so too deep to stand. Adrian shrugged; the way he floated in the water looked effortless.

"Maybe we're on one of those natural hotspots or something," he said, then smiled before diving under the water and turned so he was facing me as he swam underneath my legs. The way he moved was almost as if he was being carried by a current.

"You're an amazing swimmer," I said as he surfaced again, not even out of breath.

"Thanks, it's my favourite thing to do," he said as he slowly drifted to the lakeside, with me following him.

"You could swim rings around me, couldn't you?" I asked, unable to take my eyes off him.

"I couldn't give you a piggyback up a hill though, so I guess we're even." He laughed, but I didn't reply. Up close, there was something about his eyes now. They'd shifted; maybe it was the dappled light of the trees, but they looked like they were twinkling with their own light, and his face, it was as though he'd been carved out, and every feature seemed planned.

"Michael?" He drew a little closer. I realised I must have been staring, but I couldn't tear myself away.

"You're beautiful," I heard my voice say. It was low and breathless, and I didn't even realise I was saying it. His face flushed pink as I spoke, as a sweet smile played at his lips. He drew closer still, and he must have been on his tip toes now, looking up at me. I watched my hands go to his hips without even willing them to move. He nodded, and I lifted him to eye level. He was even lighter in the water.

"Is this okay?" I whispered. He nodded again, and we

kissed. His arms snaked around my neck, and he hung there. His lips were soft, and his body felt delicate in my hands. We held each other, it was impossible to know how long for, and then we broke apart, and my heart was thundering in my ears and my mouth was dry and I couldn't catch my breath. He looked at me with his heart-breaking eyes twinkling and I was struck dumb.

"Do you like your surprise?" he whispered. I nodded and his smile burst across his face from ear to ear.

PART TWO
THE TRUTH

CHAPTER
ONE

My heart was fluttering as I made my way down one of the many branched paths of the forest to Olivier's cottage. I didn't think it had stopped fluttering since Michael kissed me in the lake. I wasn't sure if it would ever stop, and I wasn't sure I ever wanted it to. There was just one problem; I was no expert on charges, but I was pretty sure it wasn't the done thing to kiss them in romantic lakes. Olivier would not be impressed.

As I reached her cottage, the front door was open just a crack. I crept closer and listened in.

"I'm afraid revealing the identity of my attacker has not brought the good news we'd hoped for." It was Merlin's voice; I'd recognise it anywhere.

"So, who was it?" asked Olivier, sounding as hungry for knowledge as ever.

"It was Minoty." I bit my lip to stifle a gasp. Minoty had been a minor member of the dryad court for as long as I could remember.

"It can't have been Minoty. We'd have known if it was Minoty, she'd have been declared missing. I grew up with Minoty… she wouldn't."

"It seems that the court didn't want me to know they'd been weakened by her disappearance, assuming she'd been taken," replied Merlin, sounding grave. Some members of the courts didn't like to co-operate with Merlin. They felt the fay should be ruled by the three ruling fay elemental factions, water nymphs, dryads and sylphs. This was a very old, very stupid idea if you ask me.

"So, what now? We interrogate her? Find out if more of the courts are working with mireling creatures? We can't allow our enemies to unite against us like this. They haven't done that since Morgana." I couldn't see Olivier's face, but I could imagine her steely gaze.

"I know that, of course Olivier, but we can't rush this. We can't go throwing accusations around and risk alien- ating potential allies. Some within the courts may not like me, but they like the mirelings even less." Merlin had a way of sounding frustratingly calm about things. I suppose it came with age. I was so tense with anticipation I was sure my muscles would seize at any moment.

"All the more reason to interrogate her then."

"We're already on that. She's being held at The Hut as we speak."

The Hut was one of the most important places in the fay forest, bordering mireling land and the home of the Excal- ibur system. Probably the most defended piece of territory in the whole forest.

"Any news?"

"Well, on that front, a spot of luck, it seems the pixie's brews have been most effective in loosening her tongue."

"And?"

"From what we can gather, she was never privy to the whole plan, only part of it, but the part we know about is this; the attack was a ruse. I was never their true target. They were aiming to eliminate our champions."

My mouth grew dry. If they were targeting champions, they could be targeting charges, they could be targeting Michael, and I couldn't let what happened to Cynthia happen to him.

"What! Those evil little…" Olivier's voice trailed off.

"Yes, it seems the new strategy is to destabilise me, us, the fay, by eroding that which we rely on most for our security: champions. So now it is more important than ever that we find more. How many fay do we have in the field on the hunt at this present moment Olivier?"

"Well, there are four actives at the moment… as you know, Adrian."

I jumped as I heard my name. My muscles had seized and as I tried to catch myself, I fell clean through the doorway, landing face-first on the cobbled floor.

"Ouch," I groaned, my lips vibrating from the impact and my head pounding. I looked up to see Olivier and Merlin staring down at me. Olivier looked surprised; Merlin remained unshaken.

"Adrian, just the person I needed to see," said Merlin.

"Were you listening at my door?" asked Olivier, her eyes narrowed suspiciously.

"No, of course not! You know me, I was just rushing,

never stopping to smell the flowers, and I missed my footing and wham, I'm on the ground. I thought I'd have face-planted the door, but I don't think it was shut properly," I babbled on, trying to cover my lie in nonsense before they sniffed it out.

"That'll be me, sorry Olivier," said Merlin.

Olivier seemed to accept this as she relaxed back a little.

"So, Adrian, anything to report?" she asked, as intensely as ever, but now I could feel Merlin's eyes on me too.

"No, no luck yet, no sign of anything remarkable so far, besides the whole, knowing it when I see it thing," I lied. From Michael's performance in the forest, I'd have put money on him being a woodsman. Probably a powerful one too, given his early development, but I couldn't tell them that. They'd snap him up and whisk him away and before I knew it, the song of the lost would be in the trees again.

"Well, have you tested him at all?" I could hear the frustration in Olivier's voice.

"Oh yes, I took him into the deep forest, to see how he'd fare, but he struggled just as much as me, maybe even more," I lied again.

"Oh well, you're doing all the right things Adrian. Just keep plugging along. This is important work you're doing my lad," said Merlin with a smile.

"I know, I'll do my best."

"And we're all relying on you, my boy," he said, giving my arm a squeeze and for a second, I felt his tone shift, his features darkened. His voice was heavy and the room was cold, then it had passed and he was Merlin again. A cold sweat was forming on my brow and something primal inside me wanted to hide.

"Well, I'd best be off then," I said, waving as I made my way out of the cottage. Speeding down the path as fast as I could without arousing suspicion.

TWO

"Hey, Mike, over here." Jack waved from one of the tables in the high school canteen. I waved back and made my way over. He was sitting with Alex, Jess and a girl from their year named Sam, who Jess had been hanging out with a lot recently. I sat down opposite Alex and he looked up from his phone, mischief written across his face. He had floppy brown hair, kind of like mine but longer, and he always had it styled some way or other.

"So, forgive me if I speak out of turn, but I think you've been spending a lot of time with the new kid. Adrian's his name, right?" asked Alex, pretending he didn't know full well who Adrian was. Alex probably knew about Adrian before I did, somehow. He always knew what was going on in the school – at Starkton High, all gossip-roads led to Alex. "Maybe I have," I replied, trying to fight the smile that played at my lips as I thought of Adrian.

"He's a cute little thing, isn't he?" said Alex, grinning.

"If you're into that sort of thing," said Jack with a wink.

"Oh yes, if you're into perfect skin, glossy blond hair, massive eyes, and a friendly smile. It's not for everyone after all," Alex joked. Sam and Jess sniggered.

"Are you into that sort of thing?" asked Jack, barely stifling a laugh himself.

"No, can't stand it... I'm joking! Of course I am. Who isn't?" I gave in. It was obvious what they were getting at and there was no point trying to evade Alex once he'd got his hooks in.

"And I wonder, do you think little Adrian is into six-foot athletes that stop him being bullied and give him piggyback rides home from school?" asked Alex, with so much mirth on his face I'm sure this must have been the most fun he'd had all week. I planted my head on the table and flipped him my middle finger as a blush raged across my cheeks.

"You're the absolute worst, you know that right?" I mumbled.

"You really are," added Jack. I could hear him smiling even if I couldn't see it.

"I really am," said Alex, as the entire table laughed.

"So, since we've established that Adrian likes Michael—"

"Have we established that?" I cut Alex off, raising my head from the desk.

"Obviously," replied Jack.

"So, since we've established that Adrian likes Michael, and from the colour of his cheeks, Michael clearly likes Adrian..."

I groaned.

"We were wondering if you'd like to come on a double date with us?" asked Jack.

I paused, my breath caught in my throat. I really did

want to go on a date with Adrian, and this was the perfect excuse.

"Ermm… yes."

"Victory!" declared Alex, and he took a long sip of his drink.

"Couldn't you just have asked me that? I've almost sweated through my shirt," I moaned.

"Where would be the fun in that? You've got no sense for the dramatic, Michael Tombs," Alex chuckled.

"To be fair, Alex, no-one has as much sense for the dramatic as you," Sam added.

"I take that as a compliment."

"I expected you would." The two of them fell about laughing and I sighed with relief. Alex was fun, he was a bit extra, but I'd much rather have him and Jack in the year above me than not. Somehow, he'd managed to be the first 'out' boy in the school. So he got the lion's share of all the bullying for it and still ended up the most confident person our age that I knew.

CHAPTER

THREE

When I'd enrolled in the school, picking the subjects to take had been a bit of a gamble, because the whole idea was to spend time with Michael. But of course, Olivier and I hadn't known which subjects he took. In the end we got one out of three with English, which was lucky, given how many we were picking from. That and neither of us had the foggiest idea what PE was. Otherwise, I'd ended up with economics, which turned out to be incredibly boring and drama, which had been quite fun. Alex from the year above hung around in the drama room sometimes and seemed particularly interested in me for some reason.

"So, Gawain is going on a quest to fight the Green Knight, but he's already chopped his head off, so... what?" asked Michael, glaring at his text like it had called him a rude name. I giggled; I couldn't help it, there was something charming about his utter befuddlement.

"Not quite. The knight's challenge was to exchange a blow for a blow. Gawain accepted the challenge and

71

chopped the Knight's head off. Only he didn't die, so one year later, Gawain has to go find the knight and let him chop his head off," I explained.

"But that's mental! First of all, clearly the Green Knight cheated, so Gawain should be allowed to cheat too, and also, how is he not dead anyway?"

"'Cause magic, silly," I said and grinned, not sure if Michael was playing up his frustration at this point. Every time I explained something I'm sure I could see a smile pulling at the corner of his face.

"And he has to go because it's all about honour and duty and chivalry; that's, like, the Knights of the Round Table whole thing."

"How do you know so much about it, anyway?" asked Michael as he wrote down 'honour', 'duty' and 'chivalry' in big bubbles in his workbook.

"We covered this at my old school too," I lied. The fay were on the whole middling readers, but we paid special interest when the humans wrote about us, and these Arthurian myths were *all* about us. Badly misremembered half-stories from the times we roamed the still world mostly, but it was fun to see your great, great, great...you get the idea, your however many greats grandmother turn up from time to time.

"Well in that case, smarty-pants, you won't mind if we take a break, will you?" Michael grinned as he closed my textbook, his fingers brushing over my own.

My breath faltered.

"What did you have in mind for this break?" I asked, leaning forward, finding myself drawn in.

"Alex and Jack invited us on a double date. It's on Sunday."

"A date?"

"Errm, yeah, well I mean, since we kissed at the lake, not that I presumed, I mean, I thought that maybe, if you don't want to it—"

"I'd love to," I whispered, cutting him off. It was funny at first, but I could see the doubt inching across his face and that I couldn't bear. He looked around to check no-one was looking at us — hidden as we were at the back of the class — leant forward and kissed me, just for a second. My heart leapt into my throat and I leaned forward as he was already pulling away, his amber eyes calling to me. For a while we just stared into each other's eyes, and I wished the rest of the world would just melt away.

"I've never been on an official date," I whispered, breaking the silence eventually.

"Me neither," he said, sitting back in his chair and burying his face as Mr Moore looked over at us. I returned to my work and amused myself with their woefully inaccurate depiction of Morgana.

"One more thing," he whispered once Mr Moore's beady eye had moved on.

"Yes?"

"Do you want to come to my football match on Saturday? Mum says you can stay over Friday night if you like. It'd have to be in Dan's room though."

"I'd love to. Can't wait," I replied, having not even the slightest idea what football was.

CHAPTER

FOUR

I pulled my boots on and jogged out onto the pitch ahead of the rest of the team. Usually I'd hang back, but today I had someone waiting to see me, so I'd got changed in lightning-fast time. Not being gassed by *Lynx Africa* was an added benefit.

There he was, standing by the side of the pitch in the rain. Mum was there too, in one of her huge coats.

"Sorry about the weather," I said as I reached them. "April showers – more like April monsoons." Mum chuckled at her own joke.

"Don't be sorry, I like it," said Adrian, as a raindrop dripped off his eyelashes. He was beaming.

"Aren't you cold?" I asked, grabbing him by the arm and rubbing up and down to try and warm him up.

"If you want to warm me up this is better," he said, throwing his arms around my waist and pulling me into a hug. I didn't put up much of a fight. I loved wrapping him up in my arms. It felt like we fit together, like it was meant to be. I'd have laughed at the thought of it a month ago, but I was starting to understand what all those lilting love songs were written about. Mum caught my eye with the biggest grin on her face. I rolled my eyes.

"You a big fan of football, Adrian?" she asked, after he finally let me go.

"I don't know anything about it, really," he said and shrugged.

"You don't know football?" This was even more unbelievable than the video games. Adrian shook his head and shrugged and for a second I was speechless. Out of the corner of my eye I saw mum looking just as puzzled as I felt. I couldn't quite believe he was telling the truth. But then, why would he lie?

"Should I?" he asked, shrinking back a little. He almost sounded nervous, and a pang of guilt shot through me for questioning it, even just in my head.

"No haha, I'm just wondering how you managed to go seventeen years in this country without hearing about football." I chuckled, and his face lit up again, hearing myself say it, it sounded even more ridiculous but it wasn't worth upsetting Adrian over.

"What are the big nets for?" he asked after a moment, pointing to the goal, and there was a jolt in my stomach and the urge to hug him again. He was just so adorable, in his weird way.

"All you need to know, is when I get the ball in the net, which is called a goal, you cheer."

"Got it."

"What's this, Michael, got yourself a cheerleader?" asked Coach Field, jogging up behind me.

"Got himself a boyfriend," Mum said, and I could see a cheeky grin peeking out from behind her massive scarf.

"Mum!" I barked, my cheeks burning.

"Oh, good for you, son," said Coach, giving me a slap on the shoulder.

"No, he's not... it's not like—"

"Aren't I?" Adrian interrupted me as I stumbled through the worst string of words I could have possibly come up with. The disappointment in his eyes was like a punch to the gut.

"Are you?" I whispered, drawing closer to him, my heart pounding in my ears.

"Am I?" His eyes were doing that twinkling thing again. It was a miracle steam wasn't pouring off me in this rain – I felt like I was on fire. I grabbed him and pulled him into another hug before his eyes destroyed me.

"You are," I whispered, kissing his cheek.

"Ah, young love," said Coach as he jogged off to the centre of the field.

The rain only intensified as we played, and by halftime everyone in the crowd was soaked through and looking miserable, except for Adrian, who seemed not to mind. I jogged over to Mum and Adrian as the whistle blew – the coaches' half time speeches weren't up to much, anyway.

"You scored!" said Adrian, beaming.

"I did, and you cheered." Very loudly and probably for longer than was appropriate, truth be told.

"Well, that was my whole job after all."

"So, are you two having a good time?" I asked, very aware that standing in the rain doing nothing for an hour probably wasn't much fun.

"Great, although I don't understand why no-one's using their hands except the fella in the net," said Adrian looking confused.

"Well, you see that would be a hand ball where…"

"Don't bother, I've already tried." Mum chuckled, I chuckled, Adrian still looked perplexed.

The second half started and there was something in the other team's centre half that had changed – he had a look of steely determination in his eyes. This manifested in an absolute commitment to tackling me at any and all opportunities. Ten minutes into the second half, we were both completely caked in mud. Adrian had started booing, which wasn't really in the spirit of the thing, but every time he did it I'm sure I heard Mum laughing, so at least he was keeping her spirits up. That was, until I got past the centre half, and I was running upfield. Then I was crashing through the mud, sharp white pain shooting up my leg as something tore. I could feel it ripping. All I could make out was Mum screaming over the sound of a whistle being blown. I could hardly bear to look at the source of the throbbing, pulsing pain. I screwed up my courage and winced as I opened my eyes to look, only to see Adrian knelt in the mud huddled over my leg.

"Adrian?" I asked, confused for a second, and then it hit me – the pain was ebbing away. In a matter of seconds Coach was on me, pushing Adrian aside.

"Well, I'll be damned. I was sure we'd be calling an ambulance," he said, puzzling over my leg.

"Is it bad?" I asked, the sickening tearing feeling playing back in my mind.

"Just a slight cut by the looks, you got off lucky there,

lad," said Coach before walking over to bark at the offending centre half, who was having a red card waved in his face by the ref already. Next was Mum, she was already in tears, and indecipherable; I couldn't make out if she was angry or relieved or in panic. All I could tell was "my baby" amongst other, indeterminable babble.

"Adrian, are you alright?" I asked, ignoring Mum's melodrama as I noticed he was still sitting in the mud, where he'd landed when Coach pushed him off me. At first, he didn't say anything, then he looked up and I knew something was wrong. He wasn't his normal pale, he was grey, his big twinkling eyes were half lidded and dull, and he wasn't speaking, all he could offer was an exhausting looking thumbs up.

"Mum, Mum, Mum, calm down, Mum I'm fine," I said, grabbing her hands and shaking them until she stopped crying. "Mum, could you please take Adrian to the car, I think... the excitement got to him or something I don't know."

"Oh... what? Sorry, oh actually you are looking a bit grey, dear." She said, finally noticing Adrian, slumped in the mud.

"I'm fine," he mumbled, barely sounding awake, but he didn't protest as Mum helped him off the field and took him to the carpark.

I watched them go, my heart still racing. It just didn't make sense. He'd been fine ten minutes ago. I got up and shook my leg out, the memory of tearing and white-hot pain flashing through my mind as I did. It just didn't make sense.

The rest of the game went by in a bit of a blur. Despite

being a man down the other team ended up winning, but I didn't really care. My mind was elsewhere. When it was all over and I made my way to Mum's car, I found her sat in the front with the windows all steamed up from the heating and Adrian asleep under her coat in the back.

"Out like a light, poor love."

He was so zonked out I ended up carrying him upstairs to bed. He didn't resurface until dinnertime, and even then, he didn't seem quite right.

FIVE

After spending the night and, truth be told, a lot of the previous day, in Dan's room, I crept out of the house. I had to speak to Merlin, and with the double date that night, the early morning was my only chance of slipping away unnoticed. Hopefully Michael would assume I was still sleeping off whatever he'd guessed was wrong with me. It was stupid of me to heal him like that, with everyone around. I could have been caught, but what else could I do? Watch him suffering when I knew I could help? I couldn't bear it.

I was just lucky there was so much mud and rain, so nobody got a good look at what happened before I reached him. I hadn't expected it to take quite that much out of me – whatever happened to his leg must have been worse than I'd realised.

I slipped out of Michael's front door, careful not to knock over any coats or bags or shoes, and crossed the road. There was a neighbour on the other side with a tree just big enough for me to slip through. I crept into their garden as quietly as I could and slipped into the tree.

The path to Merlin's home was largely kept secret, for obvious reasons, although luckily he'd always had a soft spot for me. From the outside it was a small circular door built into an unassuming hill, a bump in the road almost.

Knock Knock

I heard rustling inside, then the door swung open. Today, Merlin was a little stooped, his hair long and grey, and he was sweeping around in a long green silken cloak tied with golden tassels.

"Adrian my boy, what a pleasure. Come in, come in." He ushered me inside. Merlin's home started with a small entrance hall, with stairs that descended into a large open cavern that spiderwebbed out under the hill. He had laboratories, libraries, a hall. I think there was even a personal museum in there somewhere.

"So, what brings you all the way out here?" he asked, after leading me into the first room. A sort of lab-come-living-room.

"Oh, you know, I hadn't been round in a while, since I got busy in the still world really, and I thought I'd check in," I lied.

"How thoughtful. Well, how've things been going with that charge of yours?" he sounded casual, but there was an unmistakable intensity in his eyes. Just because I'd been hiding from the fay world, it didn't mean the pressure to find champions had diminished.

"Just plodding along, working out how best to test him next. You know, since working with my first charge, I've realised how complicated all this sort of stuff can get."

"Oh yes, very challenging task indeed, very nuanced. Finding them, ascertaining their skills, gaining their trust, introducing them to our world and their role in it, there can be no end of complications."

"And then there is managing your... relationship with them. I mean, what if you don't like them?"

Merlin chuckled as I tiptoed my way to the point, careful not to leave any breadcrumbs.

"Or even like them more than expected," I added as casually as I could.

"Yes, neither is ideal, though I think the latter is the more complex issue," said Merlin. I watched his face intently for any sign he might have realised my secret, but so far, he seemed more concerned with rooting through his many cloak pockets.

"Has that ever happened?" I asked.

"What, sorry?" he replied, finally pulling out a little leather-bound book.

"Someone … fallen in love with one of their charges."

"I wouldn't say fallen in love, but certainly developed that type of feeling. It's rare, but it happens, occasionally."

"What happens then?" I asked, careful not to seem desperate for answers and also somewhat curious. It certainly wasn't something I'd heard of happening before.

"Well, it depends, sometimes they move on. I can help them with that, by positioning the charge in question to the front lines, to create space, or we give the charge to someone else if things aren't too far along."

"So, they wouldn't normally stay together?" I asked, trying not to sound crushed.

"Not if I have anything to say about it," Merlin chuckled,

and for a second a flash of hate bubbled up in me. How could he laugh like that at the idea of separating loved ones?

"Well, you know best, Merlin," I laughed along with him as my fists balled in my pockets.

"Certainly do. It creates too many complications – charges are powerful assets to the fay, after all, and we couldn't have one being wasted on home-making. And think how dangerous they could become if they fell into line with a... rebellious element." I wanted to shout, to tell him that they weren't assets, they were people. That Michael wasn't his weapon, he was my boyfriend, but I didn't I just dug my nails into the palms of my hands.

"Yes, of course. Well, thanks for the chat, Merlin. I'd best be off." I smiled and got to my feet, anxious to leave before I gave too much away, or punched him.

"Before you go, take this. Might come in handy," said Merlin, passing me the little leather book.

"What is it?"

"Oh, you know, just some notes of the types of charges we come across, categorised by me, of course." I took it and made my way up the stairs, back out of the house. Merlin didn't follow.

"Bye Merlin!"

"Bye Adrian, my boy!"

CHAPTER
SIX

"There you are! Where did you disappear to?" I asked. As Adrian slipped back through the front door, he jumped and froze on the spot.

"Oh I errm, I was just getting some fresh air in the garden," he said, shifting from one foot to the other, like he needed the loo.

"Sorry, did I make you jump?" I asked.

"No, well, yes, I was trying to make sure I didn't wake anyone."

"Oh, don't worry. Mum sleeps like a log, and I was just about to go for my morning run. You feeling better?" It was a relief to see his face was no longer grey.

"Much. Sorry for worrying you," he replied, his face softening into an apologetic smile.

"Don't worry about it. What happened to you yesterday anyway? You seemed fine and then all of a sudden you just weren't." I'd been wondering about it last night, but my wondering hadn't got me anywhere.

"Oh errm, I don't know, I think the shock maybe?" he said, shifting from one foot to the other again.

"Yeah, maybe, honestly when that guy tackled me I thought for sure I was gonna be going to A&E but then I was fine, so weird."

"Yeah… so weird," replied Adrian. I'd mostly been thinking aloud, but he seemed anxious all of a sudden.

"Did it look like something bad had happened?" I asked.

"Errm, I don't know, there was so much mud, whose David anyway? I saw his name on your garden bench." A jolt shot through as he said the words. Suddenly I was cold and Adrian felt further away.

"David's your middle name, right? I remember your mum shouting it that one time," asked Adrian, talking quickly, almost rambling. His voice sounded distant now, in the background, like I was only half listening.

"He was my dad," I heard my voice say that part, it just slipped out, without a thought.

"Oh… I see." Adrian wasn't rambling anymore, he must have realised what was happening. I wasn't very good at hiding it. I hadn't had to think about the accident for a little while. The people in school had learned not to ask me about Dad I suppose. Sometimes I felt guilty for not waking up thinking about it anymore, other times I resented that guilt.

"Sorry… do you want a cup of tea? Before I go on my run?" I asked him, realising I'd been staring silently at a patch of wall behind Adrian's head for a little while now.

"Tea would be good." Adrian's voice was distant still. It barely registered as he stepped towards me, and then his hand was in mine. Warm and small and squeezing my hand, dragging me back into the now. I looked down and there his eyes were, his big blue sparkling eyes staring up at me and smiling. I didn't say anything, I just nodded and blinked a couple of tears back.

"Tea it is," I whispered. I'm not sure why I was whispering.

"You'll have to make it then. I always do it wrong," said Adrian, still smiling, almost laughing now. He was right. I'm not sure how he managed it, but he always managed to ruin the tea. As I thought of his last attempt, with burst tea bags and leaves floating in the teapot, a little laugh slipped out of me.

We made our way into the kitchen, and he perched on the counter, leaving a little brown book on the side.

"What's that then? A diary?" I asked, breathing out, only now realising how tight my chest had gotten.

"Oh errm, yes, it is actually. Good guess, don't go reading it now." He gave a little nervous chuckle and place a hand on the book. It was a funny beaten up little brown leather thing.

"Best not leave it lying around then – the temptation could be too great," I joked, almost giddy as a relief washed over. I wasn't even sure why I was relieved. I handed him a giant mug of tea, in what was effectively a cereal bowl with a handle. His eyes fell on it and he seemed to forget about the book, as a grin burst across his face.

After my run, I found Mum and Adrian chatting away. They always ended up on the subjects of gnomes one way or another. She sent us upstairs to do homework before our 'hot double date', as she cringingly called it, although we didn't exactly get much done. I swear we could talk about nothing for hours or spend the time cuddling or kissing. Thank God Mum didn't insist on us keeping the door open.

"What are Jack and Alex like?" he asked, looking up at me. He'd been laying with his head on my chest for the past half an hour or so – much longer and I think I'd have fallen asleep.

"Jack's kinda quiet, but he's funny and super smart. I think he knows how to code stuff, which basically makes him a computer god, from what I can tell. He came out a little bit after Alex, I think."

"And Alex?"

"Alex is sort of the opposite. He's a bit of a social butter-fly, very chatty. He got a lot of bullying for being gay at first, but he ended up being friends with all the boys on the foot-ball team's girlfriends, so they put a stop to all that."

"How clever – my boyfriend is friends with all the foot-ball team's girlfriends' boyfriends." Adrian said, giggling to himself.

"Are you talking nonsense?" I asked, chuckling.

"No… well, I can't say for certain, but I'm pretty sure that made sense." He laughed, rolling off me and almost off the bed. I grabbed him before he tipped off the edge.

"Where are you off to?" I laughed, dragging him back into my body and squeezing him.

"I'm trapped!" he laughed and hugged me back.

"Well, where were you off to?"

"I was gonna go get dressed for our date, isn't it nearly time?" I stretched, yawned, and checked my phone for the time.

"Oh shit!" I sat bolt upright, and nearly flung Adrian off the bed in the process, before grabbing him again.

"Sorry!" I cringed, pulling him into a hug.

"S'okay," came his muffled voice, giggling into my chest.

"What should we wear? What should I wear?" I asked, jumping off my bed and glaring at my muddy jeans discarded across my bedroom floor.

"I've got this stuff," said Adrian, pulling on a pair of pale blue chinos and a long sleeve white top decorated with blue bubbles that matched the jeans. He even had one of those little neckerchief things. Meanwhile, I'd stripped down to my boxers and was pulling a black jacket mum had got me for Christmas over a plain white t-shirt.

"You look amazing. I'm gonna look so boring next to you!" I said, grabbing him by the shoulders and pulling him in front of the mirror.

"Look at you. Who gave you permission to look like that?" I grinned as his cheeks started to flush pink.

"You think?" he asked, beaming.

"Of course, now help me find what to wear!" I smiled, planted a kiss on his cheek and then went back to glowering at my wardrobe.

"What about these?" he asked, picking up a pair of forest green jeans Alex had talked me into buying the one and only time we'd been on a shopping trip together. Only for me to never wear them.

"You think?" I asked, a little nervous to leave my trusty black, blue and grey combo behind.

"Or you could just go like that," he said, pointing to my bare legs.

"Green it is," I said, yanking them on.

CHAPTER
SEVEN

"So, what are you boys going to talk about?" asked Linda, as she dropped us off at the restaurant. Michael had begged her for a lift so we wouldn't be late. He said we'd never hear the end of it from Alex if we were.

"Probably our nosy mothers," Michael said, sticking his tongue out as he jumped out of the car. His mum chuckled and stuck hers out right back at him.

"Well, be good. I'll be here to pick you up at ten."

"Okay, Mum, love you."

"Love you too, have fun, Adrian."

"Bye, Linda." We waved as she drove off, and Michael took my hand in his and led me inside. Jack and Alex were already at the table negotiating sharing starters when we arrived. A little tingle ran up my back as we sat down. For a second, something didn't feel safe, but I couldn't put a finger on why.

"You wore the trousers we got!" said Alex, beaming.

"You know, you didn't have to wear them if you didn't like them," Jack half whispered.

"How could he not like them? They're great, also you're not whispering very quietly." I couldn't help but laugh, the way they bickered like old people.

"I see you dressed up for the occasion Adrian," said Alex, whose eyes had gone straight to my little neckerchief thing. I wasn't sure I'd tied it properly. I'd copied the complete outfit off someone I'd see in a magazine in M&S. Hopefully, he wouldn't notice.

"Doesn't he look good! Meanwhile, I'm just throwing on what's clean," said Michael grabbing a menu.

"I think you look great," I said, giving his leg a little squeeze under the table.

"Thanks babe," he whispered, leaning in and giving me a kiss on the cheek. My stomach flipped as heat rushed to the spot he'd kissed.

"Gah I love this! I love gay people." Alex clapped his hands together excitedly and again I felt that almost electric feeling. Like there was something just behind me, just outside of touching distance, watching.

"Alex, you know we're gay people, right?" asked Jack, barely stifling a laugh.

"I know, right? Isn't it fantastic?" Alex beamed. I couldn't help but laugh, and then Michael was laughing and then Jack was laughing and suddenly we were all laughing. I'd never heard the expression Michael used to describe him before, a social butterfly, but I was starting to guess what it meant.

The whole evening went on in much the same way. Alex would say something ridiculous, Jack would point out it was ridiculous, Alex would say something else, and we'd all laugh. They were like a double act. There was just one nagging feeling I couldn't get away from, that I could feel eyes on me. It was all I could do to stop myself thinking about Minoty, how she'd been disguised when she attacked Merlin. How there could be another fay in disguise waiting around the corner to strike, to hurt Michael, like they had Cynthia. To tell the truth, I hadn't done a very good job of stopping myself from thinking about it.

"So, do you think those two hate me, or fancy Jack?" asked Alex, just as the bill was placed in front of us.

"Who?" I asked.

"Those two," said Alex, almost imperceptibly nodding his head towards two men at the bar who seemed to be keeping us in their peripheral. There it was again, that shiver down my spine.

"Why do they have to hate you, or fancy Jack?" asked Michael, looking confused.

"'Cause I'm fit, obviously," joked Jack.

"Well, yes, true, but also they've been staring at us... a lot," replied Alex.

"It's probably just your imagination," said Michael.

"No, I think he's right. I've had a feeling like someone was looking at me all night." I glanced over my shoulder to look at the two men at the bar, in their late twenties by the looks. I flinched, and looked away and for a second, I was sure I'd locked eyes with one of them.

"Well, that's a bit creepy. Want me to go talk to them?" offered Michael, being admirably chivalrous. It was really a wonder he didn't understand the Green Knight.

. . .

"Nah, that's probably not the best idea. Anyway, I think they are leaving now," said Jack.

"You sure?" asked Michael.

"Quite sure, I'm fine," said Alex, although he still seemed a little tense.

We finished our drinks and to our surprise, Jack offered to pay the whole bill. Apparently, he'd started a little online business thing that was going well. I had the money, but thought it was probably a little suspicious that I had a seemingly infinite supply of cash, so didn't protest.

"Right well, we're walking back," said Jack as we left the restaurant. It was drizzling and little puddles had formed on the floor.

"You sure? Mum's picking us up in ten mins, I'm sure she wouldn't mind dropping you off," offered Michael.

"Nah, we'll be back by the time your mum gets here if we set off now," said Jack.

"Plus, it's romantic," added Alex, and Jack rolled his eyes. With that, they set off, and Michael took my hand in his as we plopped down on a bench outside the restaurant.

"That was nice, do you think?"

"Hey, faggot!"

Michael went stiff as he was cut off mid-sentence by someone shouting. He sprung to his feet and ran round to the path Alex and Jack were walking down. I followed him and looking down the lane saw Jack and Alex, and just behind them, the two men from the bar.

"Hey! Leave them alone," Michael called after them, closing the distance until there was only a couple of meters between him and the men who'd turned on the spot. I followed. Up close I could tell Jack was furious, his fists were screwed into tight balls.

"Let's all calm down," said Alex, his voice trembling slightly as he spoke.

"What did you just say to me, fag?" spat one of the men, turning back on Alex. I'd never heard that word before, but there was hate in it, I could feel it.

"Don't you talk to them like that," Michael snarled. The other man moved closer until there were only a couple of feet between them. I smirked. He'd stood in a puddle.

"Stay back Adrian," Michael said under his breath, and the man sniggered.

"Awww Adrian, is that you boyfriend … fag?" Venom dripped from his words and something in me snapped. Just as it looked like he might lunge for Michael, I focused on the puddle, flicked my wrist, and his left leg shot out behind him. Michael darted out of the way as he stumbled headfirst onto the cobbled floor. Blood sprayed out of his nose as his face hit the ground with a crunch and the other man yelled.

"What did you just do?" he snarled, glaring at Michael.

"Looks like your friend had too much to drink," said Alex.

"You what, fag?" The man wheeled round with a raised fist, but before he could strike, Michael had his arm from behind and threw him backwards. He stumbled and crashed into his friend, who was just getting back to his feet. They both went flying into the gravel.

"I'm gonna fu—"

"You're going to what exactly?" said Linda, appearing from around the corner of the pub.

"Who th—"

"Never you mind who I am, I've got 999 dialled on my phone – one more word out of either of you …" She pointed to them both as she walked around them and planted herself between me, the others and the thugs. She was the most glorious ball of coats and scarfs and rage I'd ever seen.

"One more word! And I'm calling the police. I wonder how kindly they'll take to you attacking a bunch of boys in the street."

"Y-yeah well, it's your word against ours, isn't it?" said the one I'd tripped with the puddle. Gravel marks tracked up the side of his face and he was holding his nose in his palm. Linda pointed to a white tube attached to the restaurant roof.

"I'm sure they'll be all too happy to check the restaurant's CCTV." The men's eyes grew wide and within seconds they were darting off down the street in the opposite direction.

"Are you boys, okay?" Linda asked, wheeling round on us all.

"I've had better evenings," said Alex, sagging slightly.

"Arseholes," muttered Jack, who couldn't seem to untense.

"I'll give you two a lift home. Everyone get in the car," she said. We all piled in and I ended up sitting in Michael's lap, although I wasn't complaining his arms wrapped around my waist were a welcome comfort.

"Are you okay?" he asked, after we'd dropped Jack and Alex off.

"At least we didn't get hurt," I said, and smiled, taking his hand and squeezing it. He squeezed back. His hands were so much bigger than mine.

"I liked it when you said 'stay back'." I leaned up, whispering into his ear. He smiled and kissed my cheek.

"Oh yeah? You did call me your hero that first day in class, remember?"

"Well, you were. You rescued me from falling out of the tree."

"All I did was help you up," he chuckled. I shook my head. It was more than that, there was something of safety in Michael Tombs.

"And when I nearly collapsed on you walking home, and when I slipped on that hill and tonight, you're being my hero all over the place." I grinned as a pink shadow spread across his cheeks.

"I'll always be there to rescue you," he whispered into my ear.

"Promise?"

"Promise." He crossed his finger over his heart, and we sat back into a comfortable silence, the warmth of the car heating lulling me to sleep.

"It was weird, the way that guy just went flying out of no-where," said Michael, breaking the silence just as I was nodding off.

"He was probably drunk dear," said Linda from the front seat.

CHAPTER
EIGHT

"I've got geography now, and you're in economics right?" I asked, as we got up to leave registration.

"What? Oh yeah, economics," Adrian replied, he been distracted all morning, he'd barely even touched the tea I got him from the cafeteria.

"Wanna meet up at lunch?" I asked, but he didn't respond. He was rummaging around in his bag for something, and panting slightly.

"Is something wrong?" I asked, taking him by the chin meeting his eyes with mine.

"I think I've lost my... my, errm, diary." Worry was scrawled across his face, and watching him like this flipped my stomach.

"Don't worry, you probably just left it at mine, it'll turn up," I said, pulling him into my chest and stroking his hair, softly. The tension in his body eased as he leant into me, and I kissed his forehead and let him. "We'll find it – we can go looking at lunch if you like.

Adrian let out a long sigh and nodded. "Promise?"

"I promise," I chuckled and ruffled his hair as we made to leave form. Mr Browns already had an impatient look on his face. Adrian and I separated in the corridor, I was heading down the steps to PE, when I spotted something brown out of the corner of my eye. I went back and there it was, Adrian's funny little leather-bound diary. It must have dropped out of his bag on the way to form. I snatched it up and doubled back on myself. I caught sight of the back of Adrian's blond head just as he stepped out onto the lawn. Strange, I thought, that wasn't the way to his economics class. I jogged down the corridor after him.

"What are you up to?" I said to myself as I slipped out onto the lawn, only to see Adrian push through the tree line, round to the back of the lawn, behind the blossoms.

"Adrian!" I called, but no reply. I padded along the lawn, pushed past the trees, but there was no sign of him. Just the big oak tree in the corner. There were small footprints leading up to it, but then they just stopped. I looked around, but he was no-where to be seen.

"That's weird," I said, thinking aloud. In fact, when it came to Adrian a lot of weird things had been happening. For a start, he's stayed over at my house twice now, but me and Mum have never met any of his family. We don't even know where he lives now that I think about it. And then there was his sister dying, you'd think there would have been a funeral, but he never mentioned one. And last night, outside the restaurant, that man who went flying for no reason. I was sure I'd seen Adrian do something out the corner of my eye, but what could he have done? And now this, just disappearing into thin air.

I lay back in the undergrowth and watched the sky

through the dappled tree light and there it was, in my hand, his diary.

"I shouldn't," I said aloud, raising the book to my eye line.

It'd be an invasion of his privacy, I heard my mother's voice say.

"Oh alright, just the first page," I said, flicking it open. I paused for a second, puzzled – the first page read:

"The order of Excalibur, Index for the categorisation of your charge - by Merlin"

The writing was swoopy, and it looked handwritten. I flicked past the first page and as promised there was an index.

Charges, an introduction p1-2
  The Woodsman p3-6
  The Knight p7-10
  The Hunter p11-15
  The Enchanter p16-20
  The Prince p20-28

I turned to the introduction which read:

. . .

"Once you've found your charge, it is very important to identify what capabilities they might possess. Without this knowledge the Order of Excalibur can't most effectively place them to aid in the greater work of protecting the interests of the fay. Imagine if you will, a Hunter, placed in a laboratory, or worse, a fledgling enchanter being placed on the front lines. As you can imagine, the outcome doesn't bear thinking about."

"Well, this isn't a diary," I mumbled, flicking through the pages as I skimmed the topic about testing the abilities of a woodsman by taking them into challenging forest terrain. Or inviting an enchanter to a holy service to see how she reacts, or inviting a potential prince candidate into a leadership position. Time must have slipped away from me as I heard the school bell ring for the end of first period, but I didn't care. I waited until everyone had disappeared into their second classes, careful not to be seen behind the tree line.

I picked up the book again and then I saw the strangest thing: a human hand, pocking out of the oak tree, and then an arm, and then a whole person, Adrian. I blinked, shook my head, rubbed my eyes, but he was really there. This was really happening.

"Adrian?" I breathed, I could feel my voice trembling. His head shot up, his eyes locked with mine and all the colour drained out of him.

"Michael," he whispered, wide-eyed, like a rabbit in the headlights.

CHAPTER

NINE

"I've got geography now, and you're in economics, right?"

"What? Oh yeah, economics," I mumbled, only half listening as I rooted through my bag for the fourth time in a row.

"Wanna meet up at lunch?" I didn't respond. I couldn't find Merlin's book, I'm sure I'd had it when we left Michael's house, I didn't want his mum finding it. Which meant it must have fallen out of my bag at some point, which means odds are, somewhere in this school was a book all about the order of Excalibur and the fay world.

"Is something wrong?" Michael asked. He took my face in his hands and lifted me out of my bag. There were his eyes, his warm amber eyes. My chest loosened, and I took a breath.

"I think I've lost my... my, errm, diary," I whispered, images of a teacher picking it up and using it to expose the fay world, flashing though my head.

"Don't worry, you probably just left it at mine. It'll turn

up," said Michael, pulling me into his chest. I'm pretty sure that wasn't the case, but the hug was still nice, and he was stroking my hair too. He was so big and yet so gentle and warm. He kissed my forehead and for one blissful second, I hadn't a trouble in the world. I wish I could stay cocooned in his arms forever.

"We'll find it. We can go looking at lunch if you like?" I sighed; he was right, there was no point looking through my bag a fifth time.

"Promise?" I asked.

"I promise," he chuckled and ruffled my hair as we made to leave form. He headed off down the corridor to geography and started towards economics. I hate economics. And there it was: on the way to the economics corridor you have to walk past the lawn, or alternatively, you can *not* do that. Which is what I was doing as I strode out across the lawn, slinked through the blossom trees to stand before the big old oak at the back of the lawn. The perfect gateway for me to slip into the fay world.

I stepped out onto the spiderwebbed path. I couldn't say why but I just needed to speak to Olivier and with any luck Merlin wouldn't be there hovering over us. He was getting more involved recently, I understood why, with fay allying themselves with mirelings he'd be under more pressure than ever. That didn't make his extra involvement feel any less suffocating though.

"Come in!" Olivier called, I hadn't even realised I'd reached her door. One of these days I'd remember to stop and smell the flowers. As I stepped through the doorway, Merlin's words rang in my head. *Not if I have anything to say about it.* Those words had been on my mind a lot. Merlin wasn't going to just let me and Michael be together, but I wasn't going to just let him stop us either.

"So, what brings you to my door Adrian?" asked Olivier, bringing me back to the present. She was peering past an unfurled scroll she was studying.

"I'm... not sure. I was following my instincts." I could hear how stupid it sounded as I said it, but it was true. It was nice to tell someone the unvarnished truth for once.

"Well then, you're probably in the right place, so tell me, have you made any progress with Michael?"

"Nope, not a jot. I don't think I'm very good at this." I laughed and to my surprise, so did she. "You know it took me two weeks before I even spoke to my first charge after I found them. I kept setting up situations where I could bump into them and then deciding it wasn't the perfect time."

"Really? So what happened in the end?"

"I was following her one day and lost track of her. In my panic to find her again, I ended up walking right into her," Olivier chuckled, and I chuckled too and relaxed into my chair.

"Olivier, what happens if a charge doesn't want to join us?" I asked. I knew the official line, that we make every effort to persuade them, but in the end it's their choice, but that was always so disappointingly vague.

"It depends on the charge, and why they don't want to come."

"Say they've got family they don't want to leave behind." The thought of Michael leaving Linda behind played on my mind, wracking me with guilt.

"Oh, that one's quite a common one, it depends how much family they've got. They can always visit their family, we've even brought some charges homes in the still world to act as a cover. Some told their families the truth. On very rare occasions we've even had a charge bring their family here with them. That only really works when there's only one or two family members to speak of."

"What if they told someone, and that someone decided not to keep the secret?" Her face grew a little darker, some small part of me had an idea what was coming next.

"Merlin has… in very dire situations… helped people forget things they should never have known." I nodded. Sometimes it was easier to forget that Merlin had been running our realm for hundreds of years. He made a good show of the harmless old man.

"What about… hypothetically is someone were to say… fall… for their charge?" I found myself whispering without intending to. Olivier's eyes narrowed to slits; her brows furrowed.

"Hypothetically… I'd tell them, now is a very dangerous time to be in the fay world for a charge. What I would never tell them, because it's against the Order of Excalibur, is that if I loved someone, I would keep them as far away from the Order of Excalibur as possible. For as long as I could. Things are looking like they're about to get worse before they get better." Olivier had locked her gaze on mine and there was an intensity in her face I'd never seen before. I quickly got the sense I was being warned.

"Do you, understand what I'm saying Adrian?" Now she was speaking in a whisper. I nodded and stood to leave.

"Speak soon, Adrian," said Olivier. Returning to her scroll, I nodded again, slipped out of the cottage and sagged. All we'd done was talk, but somehow it felt as though we were plotting to overthrow the entire system. At least I knew what I was doing now though, even if it was wildly illegal and I had Olivier to thank for it. Who'd have predicted that?

I meandered back to the grove and stepped through a tree, slipping into the oak on the school lawn, and heard a trembling voice.

"Adrian?" asked Michael, eyes wide, face pale. He looked terrified.

"Michael," I whispered, my heart thundering in my chest as exactly what was happening dawned on me. My legs went weak, sweat formed on my brow, my mouth went dry, and before I could say another word, he was backing away from me. He was trembling. He kept opening his mouth, but no sound was coming out.

"Wait, please, wait." Tears spilled down my cheeks. He didn't, and instead he took off running. I tried to follow but my legs gave way, I crashed headlong into the dirt and sobbed

I didn't know where I was walking; I was just walking. They say it helps you think, to walk, and I needed to think. What had I just seen? Adrian literally walked out of a tree! Either magic was real, and Adrian was magic, or I was absolutely losing my mind. And the crazy thing was I think magic might actually be real – that would explain everything. The random lake that sprung out of the middle of nowhere. Whatever Adrian did to that man to send him flying last night. My leg at the football match, I think I really did get hurt and Adrian must have fixed it.

"He… healed me." I stopped in my tracks and glanced over my shoulder for a second. I wished he was there, I wanted to see him. He'd healed me, and maybe that was why he collapsed. And the man outside the pub, he was protecting me then too, and the lake was a surprise… for me. He was doing it all for me… but then, why not just tell me? I guess it's hard to just out and out tell someone you're magic and you can walk through trees.

But then what about this? I thought, brandishing the

book, arguing with myself. He wasn't doing it all for me; he was categorising me, to work out what kind of useful I was going to be. Is that what I was to him? Some kind of asset to be put to use. That's why he couldn't tell me about it because he was using me.

Then again, it doesn't say anywhere in the book to make a romantic lake setting for your charge… or kiss them… or heal them. Maybe Adrian hadn't been following all the rules, but why would he be breaking the rules? And what about his sister? Did that even happen or was that a lie too? Would he really lie about something like that?

I lay back in the grass. My mind spinning, and it was a while before I realised where I was – looking up through the thick arched canopy. I glanced down the tunnel of trees and there was the lake. I must have walked here on auto pilot; I didn't even realise. I crawled the rest of the way down the tunnel and pulled off my shoes, dipping my feet into the lake.

"He did all this for me," I muttered, watching the dappled light dancing on the water. I needed to speak to him, but where would he be? He could be in a tree for all I know. There were trees literally everywhere. How am I supposed to know which one has Adrian in it? I leaned back on my elbows, feeling hopeless, and kicked water across the lake.

"Fuck me," I groaned, flopping back in the grass, knotting my fingers in it as I dug up great clods of earth. I lost track of time as I lay there, kicking and ripping and generally wallowing in hopelessness as the babbling wall of questions in my head gave way to white noise.

"Michael?"

I sat bolt upright, turned, and there he was. His eyes

were bloodshot red, with tear streaks down his cheeks. His trousers were muddied, one of them ripped at the knee. He was stood in the tunnel, with his hands up as if he was surrendering to me. Everything in me wanted to scoop him up in my arms and kiss his cheek and make everything better.

"Can we talk?" His voice cracked as he spoke. He was begging me, and my heart was breaking.

"I have questions," I replied, and he nodded, folding to his knees in the mouth of the tunnel. He looked exhausted.

"I errm… don't know where to start," I said, letting out a burst of nervous laughter.

"I'm so, so sorry," he said, tears rolling down his cheeks.

My stomach squirmed, I needed to hold him.

"Was it real?" I mumbled, realising that was the most important question.

"Was what real?" he asked. He sounded so afraid, he looked so small.

"Me and you? Was it real? Or was it all just a ploy to get me into the… Excalibur thingy?"

"It was real, it is real," he whispered, blinking more tears from his eyes. A wave of relief washed over me.

"But when we first met, that was for Excalibur, right?"

He nodded.

"It was my job… to find you… but as soon as I did, there was something else – you weren't just my charge, I think… I think I love you."

My heart skipped, there was a lump in my throat, and I swallowed around it.

"So why were you carrying this book with you? If I was more than just a charge?" I asked, glaring down at the book.

"Merlin gave that to me. He was trying to hurry me along, because I wasn't working fast enough." His breathing hiked, panic flashing across his face.

"Weren't going fast enough? You've already spent the night in my house, we've kissed, we're boyfriends already, so what did he want you to do?" Anger was bubbling up inside me, I could feel muscles tensing, not at Adrian but at Merlin.

"He doesn't know about any of that, I wasn't supposed to do any of it. It's all against the rules." Adrian gulped and hung his head, his shoulders trembling.

"Why?" I asked, my voice softening, as I inched closer to him.

"I didn't know what he'd do if he found out. Separate us maybe, assign someone else to you, move things along faster." He sobbed into the muddy ground.

"So you were keeping secrets from everyone?"

He must have felt so alone.

"I had to. I couldn't let what happened to Cynthia happen to you!" his breathing hiked again, he was shaking all over now.

"Your sister? Why would that happen to me?" I asked, inching closer still.

"She wasn't my sister... sorry, she was like my sister though. I'd known her all my life. She was a champion... like you would become. They made her Merlin's personal guard, and she was... murdered."

"Murdered?" I breathed. He nodded.

"And if they'd moved you onto someone else, and they'd taken you to the fay world, that could have happened to you, I couldn't let it. I couldn't, I just…" His voice trailed off. His breathing was ragged, strangled.

"You were protecting me?" I asked, and he nodded weakly, tears spilling out as he looked down.

"And you tripped that thug, didn't you?" He nodded again. I swallowed again, tears were prickling the corners of my eyes. He looked so broken I could hardly bear it.

"And you healed me at the football match, even though it made you sick, didn't you?"

"It just… wore me out," he mumbled, looking up at me again. His twinkling blue eyes were red, raw and full of tears and hurt and I couldn't take another second of it. I grabbed him and pulled him to my chest, his little arms wrapped around me, his hands clinging to me.

"I think I love you too," I whispered. His body shook in my arms for a little while until eventually he went still. I lay back, holding him and let him sleep in my arms.

ELEVEN

I woke with a start, and a bit of a headache. At first, I wasn't too sure where I was – I blinked my eyes; they were sore.

"You're awake. Are you feeling okay?" Michael's voice was soft, concerned. A pang of guilt thundered through me.

"I'm okay," I whispered, sitting up and rubbing my eyes.

"How long was I asleep for?"

"About an hour. What happened to you? You looked pretty rough when you got here." he wasn't pulling away, he didn't even seem mad at me.

"I fell down that hill on the way up here, I couldn't stop crying so I couldn't really see what I was doing." The whole thing had been a nightmare. I'd actually fallen down the hill twice but that seemed a bit too pathetic to say.

"How did you know I was here?"

"I didn't really, I just needed somewhere to go, to think and to hide."

"Me too," my body rocked a little, one of those after-shocks you get when you cry too much, he stroked my hair.

"Do you have more questions?" I was sure he must be curious.

"Well, first things first, could you just like... come through a tree rather than falling down the hill, how does that work?" he asked, curiosity scrawled across his face and perhaps even a hint of excitement.

"Fay, can use trees as doorways, between your world, and ours, but we always leave the same tree we entered through last."

"Oh, so you can just pop up anywhere on Earth then?"

"Not without help. When we pick our first tree we come out of, a dryad helps us."

"So, there are fay and then there are dryads that also help the fay?"

"Not exactly. Dryads are a type of fay, but they're particularly connected to trees. They're probably the most important fay to be honest."

"So what type are you?" he asked, wide eyes and full of wonder.

"I'm a water nymph, sometimes called a naiad."

"That makes so much sense. Are you an important kind of fay?"

"I wouldn't say important, maybe rare." I smiled.

"My boyfriend is a rare and precious naiad," he said, grabbing me and pulling me into a hug. My heart skipped, and I hugged him back.

"We're still boyfriends?" I asked, butterflies flitting in my stomach.

"Of course, we are," he said and smiled as he kissed my forehead. I willed myself not to cry again.

"So, you're not mad at me?" Against all my best intention I was getting my hopes up.

"Well, I was thinking about it all whilst you were asleep, and the way I see it, you never really had any easy choices. You were lying to everyone, which must have been lonely. And you were only lying to the other fay to protect me... so how could I be mad?"

"You're the best boyfriend ever!" I said, tackling him onto his back as I cuddled into his chest. He chuckled and ruffled my hair.

"So the next big question, we know what you are, what am I? Am I an enchanter?" he asked, grinning.

"I don't think so, I never really got to the bottom of what you are. I think maybe a woodsman or a hunter."

"Not a prince?" he asked, mock-pouting at me. I giggled.

"You could be a prince. They're just the rarest." The most typical charges were knights, followed by woodsman, hunters, enchanters and finally the rarest were princes. Merlin was an enchanter.

"What gives away a prince then?"

"Well, they're tricky, in theory, they're a bit of an every-man. Naturally skillful, like a hunter or strong like a woodsman, a leader like a knight. There is a legend that says the first ever charge was a prince, because they have the power to see the true form of a fay creature, even in the still world."

"The true form of a fay? Also, what's the still world?"

"That's just what we call the human world. Yeah, we kind of look a bit different in the fay world, not quite as human. Not crazy three eyes and seven ears or anything, just different."

"Are you bigger in the fay forest?" he asked, catching me a little off guard.

"Nope... at least, I don't think so." Truth be told, I hadn't really thought to check.

"So are all fay small, like you?" Michael asked with a teasing grin creeping across his face.

"There are some, quite a lot smaller actually," I chuckled.

"Really?"

"Yep, like gnomes, they'd only come up to your waist."

"Mum would love this, if she could believe it," Michael said.

"Why d'you think I'm always asking about her gnomes?" I chuckled.

"So you're a big fay then?" Michael asked, still full of curiosity.

"I wouldn't say that, sylphs are big, and dryads are bigger than us too. I guess we are a bit smaller than your average human," I said, talking to myself as much as anything.

"You're not human..." Michael breathed. I realised his eyes had got very wide as I said that part. I nodded, my body growing tense as I waited for him to say something else.

"I should have already picked that up. I suppose it just... it sounds mad when you say it out loud."

"I understand if you're having second thoughts," I breathed, trying to keep the heartbreak from creeping back into my thoughts.

"No, no, it's not that, come here," he said, pulling me tight to his chest again. I sighed as relief washed through me again.

"I thought I'd scared you off then," I said, breathing a sigh of relief and squeezing him back.

"I don't think you ever could," he whispered, stroking my hair. I scrunched his shirt in my hands. Holding him as close as I could as I let silent tears spill down my cheeks, listening to his heartbeat, as time slipped away.

"Can we go?" he said eventually.

"To the forest?" I asked, still muffled by his chest. He let me sit up a little so I could see his face. He was smiling, he looked excited.

"Yep," he nodded.

"You want to see it?" I asked.

"I want to see you," he grinned, rolling over so he was on top of me and kissing me on the nose.

"It could be dangerous for you to be seen there ha ah aha ahahah stop, stop." I wriggled and writhed as he tickled me, first under the arms, then the belly.

"Come on, come on, come on, for me, please, for me," he begged as the relentless onslaught of tickling continued.

"Fine!" I squealed at last when I thought I was about to wet myself from laughter.

"Yay!" He grinned and punched the air.

"But we have to put you in a disguise, hide everything recognisable about you."

"Okay, so how do we do that? Some kind of spell or ritual?" he asked, I chuckled.

"I was thinking more along the lines of a big cloak."

"Oh right, do you have any of those just lying around?"

"I thought your mum might, actually. She does seem to have a great deal of coats."

"Adrian, you're a genius!"

CHAPTER

TWELVE

"So, how do I do this? Do I need to say a spell or something?" I asked, whipping Mum's Halloween witch cloak from two years ago around me. Adrian's ruined uniform had been stowed in my backpack. He'd switched into what he was calling his fay clothes. To me they looked a bit like those posh pyjamas you see people in, a sweepy blue cloak with long droopy sleeves.

"What is it with you and spells?" Adrian chuckled.

"Well, you do magic, what's the difference?"

"Well, it's a little complicated. Most fay are connected to some element of the natural world, me water, dryad with trees, gnomes are good with mushrooms, we can manipulate that sort of stuff.

"Wait, there are gnomes? Mum would love this," I chuckled.

"Yep, there are gnomes. Why do you think I was so obsessed with your mum's garden?" Adrian giggled, and I felt a little lighter. It was good to see him smile again.

"So you were saying about spells?" I asked.

"A spell is something much more specific than what I do with water and harder to do. You could curse someone with blindness or turn them into a frog or change how someone looks drastically." I had to pick my mouth up off the floor. He explained it all so casually, as if it was just a normal thing to know magic was real. I suppose it was to him. I was still half expecting to wake up from a dream.

"So, can you do spells?" I asked.

"Not really, Merlin tried to teach me a couple, but unless you're a born enchanter, it's very hard to grasp."

"Is that what he is?"

"Yep."

"So, he was a charge then, like me?" From what Adrian said, it seemed like Merlin was the one running the show in the fay world. To think once upon a time he was just like me was strange.

"Merlin was the first charge a fay sought out, before that they'd only ever come to us. This was back when we lived amongst you all a little more openly. Although we wouldn't call him a charge now, he'd be a champion."

"A champion? What's that mean?"

"Once a charge has fully graduated, we call them a champion."

"So how did he end up in charge of everything then? Is that 'cause he's a champion?"

"Do you want to go to the fay world, or do you want to continue the history lesson?" Adrian asked, sticking his tongue out at me.

"One last question. I remembered something from a game of Dungeons and Dragons I played," I replied.

"What's that then?"

"Way too complicated to get into right now, but anyway, it's a game and it has fay in it and in that they have all these rules."

"The fay or the game?" Adrian asked, looking confused.

"Both actually, but I'm on about the fay ones, stuff like, a fay can never break their word and if they give you their true name, you can control them. Oh, and they're always out to trick you. Is any of that true?" I asked, although by the look of the grin forming on Adrian's face I could have probably guessed.

"Well, the trickster thing is half right. Remember I said we used to be much more open with the still world?" I nodded.

"Well, we ended up closing ourselves off because… things got a bit violent… to put it lightly. So the story goes anyway, but before it got to that, there was a lot of trickery that went on. Making people think our biggest weakness was learning our secret true name was a great distraction from other actual weaknesses, like being stabbed." I snorted and Adrian flashed a smile.

"So it was all a trick?" I asked.

"Yep, the name thing and the breaking deals, that was a nonsense too. We break deals all the time, I'm probably breaking three or four telling your all this." A pang of guilt shot through me and before I could think I'd pulled him into my chest and planted a kiss on his forehead.

"Thank you, for being honest with me," I whispered.

"Thank you for forgiving me," came Adrian's muffled voice from my chest.

"You're welcome. Now then, I wanna see you, in your world."

"Okay, take my hand."

I did and then he did it – he just stepped into the tree and pulled me along after him. I closed my eyes and braced myself for the hard impact of bark, but there wasn't one.

"We're here," Adrian whispered.

I unclenched, opened my eyes, and my jaw dropped. Trees spread out as far as the eye could see. The whole world was cast in green tinted light, looking up, the whole sky was a sprawling canopy. Before us spread a narrow brownish yellow path that spiderwebbed out ahead in all directions. Beside the path wildflowers grew but not like any I'd ever seen. They towered over me and Adrian, with petals as big as bin lids, in every colour you could imagine. Behind us there was what looked like a grove of particularly thick trees. I could hardly believe my eyes, but then I could smell it too, that softly damp, loamy smell. Like when you go for a walk in the woods after it rained, and I could feel it in the air, the gentle breeze, the cooling shadows the great canopy cast over us.

"Don't look too amazed. Remember, this is just the doorstep," Adrian whispered, slipping his hand into my own as we started off down the path.

"Where are we going?" I asked, just peeking out from behind my hood, careful not to expose my face.

"I thought maybe we'd go to a lake."

"You and lakes." I chuckled, giving his hand a squeeze.

"Well, I am a water nymph. What did you—"

"Lord Adrian, I'd been hoping to run into you." There was a stern voice behind us, and Adrian froze dead in his tracks, I stopped too. A figure cloaked all in blue with gold filigree passed us and rounded so that they were facing us.

They were flanked on either side by two tall, shadowy figures in black robes.

"Caspia, please, just Adrian, I'm must have said it a thousand times, there is no need for the lord stuff."

Adrian was a lord? He'd kept that one pretty quiet.

This Caspia person was quite severe looking, with a large, popped collar. They shared Adrian's almost white-blond hair and blue eyes, though theirs were tinted with green. They had the same slightness Adrian did, but they had a way of seeming imposing in spite of their stature.

"You shouldn't beg, its un-befitting of your position. On the subject of which, you're also missing your Stone of the Naiad. Regardless, as I'm sure you've noticed Merlin's already bloated influence is expanding. Some of us within the courts believe it is time to take a stand."

"I'm sure you do, but do you think now is really the time to be fighting amongst ourselves, with goblin attacks getting more deadly by the day? It's certainly a more pressing concern than my missing brooch," Adrian said. He sounded so forceful and certain, with barely disguised frustration bleeding into his voice. I'd never seen him like this.

"We can't allow Merlin to use our fear of the mireling creatures to control us further. The fate of the fay has rested outside our hands for far too long." Caspia's eyes flashed, and there was aggression in their words. I squeezed Adrian's hand. Things had gone from a cute lake date to goblin attacks and politicking real quick, and I couldn't help thinking it would be bad for Adrian if Caspia noticed I wasn't exactly meant to be here.

"That's as may be, but I'd best be off, charges to... you know, be around. Lovely chatting to you as always Caspia."

Adrian turned on the spot and I followed, although I spotted Caspia bow as we turned away.

"Are we leaving?" I whispered, wrestling panic out of my voice as we reached what felt like a safe distance.

"That was plenty close enough a call for one day, we're just lucky Caspia is snobby enough, they probably assumed you were my retainer or something."

"Which brings me to the next question, you're a lord? Why didn't you tell me you were a lord? Do I need to call you Lord Adrian now?" I grinned, watching his face contort into a cringe.

"It's meaningless rubbish honestly. Some people think that the fay should be ruled by a council of our own, headed up by the fay they consider the purest, truest fay. Purely because that's how things used to be from what I can tell. And in Caspia's case, because it would make them more powerful."

"Who are the purest then?" I asked.

"Well, that pureness thing is all rubbish anyway, but the ones they think are special are water nymphs, sylphs and of course dryads. The elemental fay they call us."

"Caspia is a water nymph, right?"

"What gave it away?" Adrian asked, smiling up at me.

"Their hair and their eyes, they looked like yours do. But if they're a water nymph too, why are they bowing to you, shouldn't you be like... equals or whatever?"

"I have a famous, great, great, great... you got the picture, a lot of greats, grandmother. She was a pretty important water nymph. What did you mean when you said she had similar eyes to mine by the way?"

"They twinkle, the same way yours do," I said, smiling

down at his twinkling eyes. Now that I was really looking at him, I realised his face looked the same as it did that day at the lake when we first kissed. His features somehow seemed carved out, like his face had been planned.

"Wow! You noticed that quick, I was going to ask you if you'd noticed any changes in my face once we'd reached the fay world," he said as we reached the grove of larger trees we'd arrived through.

"What are you talking about? They always twinkle," I chuckled, ruffling his hair.

"Really?" he asked, taking my hand and pulling me back through the tree. The world shifted around us and there we were again, back at the lake. I took his face in my hands and gazed into his eyes, his perfect twinkling blue eyes.

"Yep, still twinkling," I breathed as I leaned closer to him, his fingers laced themselves together behind my neck, my one hand threaded into his hair and our lips met. Soft and warm, my heart raced. I slipped the other arm down resting my hand in the small of his back and pressed further into the kiss. He pressed back at first and then leant back and let me dip him. Somehow, I ended up kneeling with him set on my knee.

"That was good," he breathed as we separated, his half-lidded eyes fixed on my own, his cheeks flushed red. My heart thundered in my ears.

"Let's do it again then."

PART THREE
THE LAKE

CHAPTER

ONE

"Mum is going to be furious," I said, as Adrian switched back to his ruined uniform. As good as he looked in his blue fay robes, it would probably raise too many questions.

"Why?" he asked, as he pulled on his ripped trousers, careful not to poke his foot through the kneehole.

"Skipping school twice in two weeks. We're gonna have to come up with some sort of explanation." I said, trying to think of a plausible excuse. Sadly, I'm not particularly good at that sort of thing and more often than not end up thinking about thinking about excuses.

"She wasn't angry the last time we skipped," Adrian pointed out as he pulled his ruined shirt back on. I winced at the bloodstain on the collar. He must have cut himself when he'd fallen down the hill.

"She let it go the last time 'cause of what happened with your... sister? Should I still say sister?" I asked, worried I sounded insensitive.

"Just say Cynthia." He gave a sad half-smile. I sighed and

forgot all about thinking of excuses to tell Mum as something else Adrian had said to Caspia thundered back into my mind.

"Was it the mirelings you were talking to Caspia about that... happened to Cynthia?" I couldn't quite bring myself to say murdered, it sounded so violent. Adrian nodded, his brows furrowing.

"Yes, it was a goblin attack."

"Is that what mirelings are then? Goblins?" I asked, still half expecting to wake up and have this all be a dream, talking so seriously about magic and goblins. Yesterday I'd have thought I was mad.

"Goblins are the most numerous of the mirelings, but they're not the only ones. They're like a collection of creatures opposed to the fay, we've been in an on and off war with them at the edge of our territory for as long as anyone can remember," Adrian explained, plopping down in the grass as he spoke. I got down next to him and took his hands in mine. His looked so small in mine.

"So that's why it could be dangerous for me to be a champion?"

"Yep, I don't want you to be sent off to fight goblins and ogres just because you met me. It'd be like it was my fault."

"Ogres?" I asked, a little shocked.

"Yep, goblins and ogres and dire spiders and..." He tailed off. He'd blanched a little and his hands were trembling in mine.

"And what Adrian?" I asked, coaxing him on.

"There are rumours, stories really, myths of creatures called hags." His voice shook as he said the words.

"What's a hag?" I asked, giving his hands a squeeze.

"They're like goblins, but bigger and they're supposed to live for hundreds of years. People say they do blood magic, and are the leaders of the mirelings, but I've never met someone who's seen one. The stories say they would take fay children and draw the life out of them and make them into haunted puppets to lure fay away from their homes." Adrian shuddered, his eyes had gone a little distant and glassy.

"Let's stop thinking about that," I said, giving him a peck on the cheek as I helped him to his feet.

"Probably a good idea," he said, giving one more shudder as we set off back down the tunnel of trees to civilisation.

"And hey, we still haven't thought of an excuse for Mum yet, any ideas?" I asked, but Adrian didn't respond. He was eyeing the hill nervously as we approached it.

"Climb on," I said kneeling down in front on him.

"Are you sure?"

"'Course I am, boyfriend duties isn't it, imagine how bad I'd feel if I didn't offer you a ride and you fell down and broke your neck!" I said, only half joking, he did seem particularly clumsy when it came to this hill.

"Okay then," he whispered, climbing aboard and planting a kiss on my cheek as he did.

"Besides, you really are light as a feather," I said as I started negotiating my way down the steep hill.

"I think you're just strong," he whispered in my ear and gave my bicep a little squeeze. I chuckled and flexed my arm for him.

"Oh really? And you like that, do you?"

"Well, it's certainly not a bad thing," he whispered and kissed my now burning cheek.

"Careful, if you keep flirting with me, I might just have to kiss you. Can't let you keep distracting me, we still don't know what to tell Mum!" I grinned as we made it to the bottom of the hill.

"Is that a threat or a promise?" he breathed into my ear. The hairs on my neck stood on end and a shiver ran down my spine.

"Right!" I said, reaching my arm around as I grabbed him and rotated him around my waist, so we were face to face as I carried him through the forest. He gasped as I swung him around and he clung to my neck, his legs wrapping around my waist.

"You were warned," I said as I crashed my lips into his. The kiss was warm and passionate, so much so that I didn't notice as I walked over a root, something snagged, and we were falling. I twisted in mid-air, cradling him in my arms, so we landed on my back and groaned as the wind was knocked out of me. I winced and my eyes clenched shut.

"Are you okay?" Adrian asked. I flinched, opening my eyes and there he was, his brilliant blue twinkling eyes staring back at me, full of concern.

"I'm fine," I chuckled, sitting up and pulling him into my chest.

"Are you okay? That's what I'm worried about."

"Of course I am. You saved me."

"Well, I did promise I'd always be there to rescue you," I said softly, getting up.

"You did," he mumbled as he rooted around the back of my head like a chimp.

"Can I help you with anything?"

"You've got a bump!" he wailed. Now that he mentioned

it, there was a niggling little pain, but it didn't feel like anything, and a second later it was gone.

"It's fine, I can barely feel it," I said, rounding on him, only to find him sagging a little, looking not his usual pale but grey.

"Adrian, you didn't have to do that," I whispered, bracing him at the arms and kissing his forehead. He felt cold.

"It was only a bump, not like your leg. I'll be fine in a minute," he mumbled into my chest.

"Listen, Adrian," I said, taking his face in my hands and looking him in the eye. They were half lidded and blinking slowly.

"This is serious, it was just a little bump, I'd have been okay. I don't want you wearing yourself out like this over little things. I'm worried about you." My voice cracked, and I blinked back tears as my eyes stung.

"I'm sorry, I didn't think," he whispered. My heart broke a little at that.

"I know, it's okay, don't apologise, come on, let's get you home," I said, as I scooped him back up onto my back.

"So any ideas for what we tell Mum?" I asked. All I got in response was a small sigh, I glanced over my shoulder and he was sound asleep.

"Mum, I'm home," I called, as softly as I could as I slipped through the door. There was a moment's rumbling and then there she was at the end of the hallway. She had a face like thunder and looked like she was about to shout up a lung until she noticed Adrian asleep on my back.

"What happened?" she whispered as I carried him into the living room and laid him down on the sofa. Looking at him like that, with ripped, muddied clothes, tired and grey, tear streaks still visible on his cheeks, it'd melt anyone's heart.

"What, sorry?" I whispered, completely distracted by him for a second.

"What happened to Adrian? I assume whatever it is, is why you left school after registration?" she said, sounding concerned.

"Errm, he was…" God I wished I was better at lying. I never did come up with a convincing story.

"I was mugged," came Adrian's little voice from the sofa.

"Oh, my god you poor dear, you rest sweetie," said my mum as she ushered me out of the room and closed the door behind.

"That poor love hasn't got any luck at all has he," said Mum looking back over her shoulder into the other room.

"Hopefully things turn around for him now," I said, a smile creeping across my lips as I thought about the secrets I'd learned today.

"I hope so too. I understand you wanting to look after him. Lord knows I want to wrap him up in cotton wool seeing him like that, but I don't want you skipping school."

"I'm sorry I skipped again," I apologised, although I wasn't really sorry about that. I wanted to apologise for lying to her, but she'd probably think I was losing my mind if I told her the truth anyway.

"Luckily, it's the Easter break from this Friday so you two will have plenty of time to get involved in whatever disasters take your fancy," she laughed, going on her tiptoes as she reached up and ruffled my hair.

"Love you, Mum."

"Love you too, Michael."

CHAPTER
TWO

The final days of term flew by and everyone, even the teachers, gave the impression that the Easter break couldn't come soon enough. I still wasn't entirely sure what an Easter break was.

"So, Michael, Adrian, can we put you down as a yes for Jess and Sam's Easter break party on Friday night?" asked Alex.

"Or you can just come, or not come, it's not like there will be bouncers on the door," Jack chuckled.

"Yes, but I like to know who's going to be there," said Alex.

"Because you're nosey," teased Jack.

"Yes of course, because I'm nosey, why else?" Alex replied, sticking his tongue out.

"I'd like to come," I said, looking to Michael.

"Well then, put us down as a yes Alex," said Michael.

"Adrian's first official Starkton High School house party, how exciting, and it's a Jess and Sam party too, so we're starting off strong." Alex grinned.

"Are they sisters?" I asked, and Michael, Alex and Jack all chuckled.

"Worse, we're lesbians," said either Jess or Sam, as she sat down. I'd only ever been introduced to them together, and it felt too far along now to clarify I'd never actually found out who was who.

"Oooo so you've made it official!" Alex cooed.

"Finally!" said Jack.

"Which means the population of gay couples in the school has gone up by fifty percent," said Jess or Sam.

"The gay agenda at work!" said Michael, and everyone laughed.

"Right, we'd best scoot off," said Jack as he and Alex stood to leave.

"And I need to go find Jess," said Sam, for which I was very grateful.

"See ya gang," said Michael, taking my hand as we made our way out of the school gates.

"So I've got to run some errands in the forest," I said.

"Can I come?" pleaded Michael.

"Not this time. I've got to visit a particularly observant individual, much too risky."

"Okay, well, see you tomorrow then, and you can come round to mine after so we can get ready for Sam and Jess' party together."

"Sounds fun," I whispered, leaning up to kiss him. His arms snaked around my waist, and he lifted me clean off the ground as our lips met. He held me for I don't know how long as we kissed, pressing into each other. Shivers ran down my back as I dug my fingers into his shirt. My heart thundered in my ears, his face was red, and he almost looked dazed.

"Sorry, got a bit carried away there," he said, giving a shy smile.

"We should get carried away more often," I said, reluctantly planting one last kiss on his cheek before I turned off the path towards the thickest tree I could see.

Our kiss was still playing on my mind as I reached Olivier's cottage and stepped inside.

"Ah perfect, Adrian, hold this chair steady," she said, posed awkwardly on a three-legged stool craning to reach a high shelf.

"Why do you have shelves up higher than you can reach?" I asked as I steadied her stool.

"Because there is already stuff on the shelves I can reach," she said, snatching down a large scroll and hopping off her chair.

"Take a seat, Adrian. What did you want to talk to me about?"

"I wondered if I could talk to you about something... off the record." I lowered my voice.

"As you know Adrian, everything you tell me I have a duty to report to Merlin, should he ask."

"Of course, I understand," I said, feeling defeated.

"However, memory is not a perfect thing. I can't very well report something I forgot, or misremembered. Wrong information is even more dangerous than no information, after all." As she spoke, she was running her eyes over her scroll, careful not to meet my own.

"I see... well... hypothetically speaking, if someone was to fall for a charge."

"Sorry, did you say fall on a charge?" she asked, not looking up from her scroll, although I was sure she winked, almost imperceptibly.

"And some hypothetical person was interested in keeping that charge safe… by any means necessary."

"Of course, the safety of our charges is of paramount importance."

"But what if, whilst some hypothetical person was spending time with their charge, they started to suspect their charge was a… prince type." Olivier's eyes froze. She didn't look up from her scroll, but she'd clearly stopped reading it, or stopped pretending to read it.

"Hypothetically, I would say that if anyone, on any side were to find out that information, it could be very dangerous indeed," she whispered before dropping her scroll and beginning to root through her desk drawers.

"I think you should go now, Adrian," she whispered, crossing from behind her desk, taking my hand and pressing something cold and hard into it.

"Thanks for the chat about falling princesses, Olivier," I mumbled, embarrassed at my own silly excuse for a cover story.

"One more thing, before you go."

"Yes?" I asked as she grabbed me and pulled me in for a hug.

"A prisoner dryad, involved in the death of Cynthia, was being kept in The Hut and she's escaped. She's capable of powerful disguises. Be careful Adrian, trust no one," she whispered into my ear during the most prolonged hug she had ever given me.

"See you, Adrian," she said, as if she hadn't just told me

there was a murderer in disguise on the loose, and went back to her desk.

"Bye, Olivier," I said, slipping out of her house and hurrying back, suddenly feeling on edge every time a tree rustled. Just as I reached the grove, something sharp poked my hand. I opened it and for the first time, I looked at what Olivier had given me. I froze, my eyes grew wide, and I hurtled through the tree.

CHAPTER
THREE

I couldn't get to sleep. I needed to take off my winter duvet, but I kept forgetting and now I was too tired and too hot as I shifted around under the sheets, failing to get comfortable. I'd already stripped down to my boxer shorts, but it hadn't made any difference.

As I ripped off the duvet entirely, I heard a clacking sound. I sat up blinking my eyes against the darkness, but there was nothing. Then that clacking sound again. I switched on my bedside lamp and rubbed my bleary eyes as it dazzled me. Then the clacking again, it was coming from the window. I stumbled out of bed and opened the window, poking my head out.

"Ouch!" I winced as a pebble struck me on the chin.

"Sorry!" I heard someone hiss from the front garden.

"Adrian?" I asked, just about making him out by the glow of the streetlights.

"Let me in, it's urgent," he hissed.

"Okay, wait there." I pulled on my sweatpant shorts and crept downstairs, stubbing my toe on Mum's newest addition to the garden gnome collection, which she'd not painted yet as I went. I got to the door, prayed to whoever was listening that it was quiet and unlocked it, pushing the door open. There was Adrian, in the doorway, still in his fay robes which was unusual, he'd usually change before he came back to our world.

"You look nice," he whispered as he stepped through the doorway.

"I've not got anything on."

"Exactly," he said, resting his hands on my chest as he lent up and gave me a peck on the cheek, and I chuckled.

"I thought you said there was something urgent," I whispered as my arm snaked around his waist, resting my hand on the nape of his neck.

"Oh right! Where can we go so your mum won't hear us?" he whispered. I led him through to the living room. It was the furthest we could get from Mum's room in the house.

"So, what's the urgent news?"

"Well, there's two things. I've got bad news and... well I wouldn't call it good news, but it's better than the bad news." He was fiddling with something in his hands, he seemed on edge.

"Bad news first," I said, pulling him close to me, holding his hands in my own, trying to calm him a little.

"Okay, well, when Cynthia was... you know..." already I could see his eyes going misty.

"Uhum..." I nodded encouragement.

"Well, there was a whole gang of attackers, mostly goblins, but some fay, including two dryads and a water nymph. Merlin managed to capture one of the dryads."

"Okay, I'm with you so far," I said, watching his face closely, nervousness was written all over him.

"Well, that dryad escaped, and they're on the loose. People are looking for them, I think but... they're out there somewhere." He was whispering again, like he thought someone was listening in on us.

"Okay, do you at least know who it is, who to look for? If you see them, you can just run for it, right?"

"Oh, I know who it is, its Minoty, she's a member of one of the courts, like Caspia, but that's not the problem. The problem is she can disguise herself. She could be right next to you, and you wouldn't know. She could be anyone." There was a creaking sound in the other room and Adrian jumped and cowered.

"Come 'ere, it's just the pipes," I said, sitting him in my lap as I pulled him into a tight hug.

"Promise?" he whispered.

"I promise," I said, kissing his forehead.

"Okay," he mumbled, snuggling into me as I stroked his hair.

"So, what's the other news?" I asked once he'd calmed down a little.

"Olivier gave me this," he whispered, holding out a small rock attached to a chain, like a pendant necklace.

"What is it?"

"It's a shard of Excalibur."

"The legendary sword?" I asked, confused, as it didn't look like it came from a sword.

"No, the sword wasn't Excalibur, the stone was. Every charge gets given a shard once they've graduated to become a champion. This was Cynthia's I think," he whispered, turning it over in his hand.

"So, why did she give you that?"

"I don't know really, it's super illegal, I shouldn't have this, I think Olivier wanted me to give it to you," he said, pressing it into my hand. It felt strangely warm to touch.

"What should I do with it?" I asked, rubbing my thumb over the jagged edge of the stone.

"A shard of Excalibur, in the hands of a charge or a champion, can become a kind of weapon. With a bit of practice, you'll be able to defend yourself in case… in case something bad happens," he whispered, his big, worried eyes fixed on the stone.

"Well then, I'd best hold on to it," I said, slipping the chain over my head.

"What d'ya think?"

"It suits you," he said, looking relieved as he got back to his feet and dusted his cloak off, his hands trembling.

"What are you doing?" I asked, taking his trembling hands in mine again.

"I'd better be going before your mum catches us," he whispered.

"Are you mad? I'm not letting you go back to the fay world on your own. You just said there is a crazed, disguised murderer on the loose. You're staying here with me," I said, grabbing him and pulling him back into my lap.

"Your mum will be angry," he protested feebly.

"We'll tell her you were home alone and got scared. She won't mind," I said, picking him up bridal style.

"What are you doing?" he giggled, playing with the stone which now rested on my chest.

"Carrying my boyfriend up to bed. What does it look like?" I whispered as I crept back up the stairs with him in my arms. I didn't feel right leaving him on his own in Dan's room, so Adrian slept in mine that night. He made the cutest little whistling sound when he slept.

FOUR

In the end, Mum didn't even notice. She was out the door before we even got up for school. Adrian was like my shadow that day at school. He was waiting for me outside of class at every bell. I'm not convinced he went to any of his own classes at all, but it was Easter and he was a fay lord. I don't suppose he really cared all that much about failing economics. It wasn't like I could blame him anyway. The person who'd murdered the woman he'd considered his sister was free and somewhere in disguise. I'd be a nervous wreck.

"So, what happens at these parties then?" Adrian asked as I rang Jess' parents' doorbell.

"Well, typically we play drinking games, try and fail to make cocktails, play video games with drinking game rules and one time I woke up in a field."

"Well, I love drinks, and I've never woken up in a field, but I've woken up in a tree before. Do you think they'll have tea?" asked Adrian as the door swung open.

"Course we do babe," said Sam, who was standing in the door, her hair set in two large buns.

"Your hair looks amazing!" Adrian said, smiling as she let us through the door.

"Thanks, I'd wear it like this all the time, but my form tutor says it looks unprofessional. Anyway, Jess is in the kitchen, she'll make you a brew," said Sam, ushering Adrian through the door.

"How can hair be unprofessional? It's just your hair," I said, stepping through the doorway.

"It's code," Sam snarled.

"It's bullshit is what it is," said Alex, appearing from the living room.

"Michael, did you bring gifts?" he asked, his eyes going straight to the plastic bag at my side. I chuckled.

"Want to share?" I asked, producing a bottle of vodka from the bag.

"No, I don't, as it happens, I've brought my own, but the more the merrier." He grinned and took a swig of what looked like red wine.

"How did you get drinks anyway, Michael? Aren't you only a wittle baby seventeen-year-old?"

"Yes, he is, but he's a six foot something wittle baby, with shoulders as wide as a door frame," said Alex, taking another swig.

"True, true, how do you drink that stuff anyway?" asked Sam, grimacing.

"Practice makes perfect!" He grinned, finishing the glass.

"His whole family love it, they throw these dinner parties every other week where they just get trollied," said Jack, appearing in the door.

"Family bonding!" declared Alex.

"Yes, well, we've got everything set up for a game of waterfall. You coming?" said Jack as Sam and Alex disappeared into the living room.

"I'm just gonna go find Adrian," I said, heading for the kitchen.

"So where are your parents anyway?" asked Adrian. He was swaying back and forth a little, holding a suspiciously blue bottle of something to his lips, speaking to Jess. Who looked like she was struggling to stifle a laugh.

"They've gone out for the night, left us to it," she said, sipping her own drink.

"There you are, what have you been up to?" I said, crossing to Adrian and steadying him.

"I've been trying the drinks!" he said, grinning. His teeth had gone blue.

"I see that," I chuckled.

"He drinks very fast, doesn't he?" said Jess, grinning.

"That he does," I agreed, pushing his hair out of his half-lidded eyes.

"I've never had a blue drink before," said Adrian, polishing off the bottle and plopping it onto the kitchen counter.

"How many of those have you had?" I asked.

"That was his third," said Jess, clearly enjoying the sight of fresh meat.

"Third in the time, since you came to the kitchen?"

"They were blue!" explained Adrian excitedly as he gave me a big kiss on the neck. I think he'd been aiming for my cheek, but he missed.

"Sorry he drank all those, Jess," I said as I grabbed a glass of my own.

"Oh, don't be, they're disgusting, and I gave them to him, see you in there," she said, filing out of the kitchen

"I feel much more relaxed now, Michael," whispered Adrian as she left the room.

"I bet you do," I chuckled, pouring myself a vodka and coke.

"Ooo, can I have one?"

"Okay, but you've gotta go slow with it," I said, pouring him a particularly weak drink. He nodded, making a cross over his heart with his finger.

Shortly after we joined the others in the front room playing waterfall. Which was a ridiculously complicated drinking game. Luckily Adrian couldn't follow at all, so he quickly fell asleep.

"Is he okay?" asked Alex, who'd scooted his way round to me over the course of the night as people had gradually passed out.

"Why d'ya ask?" I said, sipping my coke, with one hand rested on Adrian's back, who was now passed out in my lap.

"I saw him today in school and he seemed a bit stressed. I said hi to him, and he nearly jumped out of his skin."

"Oh yeah, he's been a bit... anxious. I'm actually dying for the loo. Do you mind watching him whilst I'm gone?" I asked, slipping a pillow under Adrian's head where my leg had been.

"Sure," he said and shrugged, and I got to my feet to nip to the loo. On the way back into the room I heard laughter, Adrian's laughter, it sounded so sweet I sat outside the door to listen.

"Hey A-Alex dy-dyou want to see a magic trick?" I heard him stumble through the sentence and chuckled to myself as his slurred words until it hit me what he'd said as he burst through the door.

"No!" I said, louder than I meant to. Adrian and Alex looked up at me shocked. Adrian, by the looks of things, was in the middle of doing a very bad job of that trick with your fingers, where you make it look like you've detached your thumb. He was just bumping his fists together.

"Something wrong?" asked Alex, looking startled.

"I err... never mind." I said scooting back over to Adrian.

"I think it's meant to be more like this," said Jack, who seemed half asleep, as he performed an impressively perfect example of the thumb trick with his eyes closed.

"T-tea anyone?" Adrian said, clumsily getting to his feet and staggering out of the room.

"He should not be around boiling water," mumbled Alex, slumping on the sofa.

"Flammable!" blurted Jack, slightly incoherently. I chuckled and followed Adrian into the kitchen, where he already had the kettle boiling.

"Close the door," he whispered, giggling as he drew a glass of water from the tap.

"What are you up to?" I asked, closing the door.

"I'm showing you a magic trick," he said and grinned, and as steam started billowing out of the kettle, he chucked the water into the air. I flinched, expecting to get splashed, but it never came. Adrian had held his hands out, water floating in the air in front of him, little droplets suspended within the kettle's steam.

"And if I just." He stuck his tongue out, concentration

written across his face as he slowly twisted his hands. The water and the steam shifted in the air in front of the kitchen light and suddenly there it was. A rainbow twinkling in the kitchen.

"For you," he said, smiling at me.

"It's beautiful," I said, grabbing him and pulling him into me before he tripped over something.

"Will you make the tea?" he asked, yawning.

"Sure thing, as long as you get all that in the sink," I chuckled.

"What a waste that would be," he mumbled, plunging his hand into the water and steam, only for it to all absorb into him.

"You can do that?" I asked, wide eyed.

"Course I can. I'm a water nymph," he mumbled as he stumbled his way out of the room. I brought the tea through and found him curled up on the sofa. I climbed on behind him and pulled him into my body as we both drifted off to sleep.

FIVE

As it turned out, Easter half term was truly bliss, no economics, no school at all, and Linda had agreed to let me stay in Dan's old room for the whole break. Michael had told her that whilst I was home alone, someone had broken in, and now I didn't feel safe sleeping alone, which was only half of a lie.

"Ice cream?" I asked, perplexed as we sat out in the park that bordered Starkton wood, on what was an unseasonably warm mid-April day.

"Yeah, it's like sugary frozen cream stuff… its much nicer than it sounds."

"I was sold at frozen. Can we get some?"

"Sure, you gonna help me up?" Michael asked, as he sat up on his elbows, squinting into the sun. He was wearing a short sleeve white shirt and blue jeans shorts and I'd not been able to take my eyes off him all day. I took his outstretched hand in both of mine and heaved with all my might, leaning back on my heels.

"Come on, put your back into it," he said and grinned, having barely moved an inch.

"I'm putting my everything into it!" I laughed as I gave up and staggered forwards, plopping down next to him in the grass.

"Am I too big for you?"

"You're too heavy," I whined, flopping my head into his lap, gazing up into his smiling amber eyes.

"That'll be on account of my big muscles," he said and grinned, flexing a bicep. It bulged, his t-shirt sleeve straining around it. My breath jumped for a second as I felt blood rush to my cheeks.

"Oh, you like that do you?" he laughed, jumping up and slinging me over his shoulder.

"Hey, what are you doing?"

"Showing off for my boyfriend," he laughed.

"I think you like that I like it," I whispered, tracing patterns on his back with my fingers as he carried me off.

"Maybe I do," he whispered, before coming to an abrupt halt and turning on the spot so I was facing the ice cream truck.

"You're ordering."

"And you're not going to put me down, are you?"

"Nope," Michael chuckled. I stifled a giggle as I looked over the ice cream menu, trying not to make eye contact with the ice cream man.

"A double scoop of chocolate with a Flake for him please, and can I have that blue bubble looking ice lolly thing?" I said, handing over some money as I fought the urge to drool looking at the shiny blue ice lolly. I'm not sure exactly what flavour it is that humans have assigned to blue, but I love it.

"How did you know my favourite flavour was chocolate?" Michael asked as he carried me back to our spot.

"Whenever you make tea, you always eat chocolate digestives," I said, planting a kiss on his cheek as he sat me back down on our picnic blanket.

"Is there any other way?" he chuckled, licking his ice cream.

"Not that I know of, but then I did learn from you," I laughed and began sucking on my blue ice pop.

"You know that'll turn your tongue blue, right?" asked Michael.

"Blue is my favourite colour," I said, smiling, and there was a pause, as something seemed to have caught Michael's eye. I looked over my shoulder but there was just a woman walking her two slightly angry looking little dogs.

"Why? Don't you like my blue tongue?" I laughed, but Michael still didn't reply. Ice cream was dripping down his hand.

"Michael, is something wrong?" I whispered, touching my hand to his chin, turning his eyes to face mine, and for a split second I could have sworn they flashed golden.

"Adrian, what does a dryad look like?" His voice was low, and his eyes had flitted back to the woman with her dogs. A shiver ran down my spine, the muscles in my chest tightening as my breath became shallow.

"Dark thick hair, almost always knotted, with green along the scalp, a bit like moss or lichen, earthy copperish skin, green eyes," I whispered, a tear trickling down my cheek as fear coursed through my stiffening body.

"Adrian, I think that woman is the dryad you were telling me about. It's like... when the sun hits her a certain way, she's this blonde lady and then she shimmers, like a holographic card and she looks just like what you're describing," he breathed, taking my trembling hands in his. "I'm guessing those dogs aren't really dogs then?" I whispered, resisting the urge to take another look.

"They're little green things with massive heads and loads of teeth... way too many teeth," he whispered.

"Goblin mutts," I whimpered, my voice trembling.

"Adrian, let's get you out of here," Michael whispered, slowly getting to his feet, his eyes still fixed on the lady behind me.

"We can't. She's trying to create chaos, to damage Merlin's ability to maintain order... she's going to attack people in the still world." I gulped, struggling to swallow around the lump in my throat as sweat beaded on my brow.

"How are we gonna stop her though? We can't very well just jump a woman in the park," he whispered, his eyes still fixed on her.

"Lead her away," I replied, my legs trembling as I got to my feet.

"Adrian, what are you doing?" Michael whispered, his eyes now back on me as panic flickered across his face. I couldn't reply, I'd screwed up all my courage for what came next.

"Hey, Minoty, you're a disgrace to the nobility of the dryad! Long live Cynthia!" I yelled, sure that'd get under her skin.

"Are you mad?" Michael said, wide-eyed.

"It worked," I whispered. Minoty's eyes were fixed on me, her angry little yappy dogs snarling.

"Merlin's favourite naiad," she snarled.

"Run!" I yelled, yanking Michael by the hand as I charged off into the forest's tree line.

"Is she following?" I called. Michael was already overtaking me, dragging me behind him.

"She's not just following, she's gaining. What's step two of the plan?" he yelled.

"I wasn't sure step one would work; I didn't get to Ahhhh—" Suddenly I was hurtling through the air, my face hit dirt and I skidded through the mud. Looking behind me a vine had twisted itself around my ankle, my fall had torn it up at the root.

"What happened?" Michael said, planting himself between me and Minoty.

"Dryads can do with trees what I do with water. Look out!" I called, struggling to get to my feet.

"Adrian, stay back," said Michael as one of her goblin mutts charged towards him. Before it could reach him, he side-stepped it and booted it through the air like a football.

"That was amazing, you're amazing," I said, watching as the mutt landed with a thud.

"So, this is your charge, Adrian." Minoty sneered, her fingers flexing as roots surged up, entwining themselves forming a staff in her hands.

"I'm his boyfriend. You leave him alone," Michael snarled as Minoty began to close on us. Her second mutt leading the charge.

"Use the shard of Excalibur," I said, drawing as much water from inside myself as I could spare and gathering it into the palm of my hand.

"Now where did you get a thing like that," said Minoty,

who'd stopped dead in her tracks, giving her mutt the order to pause.

"My boyfriend gave it to me," said Michael, a smile curling on his lips as he grabbed the shard of Excalibur from around his neck. With the mutt frozen, I took my chance and loosed my water. It impacted the stationary mutt, sending it skidding against a tree with a satisfying thud.

"Thanks for staying still for me," I attempted to taunt her, but I think the tremble in my voice gave me away.

"Adrian... how do I make it... work?" Michael hissed behind his hand as Minoty gave a venomous cackle.

"All that power and no idea what to do with it," she screeched as she charged, swinging her staff at me. Michael pushed me aside, taking the brunt of the hit to his ribs. He groaned and sagged as she delivered a jap to his stomach and swept the staff under his feet, sending Michael crashing onto his back winded.

"Leave him alone," I yelled, charging at her without a thought in my head except to get her off Michael. She swung her staff down, cracking it against my shoulder, and my vision went white as I sunk to my knees, and something was driven into my throat. I winced, choking as she pinned me to the ground, the butt of her staff pressed into my neck. I grabbed at the staff and tried to push it off, but I couldn't budge it.

"I'm going to enjoy watching Merlin mourn you," she said and grinned as she jammed it deeper into my neck. I squirmed, struggling to breathe, blackness starting to encroach on the edges of my vision.

Suddenly Minoty screamed as a glittering silver shield

slammed into her hip, sending her tumbling through the dirt.

"Adrian, Adrian, are you okay?" Michael asked, pulling me into his lap as he kneeled behind me, tears pooling in his eyes.

"Adrian, I'm so sorry I let her hurt you." I coughed, struggling to clear my throat. "You made it work, you're amazing," I croaked.

"It was watching her hurt you, I couldn't bear it and then something inside me just clicked and here was this shield. I feel like Captain America!"

I heaved myself into a sitting position, only to see one of her mutts charging at Michael over his shoulder. Minoty's illusion had dropped and the goblin mutt's rows of fangs were terrifyingly visible.

"Look out!" I yelled, as it launched itself, lodging its teeth into Michael's arm. Michael gave a howl of agony as he whipped around, ramming the shield into the mutt, it whimpered and collapsed into the dirt. "Are you okay?" I asked, my eyes filling with tears. Michael groaned tenderly, touching a finger to his bleeding arm. I gathered more water into the palm of my hand, reaching across him to his wound.

Michael pushed me aside. The next thing I knew, Minoty was on top of him, holding the staff horizontally as she pressed down on his neck. Michael managed to force her back only for her to kick him in the wounded arm, and he groaned, his arms giving way. Minoty slammed her staff triumphantly, into his throat. My blood ran cold as I watched her crush it into his neck, his face turning purple. I staggered forward, water gathering at my hand. I crept up behind her and wrapped my hand around her mouth.

"You won't hurt anyone anymore," I croaked in a hoarse, broken voice, forcing the water into her mouth and nose.

She let go of Michael, grabbing at my wrist, struggling to push me away. Cold hate coursed through me, and I kicked her in the leg. She crumpled backwards off balance and as she fell back, I forced more water in, until eventually her strength began to leave her.

"Adrian, Adrian that's enough," I heard someone say in the far distance, but I didn't respond. I couldn't.

"For Cynthia," I mumbled, as a tear trickled down my nose, dropping onto Minoty's struggling face.

"Adrian, STOP!" Michael grabbed me, pulling me away, I sagged into his arms as the hatred left me. Suddenly I was lightheaded, I felt weak, trembly and dry. Minoty was coughing and spluttering across the forest floor, and then she went still.

"Adrian, it's okay, she's passed out," Michael whispered into my ear, wrapping his good arm around me. I turned to look at him, his eyes were bloodshot, his face red, his neck was bruising, and blood was pouring from his left arm.

"You're hurt," I whimpered, then focused on the tears streaming down my face, guiding them to my fingertips.

"You're not looking so great yourself," he whispered, giving a croaky laugh.

"What a pair we are," I groaned, slowly raising my arm to Michael's wound. I knew he'd stop me if he realised what I was doing.

"How are we going to explain this one?"

"I'll leave that to you," I whispered as I forced all the

water I could muster into my hand and placed it over his wound, letting it seep in, healing him.

"Adrian, no stop, Adrian, Adrian, Adrian!" His voice grew quiet and distant as darkness enclosed around my vision. My arm went numb, and the world went black.

"Please be okay, please be okay, please be okay," I repeated, over and over as I ran through the forest, carrying Adrian bridal style; I'd never seen him this bad. He looked thin, grey, and almost hollow. I couldn't tell if I was imagining things, but he even felt lighter than usual. "Adrian, tell me what you need," I pleaded as tears prickled my eyes. "Please, Adrian." A tear dropped onto his face and to my surprise, soaked in. "Water! You need water!" I yelled, my voice still cracking and hoarse as I sprinted towards my house. It took everything in me not to kick the door down when I got home. "Mum let me in!" I yelled, my voice breaking painfully. There was a rustling behind the door, and then it swung open.

"Did you forget your keys aga — Oh my god what happened?" said Mum. Her eyes were wide with shock as I pushed past her, carrying Adrian upstairs into the bath-room, where I laid him down in the bath and started both taps running.

"What on earth are you doing? What happened to

Adrian? He needs a doctor, not a bath!" she said, reaching for her phone.

"Who are you calling?" I asked, keeping one eye on Adrian as colour slowly started to return to his cheeks.

"An ambulance, of course."

"No, Mum, you can't call an ambulance. It's too dangerous."

"Michael, I don't know what's happened, but you're clearly in shock and I am calling an ambulance." Mum's hand was trembling as she went to dial.

"No, Mum, you can't!" I yelled, slapping her phone out of her hand.

"Michael, what the hell has gotten into you?" she asked, reaching for the phone.

"Mum, he's a water nymph," I heard myself say, my mouth moving faster than my mind.

"He's a what?!" she said, looking at me as though she was looking at someone who'd just lost their mind.

"It's difficult to explain. I shouldn't have said that, can you just... just wait until he wakes up?" I slumped down onto the toilet seat as a wave of exhaustion washed over me. Mum knelt in front of me, placing her hands on my knees.

"Michael, I'm worried about you. You come barging through the house with Adrian in your arms and dump him, fully clothed, in the bath. You look like someone's choked you and you're covered in dirt, and oh my god there's blood on your shirt! Then you slap my phone out of my hand and now you're talking nonsense about water nymphs."

"It's my fault," came a tiny, strangled voice from the bath. Adrian was struggling to sit up and shivering a little.

"Adrian, it's not your fault," I said, kneeling as I took his hand and kissed it.

"Adrian, sweetie, do you want to get out of the bath?" Mum asked, kneeling next to me.

"Not just yet." His voice was so small, it tore at me.

"Adrian, why sweetie, you're shivering?" Mum asked, reaching over and turning off the cold tap.

"It's easier if I just show you," he mumbled, submerging his hands beneath the surface of the water. The bath bubbled for a second and then three large globes of water emerged and floated in the air. Adrian let go a shaky exhale and they popped, as he let himself sink back under the water.

"H-how did he do that?" stuttered Mum, as she absentmindedly swished warm water around the bath for Adrian.

"He's a water nymph, Mum."

"What does that mean?"

"Why don't we let Adrian rest and I'll explain downstairs, Mum?" I said, reaching over and kissing Adrian on the cheek as I ushered Mum back downstairs.

Mum's face was a picture.

"Okay, so Adrian lives in another world, on the other side of a tree, and he came here to find you to recruit you. Then he fell in love with you, and now he doesn't want to take you back because he says it's dangerous. Then, someone from his world came through the tree to cause trouble and he tried to lead them away and you ended up fighting. So, you got hurt, and he healed you and passed out, just like that football match in the rain. And also, he's the son of the wizard Merlin from all the legends, and also, he's a prince?" Mum asked, counting off the things she needed to remember on her fingers after about half an hour of my rambling.

"Not quite, but you're getting the main points. Merlin isn't his dad though. He's like his pushy boss," I explained.

"I don't like that getting involved with him has got you hurt, Michael," Mum said, in her rarely used stern voice, my stomach twisted anxiously.

"That's not his fault though, he was just doing his job, and he's been trying to protect me from all of it for ages."

"Well, he isn't doing a very good job is he," Mum jibed.

"If they hadn't sent Adrian, they'd have sent someone else, someone who wouldn't have risked their life to save me. I might have already been taken to the fay world and probably would have died fighting some random goblin or something. If it weren't for Adrian, I'd probably be dead," I snapped.

"Michael, don't say things like that."

"Why? It's true, Adrian's been breaking his back to keep me out of harm's way pretty much since we met." I frowned, sagging as the image of him drowning Minoty flashed through my mind.

"You know when you say about Merlin—"

"Mum, we've been over this already, he's just Adrian's boss, not his dad for the hundredth time," I said, letting exasperation get the best of me.

"No not that, I just mean, you don't think it's THE Merlin, you know, the one from all the stories, the one the BBC did that show about?" She put special emphasis on the THE.

"I hadn't really thought..." I paused for a moment. As

part of my mind began trying to convince me that we weren't dealing with a real life honest to goodness legend.

"I liked him in that show, you know, I always thought he seemed a bit gay," Mum said, absentmindedly. I agreed of course, although now didn't seem like the time to discuss our Merlin fan theories.

"I suppose he could be THE Merlin... at least in theory, but he doesn't seem much like he was on the BBC..." I said. My mind was racing as I tried to avoid the idea that I'd somehow ended up in a feud with a legendary wizard. All the while, part of me was screaming that I'd gone completely mad.

"Strange to think of Merlin as the bad guy," said Mum.

"'The bad guy' seems a bit dramatic, although Adrian certainly seems to think he's worth lying to."

"Well, the main thing is, as long as Adrian isn't trying to take my boy away from me, I suppose we can still be friends," Mum said, wrapping her arms around me as she peppered me with kisses.

"I think he's much more interested in keeping me here and sticking around our world than taking me back."

"But what about his family and friends?"

"I don't know really, he's never mentioned them, and from what I can tell, he's been pretty much lying to everyone he's close to for my sake."

"That poor love, that's a lot of weight to put on his tiny shoulders."

"That's why I've been trying to keep him around here, where he has nothing to worry about. Especially once he heard about some murderer in disguise lurking in the forest."

"But she found him anyway, right?"

"Actually, Michael kind of found her," Adrian said, making his way down the stairs in one of Mum's fluffy dressing gowns.

"How's that work then?" Mum asked.

"Michael can see what fay people truly look like, even if we've disguised ourselves," Adrian explained, slowly lowering himself into the chair. He moved gingerly, like his body was sore.

"Is that to do with you being a charger thingy?"

"I think so, we're still sort of working out what I can do," I explained, still not entirely sure how it all worked myself.

"It's to do with him being a prince," Adrian said gravely. I think we'd both sort of realised it, but we'd been avoiding saying it out loud, admitting it seemed dangerous.

"What's that mean then?" Mum asked, looking confused again. I hadn't got round to talking about the different types of champion.

"The only types of charges, or champions, that can always see the true face of a fay are prince types," said Adrian, his eyes were low, like he didn't want to look at me, it was making my stomach squirm.

"So does Adrian look different?" Mum asked, turning her gaze on Adrian, and fixing him with an analytical stare.

"What do his eyes look like to you Mum?"

"Nice, pale blue eyes, why, what do they look like to you?" I crossed the room and took Adrian's face in my hands, he resisted but only for a second. There were tears threatening to spill out as I gazed into his eyes.

"They're shimmering blue, almost… iridescent, and they twinkle," I breathed, losing myself in his eyes, a tear rolling down his cheeks as they turned a pinkish hue. "Don't cry," I whispered, as more tears tumbled out.

"Oh, like those contact lenses you see people wear!" Mum said, oblivious.

"Sort of, but if they looked... real."

"Linda, do you mind if I have a moment with Michael?" Adrian croaked. There was a certain sad softness to his voice that made my palms sweat.

"No trouble, sweetie," she said, ruffling his hair as she made her way out of the room. "I think I might take a nap; I'm half expecting to wake up and this all be a dream. Love that gown on you by the way, Adrian, you've got great taste in dressing gowns." She chuckled to herself as she made her way up the stairs.

"Well, she's taking this better than I did," I said with a little laugh, but the look on Adrian's face sapped the mirth out of the room.

"Adrian, what's wrong?" I whispered, my voice starting to tremble. I didn't even know why, he took a deep breath, his eyes were already swimming with tears again.

"I've been thinking," he breathed, his voice already shaking. "I've been thinking that maybe... you'd be better off if I went away."

"Adrian what are tal—"

"Olivier is the only person that knows you're a prince type, and with everything in the fay world being as crazy as it is right now, if you're lucky you might just slip through the cracks. I could go somewhere far away, and... and..." Tears were streaming down his cheeks, and his breathing was ragged, like he was struggling to catch his breath.

"Adrian, I don't want any of that. Why would you do

that?" I said, grabbing him by the arms, fixing his sparkling blue eyes with my own, blinking stinging tears out of my eyes. He swallowed and gulped.

"I'm ruining your life," he sobbed, tremors rocking his exhausted body.

"Since you've met me, I've been nothing but trouble, skipping school, lying to your mum. You nearly got murdered today in the woods and it could still get worse. I'm so sorry, I'm ruining your life." My stomach wrenched as he apologised, his face was twisted with guilt, it was heart-breaking.

"Adrian, just wai—"

"I've been thinking maybe it wasn't so bad, maybe I was worth it, but watching Minoty on top of you, I just know I'm not worth that. I'm so sorry, Michael, I'm going to make it right. I'm goin—"

"Adrian, please stop!" I barked. He froze, like a startled animal, tears as big as peas rolling down his cheeks, I pulled him into my chest and stroked his hair.

"Adrian, you're not going anywhere," I whispered as his sobbing tremors shook his body in my arms.

"But I—"

"Adrian please, just listen to me," I said, cutting him off. I couldn't let him say any more horrible things about himself, it was too painful. I let him go and met his eyes with mine, wiping the tears from his cheeks. "Adrian, before I met you, I was so lonely, I'd been lonely for so long I didn't even realise it anymore. I had Mum at home and friends at school, but I was alone. Nobody knew me, nobody saw me, not since Dad…" I breathed, steadying myself. "Not since Dad died. Mum did her best, but I could always see it in her eyes, this panic, that me and Dan wouldn't get what we needed, it's like she's been in a spin for the past two years. So, I didn't show her the bad parts, only a smile, because I couldn't bear to worry her anymore. And the people at school they just didn't look at me the same after that, it's like it created distance and little by little you end up alone. Surrounded by sympathetic faces but totally alone.

"Nobody knew me anymore, not really, they knew I was tall and played football and my dad died in a car crash. They didn't know how I felt, I didn't even know how I felt, I was just going through the motions, go to school, play football, come home, go to bed, rinse, and repeat. I wasn't living anymore I was just surviving. And then I met you, Adrian. I remember the day I first saw you it was like a spark, like someone lit a match in a dark room and there you were. That day with you on the lawn, I felt warm, like for years I'd be in the cold, alone in the dark and then someone brought me into the sunlight. You showed me the sun, Adrian. I look back on it now and it's like the whole world was just shades of grey and now with you, everything's in colour. I don't care if it's dangerous, I want to be with you. Please, Adrian, don't make me go back to being alone in the dark. I'd rather live one more day with you in the sun than ever go back to surviving without you."

I sank to my knees. I hadn't even noticed my shirt was wet with tears. My chest was tight, there was a lump in my throat, I could hardly swallow, I could hardly breathe. "Please, Adrian, don't leave me in the darkness." I whispered, as my voice strangled me into silence. I let my head drop. There was a pause, it seemed like it would stretch on into infinity, just trembling breaths and sobs.

"I'll stay," he said, wrapping his arms around me as I rested my head against his chest. His fingers ran through my hair and my chest started to loosen.

"Promise?"

"I promise," he whispered, kissing my cheek as he squeezed me as tight as he could, which was adorably loose.

"I love you, Adrian," I said, flopping onto my side, so we were lying face to face on the floor.

"I love you too, Michael," he whispered as he pressed his lips to mine.

SEVEN

I spent that night in Michael's room. My body was still aching all over and my head was pounding. I'd never used that much water before, and I was in no hurry to do it again. I think I'd have slept until noon, but Michael woke with a start around sevenish, the morning light just poking through his curtains.

"She's still out there!" he said, his chest heaving as a trickle of sweat ran down his neck. I sat up bleary eyed and heaved my aching arms up to rub away the sleep.

"Who is?" I yawned, smacking my dry lips together.

"Minoty," he said, reaching over me to peek out the window. It took me a moment to process what he was saying. Everything from yesterday was a little foggy.

"Oh shit," I whispered as it suddenly dawned on me and I too poked my head over to peek out the window, but there was nobody there.

"Do you think she'll come for revenge?" asked Michael as he fiddled with the window lock.

"I don't know. I don't think she'd like to face off against

you again now that you've got the hang of this though," I said, poking at the lump of Excalibur that hung around his neck.

"If anyone scared her off, I think it was you," said Michael, picking me up and moving me to the other side of the bed as he did.

"What are you doing?" I asked as he lifted me up.

"I don't want you by the window where she could get to you," he said, still glaring at the curtains. I chuckled and kissed his cheek.

"If she did come for revenge, I think she'd do it in the forest, not in your house, silly."

"Well, it's always better to be safe than sorry," he said, chuckling as he pinned me to the bed and peppered me with kisses. From then we dozed for a few more hours in between waking up for the occasional cuddle before finally rising. I took another bath to try and ease some of the aches and pains but to no avail.

"Michael, do you fancy another trip into the fay world?" I asked him when he'd finished his shower. I'd taken to flicking through some football sticker book thing in an attempt not to ogle him in a towel.

"Anything for you, but won't that be dangerous?" he asked, stretching in such a way that his body rippled. My stomach squirmed, and I nearly rammed my face into something called a David Beckham trivia page, whatever that is. I'm sure I saw a grin flick across his lips as I averted my gaze.

"I think I need to pay a visit to a special lake; I can't shake this feeling of being drained," I said, slumping against the wall.

"Are you okay?" he asked, concern shooting across his face as he paused halfway through pulling on his sweatpant shorts.

"I'm fine, just worn down. I should probably just go alone," I said, resting my eyes for a moment.

"No chance, Minoty could still be out there. I'm coming with you," said Michael, pulling on the long Halloween cloak over a hoodie.

I'm not sure what possessed us, but we ended up cutting through the forest back to where we'd fought Minoty the previous day before heading to the fay world.

"There's no sign of her," said Michael as we reached where we thought we remembered having our fight.

"There is no sign of anything," I said, scanning the forest. There was no blood, no scuff marks, no goblin mutts, no Minoty, nothing.

"Maybe we're just in the wrong place."

"Maybe, or maybe someone tidied her up. Let's not wait around to find out," I said, grabbing Michael's hand and pulling him through a tree. Something about being back there had set my teeth on edge.

"So how do we get to this lake, do you have directions?" Michael asked as he popped his hood up, careful to keep his face down.

"When you're in the fay world, you don't really need to know the way to somewhere, so much as have permission to be there," I explained.

"How do you mean?"

"It's kind of the magic of the paths, it's ancient and

confusing. The main thing is, if you have permission to be somewhere, all you need to do is think about going there and set off," I said, taking Michael's hand as we strode onto one of the many web-like paths of the forest.

"How do I get permission?"

"You have to get it from someone with authority over that place."

"Where can we find one of those then, and how do we get permission from them without, you know, giving away who I am?"

"You're holding the hand of someone with authority over this particular lake," I said, giving him a little wink.

"Oh, is this a Lord Adrian thing?" he asked, flashing me a smile from under his hood.

"I would say this place is the one and only perk of that," I chuckled, gesturing broadly to the lake.

"Oh my god, we're here, how did that happen?" Michael asked, forgetting he was supposed to be hiding his face as he looked up, surveying the lake. It stretched out far into the forest, bordered on all sides by trees with the end almost too far away to make out, like the lake edge met the canopy of the forest. In the centre stood a large, jagged stone, which glinted green in the dappled half-light.

"Like I said, think where you're going, and you just sort of end up there," I said, stripping out of my fay world robes into my blue bubble shorts I'd snuck underneath.

"Aren't we worried about me getting caught?" Michael asked, looking around nervously.

"There is only one other person here and they won't figure it out," I explained.

"Fair enough," said Michael as he began haphazardly

chucking off layers of clothes. He reminded me of his mother, shedding layers of coats and scarves as she got home from work.

"Follow me," I said, striding into the water, a tingle running up my body as my feet submerged. I shuddered and plunged deeper until the water came to my waist. Michael waded in after me splashing about as he went.

"So, where are we then?" he asked as he reached me.

"You remember the lady of the lake, from the Arthurian mythology we covered in English?" I asked, watching water trickle down my arm as I lifted it out of the water.

"Yep, the one that gave Arthur the sword Excalibur, which turned out actually to be a rock," said Michael, who was floating like a starfish on his back.

"Yep, well, this is the lake, and that is the rock," I said, pointing to the jagged stone.

"You're kidding me!" he said, standing bolt upright as he looked around, wide eyed.

"Nope, you're currently splashing around in Lake Nimueh," I said, before submerging completely in the water. I sighed, taking a deep breath as I let it fill me up, for the first time since the fight I felt life rushing through me. Michael popped his head under too, waving at me with squinty eyes and a big grin on his face, I chuckled and re-emerged.

"So this place is like, super important then?" he said, slicking his hair back.

"One of the most important places in the whole of the fay real," came a familiar, imperious voice from behind us. I turned slowly and bowed.

"Lady Nimueh," I said, nudging Michael in the rib so that he bowed too.

"Adrian, who is this that you have brought here?" asked Nimueh, her sapphire eyes appraised Michael coldly. She wore a translucent diaphanous blue gown which billowed behind her as she strode through the water, her plaited white-blonde hair dragging behind.

"My guard," I lied.

"He isn't wearing the appropriate uniform for a guard; you should rectify that."

"Yes, you're right, I'll look into it," I said, feeling myself stiffening up in her presence. Out of the corner of my eye I could see Michael, avoiding her eye contact.

"Give my regards to Olivier," said Nimueh, before she swept off towards Excalibur, quickly submerging into the water.

"Nimueh as in… the lady of the lake who gave Excalibur to Arthur, that Nimueh?" asked Michael, inching closer towards me.

"No actually, she was alive hundreds of years ago, but the name Nimueh is passed down through the women in my family." I squirted water in Michael's face, giggling, but he was frozen in shock.

"Adrian… was that your Mum?" he asked as water dripped off the end of his nose.

"Technically, yes."

"Technically, what do you mean technically? Why was she so weird? Why didn't you say something? Why didn't you tell me we'd be meeting your Mum?" Michael asked, looking back over his shoulder, I shrugged tugging his hand, so he looked back at me.

"Fay families aren't quite like human families, we're all raised by the community. Nimueh didn't really have anything to do with it to be honest. She never leaves the lake. And as for why she was weird, she's always like that."

"So, your mum and dad didn't raise you?"

"Nope, we all sort of raise each other, as there aren't very many fay born each year. Nimueh has a half-sister. She probably had the most to do with me," I explained.

"Nimueh reminded me of that Caspia person," Michael said, looking over his shoulder again.

"Oh yes, her and Caspia probably get on like a house on fire. Nimueh very much believes in royal fay bloodlines and all that rubbish," I said, descending into the water to blow bubbles, which gradually grew to the size of footballs, drifting up out of the lake.

"Okay, I have just one more question," Michael said, poking at one of my bubbles as it drifted past his face.

"Oh yes?"

"I'm your guard, am I?" he asked, grinning, as heat rushed to my face.

"I had to say something quick. It was the first thing that came to mind," I said, embarrassment curling my face into a cringe.

"Bodyguard Michael reporting for duty, sir." Michael stood to attention bolt upright and saluted.

"You're evil," I whined.

"Oh no, sir, there are hostiles incoming, but don't worry, my body shall shield you!" said Michael in a strange accent before he jumped on me. I giggled.

"Get down, sir!" he yelled as he plunged me under the water.

CHAPTER
EIGHT

Adrian had been getting better since the trip to the lake but knowing Minoty was still out there somewhere had made it hard to want to leave the house for the last couple days. Not that I was complaining about having an excuse to keep my boyfriend home with me. Especially on mornings when I woke with him in my arms, his head on my chest, his messy white, blond hair tousled in his face. When the doorbell rang, Mum had already left for work, she always left early on Monday. I slipped out from beneath Adrian, handing him a pillow to cuddle.

"What's happening?" he murmured, rubbing his dazzling blue eyes as he sat up in bed, still half asleep.

"Nothing, just somebody at the door. Go back to sleep," I whispered, giving him a kiss on the cheek before I headed for the stairs. I tried to straighten myself out a bit as I went, although I'm not sure how respectable I could really make myself look in sweatpant shorts and a vest. So I gave up and opened the door.

"Hello young man, is there a Michael Tombs here at all?" In the door stood a squat man, with receding brownish hair. He would have looked wholly unremarkable were it not for his striking grey eyes. He was wearing a police officer's uniform.

"That's me, sir," I said, my mouth going dry, as the police always made me nervous.

"I wonder, you wouldn't mind if I came in and had a few words with you, would you?" he asked in such a way that it felt more like an instruction than a request.

"Errm well, I'm under eighteen and my mum's not home at the moment, so... don't I need an adult present?" I fumbled to remember the rules from the police shows Mum had on constantly.

"Oh, it's nothing serious, we're just going to have a little chat," he said, stepping through the doorway, I froze. As the light shifted across his face, for a second, he was tall, taller than me and slim, with salt and pepper black hair, wearing a patterned leather chest plate. My breath caught in my chest. I clenched my fists, trying not to lose it as my mind started to race. Why would a fay be here, and who were they?

"Just this way," I said, leading him through into the kitchen as the hairs on my neck stood on end, my heart pounding so hard I thought for sure he'd hear it. I grabbed the chunk of Excalibur from round my neck. From where he was sitting at the counter, I could see straight through to the stairs behind him. Adrian had crept down halfway and was watching, huddled under one of my hoodies, which was way too big for him.

"So, Mickey, can I call you Mickey?" I nodded, although I'd rather he didn't.

"We've been investigating the disappearance of a certain Minty Oak. Who witnesses say was last seen following you and another boy into Starkton wood on Saturday. We believe his name was Adrian."

"How do you know that?" I asked, my fingers tightening round the jagged piece of rock in my hand. Already cursing the words as they slipped out. Why did I say that? I shouldn't have said anything, no comment, deny everything. Like on the telly.

"So, it's true then, and would that Adrian be around to speak to me?" he asked, ignoring my question. He took out a notebook and began rummaging through his pockets for something else. "You haven't got a pen to hand, have you? I seem to have misplaced mine."

"No, and no he wouldn't, not here anyway, he doesn't live here," I lied, terribly, trying to keep my eyes on the disguised man as behind him I could see Adrian creeping back up the stairs as quietly as he could.

"I see, well if you see him, let him know I'm looking for him. In the meantime, why was Minty following you into the woods that day?" he asked.

"Well… you see… it was her dog! Her dog was chasing me, and she followed it," I lied again. Something about the look on his face told me he knew I was lying.

"And what happened then?" he asked.

"I lost her and the dog in the woods and when I went back to the park, she was gone." Somehow, admitting she beat the crap out of us, and Adrian nearly drowned her in the woods didn't seem like the way to go. Although part of me wanted to rub it in his face, big bad Minoty, beat by my boyfriend.

"I see. You didn't meet her in the woods at all, did you?" he asked, his piercing eyes fixing on me. The image of the squat police officer faltering again as the taller, leather armoured man leaned across the counter towards me.

"Nope." I said, choosing not to embellish as it was getting me nowhere.

"Very well," he said, standing suddenly and starting back towards the door. I tensed, Adrian had gone back up the stairs now, but he was still walking in Adrian's direction.

"Is that all?" I asked, following just behind him, my hand balled so tightly around the shard that it was a wonder it didn't cut into my palm. If he went for the stairs I was gonna hit him. He wasn't getting to Adrian, no way.

"That's all," he said, reaching the door and turning on the spot to face me again.

"Okay, well bye then," I said, reaching across him to push the door open.

"In the meantime, if you remember anything else, you're always welcome to come and find me, and do let Adrian know I'm waiting to hear from him," he said. His eyes momentarily flicking up to the ceiling below my bedroom on the second floor, then back to me. My heart leapt into my throat and I felt like I might choke or shove him out the door, I wasn't sure which.

"Yes, sir," I said, sweat beading on my brow.

"You've been an absolute prince of a lad," he said, as he stepped out. I slammed the door behind him a little harder than I should have, as my heart jumped into my throat. I charged back up the stairs to my room, where Adrian was waiting on the bed.

"Fay?" Adrian asked, his eyes wide with panic.

"Yes. They were in disguise, like Minoty." My heart was crashing about in my chest, and this time it had nothing to do with Adrian being on my bed.

"What did they look like?" Adrian fiddled nervously with the droopy sleeves of the hoodie.

"Tall, salt and pepper hair, and wearing a leather breastplate. Oh, and grey eyes."

The colour drained from Adrian's face.

"Merlin."

CHAPTER
NINE

"Michael, I'm home," I called as I stepped through the door, discarding my shoes and my big puffer coat by the door in a heap. I unwound my scarf, draping it over the banister as I passed and dropped my bag with a thud as I stepped into the kitchen. Wreckage strewn all about, old tea bags piled hire next to the tea bag dish rather than on it. Empty biscuit wrappers and crumbs all around, milk splashes on the counter. Like a tea making tornado had passed through here. Still, no-one had replied to my calls so I followed the wreckage into the living room. There I found Adrian and Michael. Adrian had a large mug of tea in his hands and was staring into it so intently it was as if he was expecting it to unveil hidden secrets. Michael was pacing up and down the room and from the looks of it, had a bit of a sweat on. Neither of them seemed to have noticed my arrival.

"There is no way he actually interviewed real witnesses right, that's crazy, can we at least establish that much," said

Michael, gesturing as if he was drawing on some imaginary whiteboard.

"He's got Minoty, I'm sure of it. That's why there was no sign of her in the woods," said Adrian, pulling down Michael's hoodie over his face so he became a single black lump on the sofa. Poor love didn't seem to have any clothes of his own.

"So, he didn't come here to learn anything about that anyway, that was a whole pack of lies."

"For sure," said Adrian the lump.

"Which means he came here for some other reason."

"I'm telling you; it was to intimidate us and let us know he knows what we're up to, he's trying to scare us," said Adrian, flopping over backwards onto the sofa.

"But would he really reveal his hand like that? Wouldn't it be better if we didn't know he knew we were lying?"

"It doesn't matter if we know because it's hopeless. There's nothing we can do about it," moaned Adrian, slapping his sleeved hands over his face.

"It can't be, I'm not letting him take you back there without me."

"And I'm not letting him force you into our stupid war with the mireling creatures, no way," said Adrian, sitting up again and taking a huge gulp of tea.

"So, what do we do then?" said Michael, flopping down on the floor.

"I don't know, we're going in circles," said Adrian, discarding his empty mug.

"You could always flee to Mexico. That's what they do in the movies," I joked, announcing my presence.

"Mum! When did you get here?" asked Michael, looking shocked.

"Hello, Linda," said Adrian, who'd again completely wrapped himself up in the hoodie.

"Long enough to know you boys are in a bit of a panic. Wanna tell me what's up?" I asked, heading for the kettle to make everyone another cup of tea.

"Merlin came to the house, Mum, disguised as a police officer. I spoke to him, Adrian was hiding," Michael said.

"But he knew I was here," said Adrian the lump.

"And he knows I'm a prince type, I can just tell."

"And he knows I've been lying to him about Michael."

"And we don't know what to do about it," said Michael, flopping back on the floor.

"Well, Michael, first things first. You need a shower, you've got a right sweat on, and maybe you'll have an idea. I do all my best thinking in the shower," I said, pouring Adrian a new giant mug of tea. Michael gave his pits a sniff and then recoiled in disgust which elicited a giggle from Adrian. The two of them really were adorable together.

"Right Adrian, let me see if I can get to the bottom of this then," I said, handing him his tea as Michael padded upstairs.

"Okay then," Adrian said, sipping his tea.

"So, this Merlin fella, is he the king or something, of the fay?" I asked, trying to get an idea of just how important he was.

"Not really, we haven't had a ruling king or queen for hundreds of years," said Adrian.

"So, what is he then?"

"He is the person in charge of the Excalibur system and the Excalibur system is in charge of our military, so he's sort of in charge of our military."

"So you were part of the military then? Don't take this the wrong way Adrian, but you don't seem like much of a soldier." A little smile tugged at his lips.

"The Excalibur system finds charges that become champions, and champions are Merlin's weapon of choice. He funnels them into the military. I'm not in it myself, I'm just an agent."

"How did you get that job then?" I asked, curiosity getting the better of me.

"Would you believe it was my boyish looks?" he asked, his shoulders finally relaxing slightly he gulped his tea.

"No really, go one, tell me, did you have to write a CV?"

"No really, it was my boyish looks, a lot of its to do with being a type of fay that can pass for human, which means water nymphs and dryads usually. We tried it with sylphs but they're sort off... long in all the wrong places."

"How d'you mean?"

"Their arms and legs are a bit... spidery, hands tend to dangle passed their knees," he said with a distant look in his eye.

"Oh, I see how that could be a problem," I chuckled, imagining spindly men with arms like orangutans. Adrian didn't laugh along with me, he'd gone quiet. "So, once they'd narrowed it down to water nymphs and dryads, they decided you were the best one for the job, did they?" I asked, trying to tease the smile back onto his face.

"Not really, I wouldn't have said so anyway. I got the job because Merlin wanted me to," he said as his eyes dropped.

"Why's that then?"

"I was his favourite," he whispered, his voice shaking. I couldn't put my finger on what it was I could hear, fear, sadness, nothing good. I didn't think it was a good idea to press him on that anymore.

"So, he wants my Michael to join his military?" I asked, trying to get up back on track. He nodded; his eyes were still down, and he was at risk of crying into his tea.

"But you don't want that," I whispered, putting a hand on his shoulder. He took a deep, shaky breath and then it all spilled out.

"It's dangerous. Mirelings are more dangerous than ever, champions are dying, my friend died, I don't want Michael to die fighting some pointless skirmish with an ogre, all because he met me. I can't let Merlin have him, I won't." He took another sip of his tea, his hands shaking, and my stomach was churning. Whoever this Merlin bloke was, he wanted to take my Michael. There's no way I could let that happen.

"So, how do they normally get people like Michael to come with them willingly?" I asked, trying to keep him talking.

"Some of them want to. They get to see a whole new world and they get to be important, and they get magical powers, that's enough for some people. Some of them live sort of half-lives, half with us and half in the human world. And then there are the rumours." Adrian gulped another mouthful of tea.

"Rumours of what?" I asked, a knot twisting in my stomach.

"There are stories of Merlin... messing with people's

memories. To make them forget families they might be leaving behind. I don't know if it's true but... I think it is. I think he'd be capable of that." Adrian's breath started to quicken and become irregular.

"But you said he has lots of enemies, people who don't agree with the way he does things? People who think someone else should be in charge?" I asked, trying to distract him from whatever scary story he was obviously remembering.

"Well, yes, there are some within the major courts, they're related to the families that used to run the fay before Merlin. They still have a lot of respect, Merlin can't completely ignore them. The whole place kind of runs on who has the most authority and respect. There're a couple of underground groups too, that are more... violent, the followers of the fairy queen. They are the people who lost the civil war Merlin won to gain control of the fay. There's also the never king people. They think the Excalibur system is waiting for a charge to be found to supplant Merlin. They believe Merlin is trying to stop that happening. Then there are the mirelings, who hate all fay."

"Sounds like he's not all that popular at all then."

"He's getting less and less recently. The underground groups have been getting more active and the mirelings have been getting more violent. Some people think he's losing control." My heart leapt.

"Hang on a second, Adrian. You said there are under-ground groups, as in ones that Merlin can't find that are defying him, inside the fay world?" Adrian nodded, putting down as his tea. I could see the penny dropping for him.

"So, you just need to find out how they're doing it. Is there anyone you could talk to who would know?" I asked, watching Adrian's face, you could see the gears turning, the seed of an idea germinating. "Anyone who knows everyone? Who's plugged into what's happening, current events and all that? Who might be willing to help you?"

"Olivier... Olivier might know something," Adrian whispered.

"Who's that?" I asked.

"She's... my friend. She's my boss actually. She monitors all the fay going on their first mission to find charges, but she's sort of an information hub too."

"And would she help you? With Michael?" I asked, excitement building in my chest.

"I think she would... she sort of already has," Adrian said.

"Any progress?" Michael shouted padding back down the stairs in only a towel. He'd never admit it but I'm sure he did that to show off for Adrian.

"We're going to see Olivier," Adrian said, a cute little blush had appeared on his cheeks now Michael had presented himself looking all wet, and I chuckled.

"Well, you two, be careful, look after each other. For heaven's sake, put some clothes on Michael before you give poor Adrian a heart attack."

"Muuummm." Michael gave his embarrassed groan, setting me off laughing as I left them to it. I knew what they were doing was dangerous, but if there was anything I learned from my time with my David, it was this. Once you've found your person, you've got to fight for every second you can get with them, you'll regret it if you don't. A tear rolled down my cheek, and I touched a hand to the picture of David I kept by my bed.

"You'd be so proud of him, David," I whispered, as I lay back on my bed and let out a shaky sigh.

TEN

"Okay, so when we get to Olivier's, let me do the talking. I think she'll be on our side, but she is a bit of a stickler. The less we remind her how many rules we're breaking, the better," I said.

"Is she a water nymph too?" Michael asked, barely bothering to conceal his excitement as he pulled on the Halloween cloak.

"She's actually half water nymph, half gnome, which is pretty rare."

"Is it rare because water nymphs are supposed to be elemental fay, or whatever which are super special, and gnomes aren't?"

"Yep, although some of us think that's a load of rubbish, I certainly do. Still, there are some stupid hang-ups about mingling, but Olivier is probably the best fay I know," I said as I looked around to make sure we weren't being watched and dragged Michael through the tree.

"What's she like?" Michael asked, keeping his head bowed as we made our way down one of the many sprawling paths. He took my hand, his were firm, strong and rough, with callused palms. He said he got them from visiting Jim. I'd yet to get to the bottom of who Jim was, but Michael always got a cheeky grin on his face when he said it. So I guessed Jim must be funny.

"She's strict, she's nosey, she's a stickler for the rules. She's smart, she never says more than she needs to, she doesn't like it when people linger outside her cottage."

"Come in!" called Olivier's voice from inside.

"That was quick," said Michael, looking around bewildered.

"Oh yeah, I'm not sure how she managed to swing it, but I swear you can't get anywhere quicker than you can to her cottage. It's like she lives round every corner." I laughed as I pushed the cottage door open.

"So, what brings you here today, Adrian, and I assume this is the guard Nimueh sent a uniform for," said Olivier, gesturing to a set of weaved leather armour with blue accents that bore the family crest. A jagged rock in the centre of a rippling pool.

"That was nice of her," said Michael, who was already stripping out of the Halloween cloak. I averted my gaze as best I could, but there is only so much you can do to stop wandering eyes. Heat burnt across my cheeks as I took in his physique, a little hair across the chest and torso, muscled but not bulky. He was a bit like a statue, one that was warm and gave good hugs.

"She probably just didn't want me embarrassing her by having an inappropriately outfitted guard," I said, distracting myself.

"Ahem!" Olivier cleared her throat, not especially subtly reminding us she was there.

"Ah right... yes, why we're here, well... you see, you remember the secret hypothetical prince charge that someone might have hypothetically fallen for... that would be best kept a hypothetical secret?" I asked. Olivier rolled her eyes and nodded. "Well, imagine a certain powerful... grey-eyed person knew about them now, and we were trying to work out what to do next... hypothetically!"

"Yes, I think we all get that it's hypothetical Adrian, so let me get this straight. The hypothetical secret is not a secret anymore and now you want to know how to defy a ruling power?" she asked with a raised eyebrow.

"Would it help if I said I was hypothetically completely lost?" asked Michael and he shoved his head through one of the sleeve holes of his new armour. I giggled and started helping him put it on properly.

"Adrian, what are you asking me for?" asked Olivier, clearly less amused.

"Well, I don't know how to keep Michael away from Merlin anymore, but I still don't want him being shipped off to the frontline to die in some pointless skirmish with an ogre. So I got to thinking well, and I realised we can hide from him. It's clearly possible because of, well, you know, The Fairy Queen lot and the Once and Never King bunch."

"So, what you're asking me is if I, one of Merlin's trusted lieutenants, am connected to his most dangerous and secretive opponents. So that you and your boyfriend can go and live in hiding."

"Well... when you put it like that, it does sound a little—"

"Sounds mad, doesn't it," said Michael, finally popping his head through the head hole.

"So, you're saying you don't have any idea how to reach out to them?" I asked, watching her expression carefully, noting she hadn't denied having those connections.

"What I'm saying is I think you've overlooked a simpler solution," said Olivier, deftly dodging my question.

"What's that then?" asked Michael, plopping down in the seat opposite Olivier's desk. Obviously forgetting to let me do the talking, not that I was making much progress, anyway.

"Well, whilst Merlin does hold the most authority among the fay, there are still select members of the community who it would cost him to oppose."

"And who are they?" Michael asked.

"Well, the keeper of the grove and chief authority of the dryads, for one. The matriarch of the Sylvens who're responsible for fay intelligence networks and finally—"

"Nimueh…" I breathed as the penny began to drop.

"Exactly, surely it's worth speaking to her before you become an underground rebel. I heard she was in the market for a new guard after what happened at the lake with Cynthia," said Olivier.

"Do you think she'd help us? She seemed a bit… distant," Michael said, frowning.

"We could present it as us doing her a favour," I said, thinking aloud as an idea took shape in my mind.

"How so?" Michael asked.

"If there is one thing Nimueh cares about it's her status, and there could be no better status symbol then her personal guard being not only a champion, but a prince."

"The first prince champion to be declared in decades," added Olivier.

"You mean I'd become her personal guard?" Michael asked, looking confused.

"Exactly. If Merlin ever tried to take her personal guard off her it would kick up a right fuss and you'd be kept away from the front lines and me and you could have constant access," I said, excitement washing through me.

"And it would be easy for Adrian to get you back to your mother, when it suited," added Olivier.

"You know about my mother?" Michael asked.

"Oh, course I do, Michael Tombs, it is a pleasure to meet you at long last," said Olivier, winking over her spectacles.

ELEVEN

"Well, I like her," I said as I fiddled with the straps on my new chest plate. It was nice not having to keep my head under a hood, I got to have a look around. The fay forest was wild, trees that reached up into the sky, blanketing the world in green. It wasn't dark, but it was cast in half-light, with the occasionally twinkling shaft of pure light peeking through. The floor was a field of moss-covered stones, tall grass and an ever-present yellow path. Wildflowers as big as a traffic light and mushrooms the size of stools lined it's edges. Back home the forest was mostly brown and usually wet and muddy, here everything felt so alive.

"And she's a genius! I can't believe I didn't think of this before," said Adrian, who had only let go of my hand for a moment since we'd left the cottage, to shove a little sparkling sapphire brooch onto his chest; otherwise, he'd had my fingers in a death grip. He wasn't enjoying the forest like me. He was constantly looking over his shoulder, jumping at every creaking tree trunk or snapping twig.

"Yeah, you'd think we'd have thought to go to your mother before now," I said with a chuckle.

"The fact I'm her son will have very little sway on the situation," said Adrian, before freezing and ducking down behind a rock, dragging me down with him.

"What is it?" I hissed.

"I don't know… maybe just the wind." He spoke slowly, his eyes wild. Looking out for Merlin constantly was starting to get to him.

"Adrian, look," I said as I picked a flower, a little purple one, with a yellow centre, and held it up for him to smell. I wasn't sure exactly what I was doing, but Adrian definitely needed a distraction. He paused for a second and then breathed in the scent, letting out a long shaky sigh.

"I never do stop and smell the flowers," he said, his eyes going a little misty as he straightened up again.

"Well, you've had a lot of plates to keep spinning," I said.

"What? I've never spun a plate," said Adrian, looking utterly bewildered.

"You don't have plate spinning here?" I asked, shocked. I think I'd just started assuming everything you did at a summer fete happened in the fay world. Summer fetes somehow seemed very fay.

"We barely even eat off them," Adrian chuckled as we crested a hill, and the lake came into view.

"It is beautiful," I said, imagining a future where I worked there wasn't so bad really and Adrian could feel safe.

"Do you think Mum could visit?" I asked.

"I don't see why not, we'd just have to keep her out of

Nimueh's way," said Adrian as he started down the hill, tripped on a rock and almost fell.

"Careful there, Lord Adrian," I said, grabbing him and scooping him up in my arms bridal style. A blush burned its way across his face almost instantly.

"You don't have to call me that," he said, burying his face in my chest plate.

"I see you like the new armour," I chuckled

"It does sort of show off your... well, everything," he mumbled, running his fingers along the straps.

"It's good to see the crest on a suitable bearer again," Nimueh's voice cut through the air like a knife.

"Nimueh," Adrian said, I hesitated before planting him on the floor, he bowed, and I quickly copied. It didn't make sense to me that Adrian had to bow to his own mother, but we were trying to win her over after all.

"So, what brings you here again, so soon after your last visit?" Nimueh asked, turning her back to us as she made her way to the lake. We followed.

"I've heard that you were considering bringing on a permanent guard. Since the attack on Merlin near the lake," Adrian said, his tone changed around her. He seemed distant, it was like watching a wall go up. I hated it.

"That's true, but finding the right champion that's befitting of the position has proved challenging," said Nimueh, stepping into the water, allowing her flowing blue gown to billow behind her.

"Well, I believe I might have a solution for you, Michael. Michael Tombs might be the perfect candidate," he said, giving my hand a squeeze. I squeezed back.

"And why would your charge be the perfect candidate,

Adrian? As far as I know he hasn't even graduated to a champion as yet?" she said, slowly drifting further into the water, she was up to her shoulders now.

"He's a prince." As the words left Adrian's lips something changed; the air was suddenly charged. She wheeled around and for the first time, she was truly looking at me. Her eyes were just like Adrian's, perhaps a hair lighter, but with none of his kindness, and they didn't sparkle, they flashed. When she looked at me now, it wasn't like she was looking at a person, it was as though she'd seen something she was hungry for.

"And Merlin hasn't claimed you yet? Michael Tombs?" My name dripped off her tongue like venom. It made my skin crawl, as she drew closer, out of the water, her movements slow and measured, like a cat prowling.

"Not yet, but I think he wants to, and will do soon. He wants to keep us apart." As he spoke a little softness re-entered Adrian's voice.

"Has he found his voice yet?" she asked, her eyes unblinking, eerily focused.

"What do you mean, his voice?" Adrian asked, slowly moving himself between me and her.

"The true power of a prince is in his voice," she said, looking at Adrian with scathing disappointment, as though this was something he should know. She drew herself up to her full height, standing over Adrian. It took everything in me not to push her away from him.

"Nothing in the texts mentioned a voice, just the ability to see the true form of a fay. He even saw through Merlin's illusions."

"Of course, Merlin wouldn't want you to know the true

power of a prince, it's too dangerous. The ability to command lies within princes, to bend the fay to their power." Her voice was full of cold hunger, and her features grew dark, taking on a blueish hue. I'd seen this only once before; it's how Adrian had looked as he was drowning Minoty.

"Michael's never done anything like that. He wouldn't command people," Adrian protested.

"But he could," breathed Nimueh, ambition dripped from her voice.

"So, you're interested then?" I said, taking Adrian and moving him out of her path. I couldn't take her towering over him like that anymore.

"With me you'll find your true voice," she whispered. Her breath was cold against my skin, her face inches from mine.

"Whatever, but I have conditions," I said, drawing myself up to my full height.

"Oh, yes? And what might those be?" She recoiled slightly.

"Me and Adrian can't be split up and I need to be able to leave, to go home, to be with my family." Her eyes narrowed. There was something calculating in her face. "That could be—"

"Something's coming," Adrian said, cutting her off. His hand was outstretched, pointing to the lake, there were vibrations on the water surface. Nimueh stiffened, bolting towards the water, instinctively I reached for the lump of Excalibur around my neck, the shield burst forth into my hand.

"Adrian, get behind me," I yelled, turning to face the

rustling tree line, water had started streaming out of the lake, pooling at his hands.

"Michael, be careful." He sounded scared, small. The ground was starting to tremble, and there was a distant thudding drawing closer.

"Merlin?" I called behind to Adrian.

"No, I think this is—" A tremendous roar thundered through the forest and the cracking of wood drowned out Adrian as the tree line erupted. A hulking monster emerged. It must have been fifteen feet tall, with legs like tree trunks and a potbelly, wearing a loincloth and wielding a huge club, the size of a tree.

"Ogre!" Nimueh's voice called over the crashing of trees.

"RUN!" Adrian began firing jets of water in the direction of the Ogre's face. Goblins spilled out from between the beasts' legs, wielding spears and bows. An arrow whistled past my head and then another, I raised my shield and a third shattered across it.

"You are my guard, and this is my home. You may not leave!" bellowed Nimueh. Sharp bolts of water coalescing around her before surging towards four of the goblins. They were blasted clean off their feet, sending them sailing back through the air.

Adrian's jets didn't seem to stall the lumbering ogre. It swung towards me and I dived. There was a crunch as an ill-placed goblin was pounded into the ground. The ogre howled at me, foul smelling spittle splattering across my face as a huge funnel of water crashed into its mouth, forcing it back. I looked over my shoulder, it was Nimueh, drawing multiple streams out of the lake.

Goblins screamed, charging towards me, spears and

knives brandished, but their movements were wild and clumsy. I danced around them, deflecting blows, crashing my shield into their bodies, sending them flying. It was like dribbling a ball past defenders in a game of football. Only if the defenders tackled you, you'd get stabbed to death.

Nimueh's water funnel had knocked the ogre off balance. I saw my chance, I ducked between its legs and thrust my shield into its ankle. An ear piercing roar rang out as the ogre sank to its knees. I circled round and let loose my shield towards the ogre's forehead. It crumpled back, and the earth shook as it crashed into the ground. Next thing I know there was a stabbing pain at my leg. It went heavy and cold, and I sunk to one knee. Just past the ogre there was a goblin, levelling a second arrow at me, I raised my shield deflecting the shot.

"Duck, Michael!" Adrian's voice rang out. I ducked, and a jet of water shot over my head, crashing into the archer's face, sending it tumbling backwards. Adrian broke from the lake, charging to my side, a ribbon of water trailing behind each of his hands.

"Keep your shield up," he whispered, taking one ribbon of water and bathing my leg in it. There was a tingling warmth, and then the stabbing pain and the numbness began to fade.

"Feel better?" he asked. For a moment the chaos stopped as his twinkling blue eyes met mine there was calm. Then an arrow flew between us, just missing us by an inch. Suddenly Adrian's eyes were cold, his face snapped round, it was that same goblin again.

Adrian leapt to his feet, charging the goblin, the other

ribbon of water coiling around his wrist. I struggled to my feet, limping to follow him, my leg still recovering.

He reached the goblin, another arrow missing him by inches as he grabbed it by the face and funneled water into it. That same blue grey darkness had overtaken him again.

"Adrian, it's not worth it. We've got to go," I called. He looked up, his eyes found me, and the blue-grey drained out of his face. He let go of the goblin, which fell spluttering to the ground. That's when the world started to move in slow motion.

"Adrian, look out!" I called, but he was too stunned to move, having just fallen out of whatever that trance was. Two more goblins charged at him from behind, I struggled to reach him my leg was dragging. I watched as a spear punched through his calf, pinning him to the ground, his mouth dropped open, into a scream but no noise came out. The second punched through at his shoulder, driving him down into the dirt.

"Get off him!" I spat, my blood boiling, rage coursing through me. The goblins paused and withdrew their spears as I charged them. I swung my shield around, crashing it into the first goblin's chin, only it wasn't a shield anymore, it was some kind of a hammer. There was a sickening crunch as it impacted the goblin, lifting it off the ground, sending it flying. I spun in a flurry of rage, crashing the hammer through the second goblins spear, into its chest. It crumpled to the floor, and I grabbed it and tossed it aside before turning Adrian over onto his back.

He was white, his face twisted in agony. I scooped him up in my arms, tears stung my eyes as I carried him back towards the lake and submerged him up to the neck in the water.

"Adrian? Adrian, please be okay," I whimpered, my voice strangled as a lump formed in my throat. He shook his head and groaned.

"Use the water to heal yourself," I whispered, pushing his fringe out of his eyes as he struggled in my arms.

"Leave him, they're gaining ground," I heard Nimueh call from behind. I looked back, she was right, the ogre was back on its feet, black ichor trickling into its eyes from the gash on its forehead. Goblins were charging towards the lake from all directions.

"Why isn't the water helping him?" My voice shook as I yelled over the chattering of goblins and roar of the ogre.

"Poison arrows," Adrian groaned, squirming in my arms. He seemed to be drifting in and out. I looked back at Nimueh. She was unflinching, she had no intention of leaving her home. I looked at the goblins surging forth and took off running, wading away from the lake.

"Where are you going?" Nimueh screeched. I ignored her, sprinting out of the water. Adrian had gone still in my arms. He needed help and I could only think of one person who might be able to save him.

I didn't know how to get to Merlin, but his words echoed in my head from the day he visited us at my house. *You're always welcome to come and find me.* He'd given me permission.

PART FOUR
RESCUE

CHAPTER
ONE

Adrian's breath was shallow, his face constantly shifting, from still and peaceful to screwed up in pain. The fingers of one hand kept wrapping tightly around my wrist and then going loose.

"Just hold on," I whispered around the lump in my throat. Thoughts of Merlin's home rushing through my mind as I ran down the path. Just think of the place you're going, and you'll get there. That's what Adrian said. I almost didn't notice it as I sprinted down the path It was barely a hill, just a bump in the road appeared on the horizon. Drawing near, I spotted a small circular door built into an unassuming the grassy mound.

"MERLIN! OPEN THE DOOR!" I yelled and kicked at it, as Adrian squirmed in my arms. There was a pause, I panted, Adrian groaned, and the door swung open. There he was, not the squat man in a police uniform, but the tall, salt and pepper-haired, leather armour-wearing man, with flashing grey eyes.

"What happened to him?" Merlin asked, turning on the

spot and ushering me down a staircase into a large open room.

"He got stabbed, goblins stabbed him, I took him into the water, but it didn't work and Nimueh wouldn't help. I think Adrian said something about poison." Merlin nodded, grabbing a small, jagged chunk of green rock that was dangled around his neck and threw it into the ground. Suddenly, it was a glistening silver cauldron.

"Put him in," he said. I laid Adrian down in the cauldron, supporting his head as Merlin began to chant in tongues. The light in the room receded as darkness took its place. Merlin's voice grew deeper and yet rang in my ears as the air grew thick and dank. The cauldron trembled; some strange purple mist beginning to issue from it. Suddenly objects started flying off the shelves, dumping things into the cauldron. Crashing crystals together, creating powders, liquids mixing in mid-air as they sloshed over Adrian's trembling body. Then the chanting stopped, everything still in the air clattered to the ground and light slowly returned to the room. Inside the cauldron lay Adrian, in a crystalline purple liquid, that was bubbling softy.

"What was that?"

"That was magic," said Merlin, flexing his fingers as he peered over Adrian lying still in the cauldron.

"Will he be, okay?" I asked as I stroked his hair, wiping the tear streaks from his face. Flinching for a second as I caught a flicker of a smile curling Merlin's lip, his eyes lingering on me, cradling Adrian's head. It wasn't the kind of smile someone had on their face when they were happy for you. It was the kind of smile a predator might wear, when they caught sight of a fresh meal.

"Yes, you did the right thing coming here, he'd not have lasted much longer," said Merlin, grabbing a book off a high shelf and flicking through it. I leaned down and kissed Adrian on the forehead.

"You're gonna be okay," I whispered.

"It's just a shame that Adrian never brought you to see me under better circumstances," Merlin said, rounding on me. His tone hadn't changed, but something in the air had shifted.

"Yes, well, we're here now," I said, avoiding his gaze.

"And you said you were at Lake Nimueh when mireling creatures attacked, correct?" I nodded.

"And what happened to Nimueh herself?"

"I don't know, she wouldn't leave," I said as a pang of guilt washed over me as I thought about her there, fighting alone. Which was quickly washed away as I remembered her telling me to leave Adrian. I glanced across at him, still laying in the cauldron, the liquid was slowly taking on a murky green colour.

"No, I can't imagine she would, so that means, the mirelings have captured the lake, Excalibur and Nimueh." Merlin's eyes flashed as he began again to chant, this time the walls trembled. His voice became momentarily deafening and then he halted; I winced, covering my ears, but it was already over.

"What was that?" I asked.

"He's called a meeting of all the fay lords," Adrian whispered, struggling to sit up in the cauldron.

"Adrian, you're awake!" I rushed to his side and pulled him into a hug, purplish green liquid sloshing all over me.

He wrapped his arms around me and clung to me, he felt weak, I scooped him up lifting him out of the cauldron.

"Put him back, he's not finished yet," Merlin snapped, looking up from another book he was riffling through.

"But we should be going now," Adrian said, still struggling to get out on his own.

"Oh no, you're not going anywhere, with Nimueh captured that makes you the de facto leader of the naiads. I can't risk your safety being left in the hands of anyone else," Merlin said, as he gave a lazy flick of the wrist and all the doors in and out of the room suddenly slammed shut.

"But—"

"And what's more, you'll be needed at the meeting I'm calling, I'll take you there myself and we can bring Michael along too. A new prince, well on the way to being confirmed as a champion. I can think of no one better to lead our newly renewed attacks on the mirelings' territory." Merlin's eyes glinted cruelly as he cut me off.

"Michael isn't going to the front," Adrian said, struggling to get to his feet as his legs trembled I held his hand steadying him.

"I'm afraid he most certainly is," said Merlin, flicking his wrist again. The cauldron lifted off the ground and floated towards him, Adrian stumbled losing his balance and fell back in.

"Or what?" I barked, grabbing the cauldron, and pulling it back to my side, as a cruel smile curled at Merlin's lips.

"Oh, dear boy, don't think I'm threatening you. No, no, I'm just trying to keep everyone safe, if you don't go to the front lines, to protect us all, just imagine what could happen. Any number of nasty accidents could befall poor

Adrian if the mirelings continue to gain power. Or heaven forbid, they could reach the still world. I wouldn't want something bad to happen to your dear mother, Linda," he crooned, not looking up from his book for a moment. My grip loosened and the cauldron shot out of my hands to Merlin's side, Adrian had blanched white. I wondered, was he feeling the same cold dread that was overtaking me?

CHAPTER

TWO

I turned my back to the door as Caspia left. They'd been looking for Adrian again, some nonsense about wanting to solidify the position of the naiad among the other ruling fay classes. You'd think by now they'd have realised Adrian couldn't care less about that. He'd never had much inclination towards ruling, if anything I got the impression he was a bit embarrassed by the idea. He couldn't be more different from his mother, thank goodness.

I was flicking through my ledger when I froze, a shiver running down my spine. Merlin's voice thundered through me.

All senior members of the fay courts, Excalibur system, military leaders and home stationed champions must assemble at Grandfather Tree.

I threw on my ceremonial naiad robe and gnomish broach as I swept out of my door. The forest was abuzz with life. Sylphs flitted through the air as gnomes and elves meandered down the many sprawling pathways. Loitering to gawk as the great and the good of the fay world made their way to Grandfather Tree. The oldest and greatest tree of the fay world, its seedlings made up the grove through which we travel to the still world. For Merlin to call a meeting at Grandfather Tree in this manner meant something huge had to be happening. I picked at my fingers anxiously as I tried not to think about the Adrian and Michael's last conversation. Could the meeting be about them?

The betrayal of a fay lord and his prince type charge would certainly merit such a meeting. Said an unhelpful voice in my head, the words repeating themselves so many times that they almost lost their meaning all together.

All paths in the fay forest start here, linking into one, great road. Trees arch across the great road creating a tunnel, at the end of the tunnel is a clearing and in the centre of it, Grandfather Tree. The ground bulges as its tremendous roots run under and over like the veins of the forest. Its great trunk reached up to the canopy ceiling, spreading out so far it almost seems to cover the world. In the centre, before the impossibly thick tree, stood Merlin. On his left, Adrian, looking drained, his robes torn and wet, his eyes sunken. I could see his mind racing; it was written all over his face. Behind him, Michael, still in his leather armour, there is a cut across one leg, and what looked like dried blood. My stomach lurched; this could only mean they'd been caught.

I took my place with the other keepers of Excalibur to Merlin's right. Adrian locked eyes with me as I passed, and it was like I could hear him screaming into my head.

HELP. Part of me wanted to, to make a break for it, grab

him and run, but what would be the point? We wouldn't get away. I had to be smart.

A whisper broke through the crowd and several in attendance bowed as the keeper of the grove, Mu-terra passed, followed by Wynda, mistress of the sylphs, finally the gnomish and elvish members of the courts filed in.

"Let us begin," said Merlin, silencing the hubbub. As I glanced through the throngs there was one notable absentee. My half-sister Nimueh, she wouldn't miss this kind of occasion for the world.

"Why have you called us here?" Mu-terra bristled, never one to appreciate a summons.

"The mirelings have launched their largest attack in decades. They have taken Lake Nimueh." A thunder of whispers broke out amongst the crowd. My mind raced, with the lake in their hands we would lose access to Excalibur, Nimueh was almost certainly their prisoner, if not worse. Adrian and Michael had probably been there when it happened. For all the disastrous implications, relief was coursing through me. Merlin hadn't caught them in the act of betrayal, they were safe... Ish.

"What about our lady?" called Caspia from the audience. My eyes rolled reflexively.

"At this time, we do not know her status. For which reason, until such a time as we can reclaim the lake and learn her fate, Lord Adrian shall take up her position within the water nymph community. I craned my neck back behind Merlin to look at Adrian, he was unsteady on his feet. Michael had a hand at the small of his back, supporting him.

"He's just a boy," barked one of the gnomish chiefs.

"He is young and for that reason, he shall be staying with me, under my direct supervision, until we have pushed back the mirelings." Another wave of whispers broke through the crowd and again my stomach lurched. He may not have caught them red handed, but if he wanted Adrian under his thumb like that, then he definitely had his suspicions.

"And how do you intend to push them back then?" a voice from the back called, followed by a chorus of agreement. In the face of this dissent a smile curled Merlin's lips and I got a very bad feeling. He grabbed Michael, thrusting him forwards, Adrian held onto him for a second, but his hands fell as Michael was ripped through his fingers.

"On the subject of how, I shall take this moment to introduce you all to our newest and greatest hope, this is Michael, Lord Adrian's charge, a prince type." Michael shifted uncomfortably on the spot as an eerie quiet blanketed the crowd, everyone's eyes fixed on him, drinking him in. Michael seemed almost to shrink from them, I suppose to be the object of so much fear would be itself, terrifying.

"Michael will, with the help of our other champions take back Lake Nimueh and then push into the mireling territories. Finally we shall be able to strike a decisive blow to the mirelings. With his help, we shall usher in a new age of stability for the fay." Merlin's eyes flashed in the dappled light and slowly the silence dissolved into whispers. Fear in the eyes of some, excitement sparking in patches and defiance in others.

"Now we must begin preparations," said Merlin. Taking a step forward, the audience took a step back, opening a path back to the tunnel of trees for him. Which he strode down, followed by Adrian and Michael, as he passed some fay reached out, desperate to touch Michael, and in the chaos, I saw my chance. I closed in and took Adrian's hand, pressing a whispering stone into it. He froze for a second before his fingers wrapped around it, looking over his shoulder our eyes met.

"I'll come when you call." I mouthed the words, before melting back into the crowd.

THREE

My feet were moving, carrying me past all the most important fay in the world. Some of them were cheering for Michael, others had hatred in their eyes, occasionally I got the odd sympathetic look. Then something cold was pressed into the palm of my hand. I turned, there was Olivier, intensity written across her face, dragging me back into my body.

"Speak into it before you make your move," she said as she disappeared into the crowd. My fingers wrapped around the cool smooth thing in my hand, and I followed Merlin out of the tunnel of trees. Two champions were leading us now, Jamie, a hunter and Alisha, a knight. I remembered the ceremony when they were given their shards of Excalibur. That seemed a lifetime ago now.

"Home sweet home," said Alisha, as we arrived at The Hut. I shuddered as I took it in. The Hut wasn't like other fay structures, it existed far outside the normal perimeter of the forest, right on the mireling boarder. It carried none of our arches or gentle curves and twists. It was knotted and curled and thorned, as big as Grandfather Tree and twice as imposing. A huge wooden stronghold, carved out of intertwined iron wood roots, thicker than any tree trunk in the still world. There was no dappled light here, its canopy cast us in shadow. Within its dark and twisted halls and chambers, Merlin ran the whole Excalibur system, the most fortified places in all the fay world. I'd always done everything in my power to spend as little time here as possible. We were led down winding corridors, lit in sickly yellow half-light from glowing specks in the woodwork. Gnarled roots riddled the walls and the floor until Alisha and Jamie separated.

"This way," said Alisha, taking my hand, as Jamie led Merlin and Michael down a different corridor. Michael stopped, spinning on the spot, our eyes locked. He looked lost, and guilt washed over me like a wave.

"I'm not leaving him," he said, as he started back towards me. They didn't stop him, and as my hand slid from Alisha's grasp, I stepped forward and I was in his arms. I sighed. I could breathe again, and as exhaustion rocked my body, I was melting into him, his warmth, his smell.

"Are you okay," he whispered, his voice trembling.

"I'm gonna save you," I whispered, clarity rushing into me like an icy breeze. My fingers wrapped tighter around the stone in my hand and suddenly I knew what it was.

"Come on, you're only gonna be down the corridor," said Alisha, her hand on my back, pulling me away. Michael stiffened.

"Trust me," I breathed. He held tight for a second and then let me go, we shared one last long glance as we were led away. As we separated I caught a glance of Merlin. He was watching us, appraising, assessing, if he didn't already, he knew now. He knew what I'd done, every rule I'd broken, every time I'd lied to him, he knew I'd fallen for my charge. I'd fallen for his precious champion.

As she led me off, Alisha took her shard of Excalibur, dangling from a loose bracelet at her wrist and brushed it along a root running sprawled across the gnarled wall. There was a creaking sound, shifting and a knot in the wood was revealed, leading into a small hollowed out room, one of The Hut's many chambers. There was a bed, a steaming bath in the corner and not much else. I stepped through the knot; she didn't follow me.

"See you in the morning Lord Adrian, Merlin's got big plans for you," she said and smiled, then tapped the wood twice more and the knot closed. My fingers uncoiled, revealing a small, round black stone, a whispering stone. A way to talk to Olivier, to tell her we were making a break for it.

I took a deep breath and plunged my hand into the hot bath, gathering some water around my wrist. I whipped it out against one of the root laden walls, it splashed ineffectually against the wall. I squinted drawing near, running my finger across my target. Looking for a mark, a slash, a sign of damage, I didn't find one.

"If at first you don't succeed, try, try again," I muttered, gathering the water up again, wreathing my hand in it as I slashed it across the same spot. I tried again, sweat forming across my brow. I plunged both hands into the hot water, slashing them across the wall again and again, coiled whips of water colliding with the wall. I imagined cutting away the iron wood, bursting into the adjacent chamber. Taking

Alisha by surprise, seizing her shard of Excalibur, freeing Michael and fleeing The Hut before Merlin even knew anything had happened. I let my water wreathed arms drop as they grew heavy and my lungs burned and again approached the wall, inspecting my work. Still nothing. I lifted my aching arms and let the water twist around my fists like drills.

I lost track of time as I railed against the wall. My head pounded and suddenly the world shifted. I stumbled and fell back with a thud. I was dizzy, and struggled to get to my knees, panting. My heart thundered in my ears as I heaved myself to my feet, falling into the bed as I looked around the room. There had to be something else I could use. My head ached. I closed my eyes and thoughts of Michael alone in his room started to form in my mind. Then Michael again, this time surrounded by other champions, charging into battle. Michael, bloodied and bruised, surrounded by ogres. I shook my head.

"Don't think about that!" I shouted at myself, louder than I meant to.

"Everything alright in there?" came Alisha's muffled voice.

"Fine!" I shouted before I could think, then there was silence. My eyes fell on the bath... watched the steam coil in the air, and it hit me.

I hope you're ready Olivier.

I bolted across the room and plunged my hands into the bath. Thoughts of cruel men taunting Alex and Jack, thoughts of Merlin's malicious smile, of Minoty choking the life out of Michael. I let every awful image of dread fill me up as rage bubbled out of me and funneled into the water. It sizzled and fizzed, heating the water until the room filled with steam and you couldn't see a hand in front of your face. I crept blindly to the wall, pulling the steam with me, gathering it as densely as I could before. Then I put the whispering stone to my lips and spoke aloud.

"It's now, I'm getting us out." Then I dropped the stone at my feet and stomped on it, shattering it, releasing the storm of whispers trapped inside. They filled the room as I banged on the wall.

"HELP! HELP!" I screamed, hoping against hope that Alisha would fall for it. I held my breath; there was a pause and then the cracking, screeching of iron wood twisting.

"What the hell?" Alisha's voice pierced the room as I squinted through the steam at her peering in. There was a tap as her feet touched down on this side of the knotted doorway to my chamber and I lunged. Feeling for her wrist, I dragged the hot steam with me. She screamed as it engulfed her. As she writhed within the steam, my fingers brushed against the bracelet and I grabbed it, slipping it off her wrist as I jumped out of the porthole.

"Hey what's happening? Wait!" Alisha's voice shot out of the cloud as I landed on the other side of the knot. Dragging steam with me, I slammed the shard against the wood twice and watched the knot close. Looking up, I caught sight of Jamie, already charging in my direction, a glistening silver axe in his hand. I took my steam and focused it, breathed in, the world slowed, Jamie was fifteen feet away and closing. The steam condensed in my hand, it was water again, boiling water. Jamie slashed, coming within inches of cutting me as I threw myself out of his reach, slamming into the wall knocking the wind out of me. I grabbed desperately at his wrist with my boiling hand and yanked him down. Jamie grunted, pulling away clutching his blistering wrist as I bolted, scrabbling down the corridor.

"Michael, I'm com—" I groaned as something heavy crashed into me from behind. Jamie was on top of me, his hand on the back of my head. My face crushed into the hard ground as I ran Alisha's shard across the root wall.

"So, what was the big plan, Adrian?" Jamie snarled, his knee pressing into me, I squirmed but I couldn't move, he was too heavy.

"Did you really think you couArghh," I gasped, suddenly free as Jamie's weight was lifted clean off me. I rolled onto my back panting and Michael was standing over me, with Jamie pinned against a wall.

"Here." I reached up, handing him Alisha's bracelet. Michael's finger brushed across it and a silver glittering shield exploded into his hand. Jamie tore free of Michael and lunged. Michael stepped aside, smashing the shield into Jamie's back. He gasped and crumpled to the ground.

"Adrian, are you okay?" Michael offered me a hand, lifting me to my feet, pulling me close, and I breathed a deep slow breath. Aching pain wracked my body, my back pulsed, my chest stabbed, and my head was on fire.

"Let's go home," I mumbled, slumping against his chest momentarily as I struggled to catch my breath. I could hear his heart thunder, his arm wrapped around me and his lips pressed into my forehead.

"This way then?" he said, propping me up with his free arm as we set off down a corridor.

"Do you know the way?" I asked, looking desperately through the endless knotted iron wood tunnels of The Hut.

"I memorised the route they led us down," he said, stopping before a corner and peeking his head around it. I held my breath.

"I think we're clear," he said and pulled me along, turning down the corridor. I looked back behind us but there was nothing.

"Michael, I'm so sorry," I whispered as we crept through the darkness, every footstep sounded like a stomp.

"None of this is your fault." Michael rounded on me, his amber eyes flashing golden in the darkness for a second.

"But I—"

"But nothing, you didn't choose to go to Merlin. I did and the only reason we were at the lake is because you decided to rebel against your whole world for me." Michael's voice shook as he spoke, his face inches from my own, his breath warm against my cheek. "We're going to leave this place and go home and have cups of tea and I'm going to teach you how video games work and you're going to show me magic tricks and we're going to be together forever." Tears sparkled in his eyes.

"Promise?" I whispered, struggling as my voice choked in my chest.

"Promise," he breathed as he kissed me, my legs went to jelly and he held me in his arms. Time melted into nothing, there was just Michael's warmth and me as the whole world dropped away and only we remained.

"I think they went this way." Jamie's voice brought the world screaming back into focus as it clanged through The Hut. We broke our kiss. Michael's hand wrapped around my wrist, and he took off, sprinting down the corridor, dragging me behind him.

CHAPTER
FOUR

L eft, then right, straight on until the big moss path, then left again. I recounted the directions in my head as I sprinted through the bowels of The Hut. More and more footsteps joined the chorus of those chasing behind us, or maybe it was just an echo. I couldn't say for sure, but I didn't want to wait to find out.

Adrian was struggling, I could feel his steps tripping behind me. He could barely keep his legs underneath him. I had to get him out of here fast.

"Michael, look out," I heard him gasp, just ahead at a turning a dryad had appeared. Instinctually I hurled the shield, it spun through the air like a frisbee and caught them clean on the chest. They crumpled to the floor, and I snatched it up. I'd be celebrating my Captain American style moves if there weren't a gang of kidnappers chasing us. I twisted, careering left down another corridor, two more ahead, another dryad, and what I was guessing was probably a gnome.

"Hold your breath," Adrian called as mushrooms

bloomed along the path ahead of us, releasing little puffs of yellow spores. I did, covering my mouth as I picked up speed, ramming the gnome clean out of the way. Seconds later there was a tug at my hand, I looked back. Adrian was caught in a root, more wrapping around him every second. The dryad behind us had her arms held aloft, her fingers pressed into the knotted roots that made up the wall of The Hut. I slammed the shield into a root smashing it off Adrian, but two more hands had taken its place.

"Leave me," he whimpered, tears streaming down his face as he tried to pull his hand free of me. Something flipped inside me, rage thundered through me like a shot.

"Let him go!" I commanded in a voice I didn't recognise. The sound radiated through walls, the dryad froze and then slowly withdrew, her roots recoiling. I grabbed Adrian and again we were running, I shuddered as the thought of that voice echoed in my mind. We took a right, the path ahead was clear for now and behind us the sounds of footsteps were fading. Left again and there he was, Jamie standing in our path, silvery axe in hand. He took off at a sprint towards us.

"Move!" I bellowed, but the voice didn't come, and Jamie took a swing. I let go of Adrian deflecting the axe into the wall. Jamie hooked his leg around, smashing his knee into me, slamming me against the wall, the air knocked out of me. Jamie sliced his axe down towards me as something forced me to the side. Adrian had shoved me clear. Behind him the dryad and the gnome had just rounded the corner. I grabbed Adrian and made a run for it, raising my shield, as a figure in a long black cloak took up the path ahead of us. We didn't get far — Adrian yelped.

He was caught, his wrist in my hand, his ankle in Jamie's. I faltered and Jamie yanked him clear. I winced as Adrian skidded across the hard ground. I charged, and Jamie sneered, his axe raised, but before we clashed, a huge mushroom erupted out of one side of the tunnel, crushing him against the opposite wall. I grabbed for Adrian and caught a hand just as the dryads' roots started dragging him back under the mushroom, which now took up most of the corridor. More tiny mushrooms were springing up around us, releasing yellow puffs. I held my breath. Adrian's eyes were going dull and glassy, his grip was loose.

"Run," he breathed, as his eyes shut, and his fingers went loose.

"No, let him go." I tried for the strange voice again, but could only muster a whimper as I struggled to keep hold of him against the roots. Something wrapped around my collar, dragging me back, and Adrian slipped from my grip. My eyes widened as I watched him disappear into the mushroom cloud... but then there was something behind me, pulling me away.

"We've got to get you out," came a familiar voice. I couldn't place it. I looked round, struggling to my feet. The cloaked figure was dragging me, and all I could make out was a flash of blonde hair beneath the hood.

"Nimueh?" I croaked, gasping for air as I was pulled clear of the cloud.

"Half right," said the figure, raising their arms with force as more giant mushrooms bloomed out of the roots behind us, blocking our path.

"Time to go," they said, taking off towards the exit.

"I'm not leaving him," I struggled to my feet. There was a

rustle of cloaks, and the figure was inches from my face, the hood barely covering them.

"If you don't leave now, you won't save him later." The voice was low, cold, and calculated, and I was stunned into silence as Olivier's eyes flashed at me from beneath the hood. "We're leaving," she barked, dragging me. I staggered forwards, and we were running, clear of the corridors of The Hut. Another dryad spotted us as we tore out into the forest, but before it could raise a finger, it was surrounded by a bloom of tiny mushrooms puffing yellow clouds all around it.

"How did you know to come?" I called as we entered one of the webbed paths of the forest.

"Adrian called to me; told me you were making your escape," she yelled, the cloak which I now recognised, my old Halloween costume, billowing behind her. I'd been wondered where I'd left that.

"We've got to go back for him," I said, grabbing her by the cloak to slow her down as I struggled to catch my breath.

"We will get Adrian back, but first we need to gather some reinforcements."

"But I promised I would get him out and take him home," I whispered, my stomach churning at the thought of him waking up alone, realising I'd abandoned him.

"I'm not about to lose a fight today that I could win tomorrow," Olivier snapped, still speed-walking ahead of me.

"But what if he thinks I've left him," I struggled to keep up, almost choking on the words.

"So, what if he does? We're coming back for him," said

Olivier, turning back to face me as she pulled back the hood.

"What if he doesn't... trust me anymore?" My mind raced; I'd promised him, I'd told him I'd get him out, the hope sparkling in his eyes. I felt like I was about to be sick. My body trembled as guilt crashed over me and I sank to my knees. Olivier gave a sigh and knelt before me.

"How would you describe Adrian to me?" she asked, her face softening.

"What? You know Adrian."

"Just describe him."

"Okay, well... Adrian is... blond and short, and he's funny and he's kind, brave, although he doesn't think he is. Clever, too clever for me probably, he's gentle, and so open and loving... selfless. Adrian is the best person I've ever met." I smiled as tears tumbled down my cheeks.

"Do you know how most folks round here would describe him?" I shook my head, and sniffled.

"They would tell you Adrian is withdrawn, aloof, distant, shy and quiet."

"But he's nothing like that."

"He's nothing like that around you, Michael. You've brought more out of Adrian in a month than we did in seventeen years. He's not about to stop trusting you overnight. Especially when you're about to rescue him from a thousand-year-old wizard," she said, giving me a warm smile as she helped me to my feet.

"And how are we going to do that?" I asked, as she led whilst I let happier images of Adrian wash through me. Mostly revolving around him enjoying a ludicrous amount of tea.

"With reinforcements," she said, stopping outside a particularly thick tree. She took the shield from my hand, and it popped back into a shard, which she tapped against the tree. It shuddered and twisted, and a knot opened in its centre, leading to a spiral staircase.

"Where are we?" I asked, as we climbed the staircase up into the branches.

"You're in the private quarters of the royal host," came a familiar voice. I looked around and there was Caspia, alongside another Naiad, a dryad, and two slight, spindly looking men with white hair, faintly lilac skin and extremely long arms. They looked distinctly like they might have an extra set of elbows. I guessed they were sylphs based on Adrian's description.

"What's going on?" I asked, bewildered.

"We don't like the idea of Merlin holding a royal water nymph hostage," said Caspia.

"Or wielding your princely powers with impunity," the dryad's deep voice rumbled.

"So, we're... resisting," said one of the sylphs, grinning eerily.

"Michael, you'll be safe here for now, this is one of the last places Merlin would think to look," said Olivier.

"Because typically we do not like champions," chuckled the other sylph.

"Are you going somewhere, Olivier?" I said, doing my best to ignore the four pairs of eyes drilling into the back of my head.

"I've got more reinforcements to gather," said Olivier as she descended the spiral staircase without another word.

"So, you've met me. To my left you will find Lord Aechor

of the dryads, Ionia, my sister, and the twins Ephyr and Rocco," said Caspia, imperiously.

"I'm Michael," I said, offering a hand.

"We know who you are, you're Adrian's... charge." Mischief flickered across Ionia's face.

"Why do you say it like that?" I asked, shifting on the spot.

"We noticed Adrian was spending more time in the still world than most fay do, is all," said Aechor.

"A lot more time than usual," said one twin as the other gave me I wink. I could feel my cheeks burning.

"We got pretty... close," I mumbled, not sure how much to admit to them.

"I bet you did," crooned Ionia.

"Every fay gets close to their charge," Caspia said, looking almost as flustered as me.

"Of course."

"Totally professional," the twins said in a sort of rhythm. I couldn't tell if they were doing it to put me off or if they were just like that.

"Regardless, if Lady Nimueh has truly been captured, then Adrian is the leader of the naiad. It doesn't matter how important Merlin thinks he is, he doesn't have the authority to just keep a fay lord locked up.

"Well, don't worry about that cause I'm getting him back," I said, as I fought the image of Adrian being chained up somewhere in the bowels of The Hut out of my head.

FIVE

There was a thud, I jumped, as something like electricity rushed up my spine. I reached for a tree branch, but I was too slow. I was falling, wind rushed around me as my outstretched fingers fell away from the tree. I tensed up, bracing for impact but it didn't come.

"You want to be careful, climbing trees like that, might not always be someone there to catch you when you fall." I squinted into the light and there he was, Michael, his amber eyes glinted as he smiled down at me and gently set me down on my feet.

"You caught me," I whispered, planting a kiss on his cheek.

"Of course I did, what else am I gonna do, just leave you to fall?" He took my hand and we set off through the woods.

"Where are we going?"

"That's a surprise," he said as our path started to steepen. Michael bent to one knee in front of me and looked back over his shoulder.

"Climb aboard, I know what you're like with hills." He gave me a wink as I hopped onto his back, looping my arms around his neck.

"You're gonna get sick of carrying me one of these days," I said, twisting some of his hair around my fingers.

"Don't be daft, it's the highlight of my day," Michael chuckled as we crested the hill and he set me down.

"So, what do you think?" he asked, gesturing to the view. I looked out and my breath faltered, my body tensed, my chest suddenly tightening. A twisting tower of roots sprawled out before us, a symphony of black and brown and thorns. Goblins and ogres teamed around the massive structure of black thorned iron wood.

"Michael, why are we here?" I asked, hairs on my neck standing on end as my feet rooted to the spot, everything in me screaming "run", but I couldn't move.

"Wake up, Adrian." Michael's lips were moving, but it wasn't his voice I could hear. I closed my eyes and covered my ears and shook my head.

"No, no, no, I don't want to," I pleaded, tears prickling my eyes, something shook me, and I froze, slowly peeking open on eye, and there he was, Merlin.

"You've caused me a lot of trouble, Adrian." His voice was flat and dry, almost unrecognisable. I looked around the room, it didn't look like The Hut. The walls were cobbled and flickered in the light of four ornate torches burning in each corner of the room. There was one entrance, dead ahead of me, with guards stood in shadow at either side. I was back in Merlin's cauldron, in the centre of the room.

"What are you going to do to me?" I asked, struggling to

climb out of the cauldron, to move at all. My body was heavy, too heavy to move, and it ached. My throat was scratchy, I felt dry, and my back was sore where Jamie had pinned me to the ground.

"I'm going to use you, Adrian."

"For what?" I squeaked, fear strangling my voice.

"I need to know what's happening at Lake Nimueh, what's happening to Nimueh herself, and I can't very well just march in there, besieged as it is with goblins and ogres."

"So, you're going to send me?" he laughed, and it was a cruel, mirthless laugh.

"I'm not letting you out of my sight Adrian, you've proven far too slippery for that. Oh no, I'm going to use your connection to the Lake to look through your eyes and see it."

"You can do that?" I asked, malevolence emanating from him, my body beginning to tremble.

"You'd be amazed at the things I can do when I set my mind to it Adrian." As he spoke, he started to wave his arms, like an orchestral conductor. Blue smoke began to bubble up around me inside the cauldron. At the same time, black smoke was billowing out of the torches that lit the corners of the room. My vision started to blur as the black smoke funneled towards Merlin. He breathed it into himself and closed towards me. My head was heavy, my body was numbing, Merlin grabbed my neck, pulled me close to him and blew black smoke into my mouth. Suddenly my body was alive, my nerves were crackling, I was tense, my skin prickled like I'd touched a live wire. Then there was a searing pain behind my eyes and my vision faded to black and then blue. There was blue all around me, my head pounded as my vision came back into focus.

"Where am I?"

"Look around and see." Merlin's voice thundered through my head like a drum. I winced and looked about myself.

"The lake," I whispered. I was floating, just above the water, sparkling in the dappled half-light of the fay world. In the centre of the lake was Excalibur, twinkling black green and crawling with goblins, chipping and chiseling away at it.

"Go to the land." Merlin's voice boomed in my mind, his every word agony, like it was grinding into my bones. I screwed up my focus as steadily my consciousness floated over the lake to the land. The full length of the tree line was guarded with ogres and more goblins, gigantic spiders as big as Alsatians skittered across the grassy lake side, dragging wood and rocks. There was a large structure being erected in the centre.

"Find Nimueh!" he commanded. I gasped as his voice slammed into me like a hammer. The vision was fading. I willed myself towards the structure, but I was slowing. I passed over small camps, with goblins around fires, some with little chunks of what looked like Excalibur between them.

"Focus Adrian!" I groaned as his voice tore through me. I could barely move at all now. My vision faded to black, and I collapsed into the cauldron, pain filling up my senses.

"That was a good first effort, we'll try again in a little bit," I heard Merlin say, and now there was mirth in his voice.

SIX

" I should never have suggested them going to find that Olive who's it woman, what was I thinking? This is madness. They're just boys, they shouldn't be messed up in nonsense like this, they should be getting in trouble at school. Not fighting wizards and starting rebellions."

I sound insane; if anyone heard me, they'd lock me up.

I'd been pacing through the kitchen all morning and most of the night. Adrian and Michael hadn't come home last night, and I didn't know where they were. I'd even tried squashing myself into a tree a couple times, but that'd only served to snag my best coat. I don't think it works without Adrian there to do the magic.

"Who am I kidding? I don't know how any of this stuff works," I said aloud, arguing with myself again.

Knock Knock

I jumped halfway out of my skin as someone knocked on the door, harder than was necessary.

"No visitors today, thank you," I shouted as I started rooting around in the cupboards for biscuits.

Knock Knock Knock

"Alright, alright, I'm coming," I grumbled as I made my way to the door, navigating through the mess of coats, bags and shoes that seemed to be breeding in the entrance hall. "Can I help you?" I asked the shortish figure in the long cloak that was standing in my doorway.

"Hang on, is that my Halloween cloak from last year? Adrian… is that you?" My stomach flipped as I leaned in to hug him.

"Not quite," came a much harsher voice than I was expecting as the cloaked figure stepped past me into the hall and closed the door behind them. "Are you alone?" they asked.

"Errm, yes?"

"Good, I'm Olivier and I'm here because I need your help." She pulled down the hood of the cloak, revealing a petite woman with a shock of white-blonde hair and slightly odd facial features. Her smile was unusually wide, and her nose was like a button.

"Olivier, you're who the boys were going to see, so did they find you okay? Are they okay? Is Michael okay? Wait, why would you need my help?"

"Correct, yes, yes and no, yes and to help get Adrian back."

"Back, back from where? What happened to Adrian? Is he okay?" My heart was pounding as sweat started beading and I put the kettle on, almost instinctively.

"Merlin has him. He had them both, briefly, but we

managed to get Michael back. I think Adrian is safe though, Merlin wouldn't do anything to risk his life."

"If you got Michael back, where is he now?"

"He's in hiding, whilst we formulate a plan to rescue Adrian," said Olivier, watching with interest as I absent-mindedly shoveled sugar into two mugs of tea.

"So how do we do that then?" I said, handing her a tea that was sixty percent sugar at this point and I grimaced as I sipped my own.

"Well, Adrian has already managed a semi-successful break out of The Hut. So I'm betting he's been moved to be under Merlin's personal supervision."

"What's The Hut and how do you semi-successfully break out of it?" I asked as I started on the biscuits.

"The Hut is a sort of fay military installation, and you semi successfully break out by getting Michael out but not yourself."

"Poor Adrian." I sagged as I anxiously munched through a digestive.

"Indeed, which is why I come to you," said Olivier, taking a second mug as I offered her a fresher, sugar-free cup of tea.

"What good am I going to be in the face of a wizard?"

"No good at all, but you could provide the ingredients I need to help Michael?"

"I've not got much in I'm afraid, lovely. I was gonna order takeaway," I said, looking to my embarrassingly ill-stocked fridge. Olivier rolled her eyes.

"For a spell, not a sandwich."

"Oh, are you a wizard too?"

"No and Merlin isn't either, he's an enchanter, but that's

beside the point. Any fay can cast a spell, it's just easier for an enchanter and I've been studying this one for a while. Since Adrian first started falling for Michael actually." She'd pulled out a scroll and was scanning it.

"Okay lovely, so what can I give ya?" I asked.

"Well, first things first, we need a big pot."

"That I can do," I said, rooting through the draws for the big pot that I only ever used to make mulled wine at Christmas.

"Now the spell calls for the virgin blood of the intended target's mother," said Olivier as casually as if she'd asked for a half cup of sugar.

"I'm afraid the ship has sailed on the old... you know... *virgin* front," I mouthed as my cheeks burned. You'd think she'd have figured that out already given that I was Michael's mother.

"Virgin, in this instance, just means the person in question's blood hasn't been used for a spell before," Olivier explained.

"Oh... so you just need... some of my... blood. How much exactly?"

"A litre should do."

"A litre?"

"That was a joke," Olivier deadpanned as she dumped a mound of sage into the pot and a whole nutmeg from a bag hidden inside her cloak.

"Oh, should I... slice across the palm?" I asked, eyeing my kitchen knife block with a newfound fear.

"Whatever you think is best. I'd prick a finger myself. Palm seems like a terrible place to start." Olivier was barely looking at me now as she dumped two whole apples and four bay leaves into the pot and put the kettle back on for a third time.

"Oh, right, good, yes, need anything else?" I mumbled desperately, trying to distract myself as I pricked my fingertip with a knife, which I suddenly felt was unnecessarily large.

"Well, there is one other thing I could use from you," said Olivier, as she grabbed my hand, squeezing my finger over the pot, as casually as if she'd been handing me a cup of tea.

"Oh, what's that then? I think I've got half an onion going spare in the fridge." I chuckled nervously.

"I need something of his father's, ideally something that won't melt," she said, dumping the kettle into the pot as she switched on the burner. David's smiling face flashed through my mind, followed by a pang of grief.

"Oh erm, I think I have just the thing," I said, bustling off upstairs as Olivier dropped a small black rock into the pot and started poking at it with my good sangria spoon. I had never really gotten rid of David's things, not all of them anyway, the bits and pieces he kept in his bedside table at least. I know people say you have to get rid and move on but in the end I just thought, stuff 'em.

"You wouldn't mind would you, David?" I said to the room as I pulled out his end table drawer. David kept his wedding ring on a silver chain.

"I don't think I've seen you for two years," I said, running the chain through my fingers. I sniffled and headed back downstairs.

"Will this do?" I asked, peeping my head back into the kitchen, which seemed to be filling with brown steam.

251

"Looks perfect," said Olivier, who appeared to be sprouting a mushroom out of my window plants.

"Should I open a window, lovely?" I asked, already wafting steam out of the kitchen.

"Whatever you think is best," said Olivier, mashing the mushroom into the pot.

"I will get this back, won't I?" I asked as I handed her the chain.

"Absolutely," she said, taking the chain and dunking it ring first into the pot.

"So what's this going to do then?"

"Well, in theory, whoever wears the charm will be protected from the target the spell is bound to and in turn, the target will be protected from whomsoever wears the charm."

"The charm being David's ring?"

"Correct."

"And who is the target of the spell?"

"The proud owner of this, quill," said Olivier as she dropped one of those fancy feathers tipped quills into a pot.

"And whose pen is that?" I asked, craning over the pot into the murky bubbling broth, which was weirdly scentless.

"This pen? Merlin misplaced it just last week," Olivier said, giving me a cheeky wink.

"You know Olivier, I think we could be good friends in another life," I said as she placed the lid onto the pot.

"Why not this one?"

SEVEN

"Right, so does everyone know their part in the plan?" Olivier asked. She was still in the long Halloween cloak. Beneath it, she wore a twisted suit of rope and leather, which she said was gnomish.

"We draw the door guards to you, Olivier," said the twins in unison.

"I rock the lower chamber, to draw out the inner guards," said Aechor, who was wearing some thick bark plated armour.

"And I get Adrian back," I said, as I took the shard of Excalibur from around my neck squeezing it, as my silvery hammer burst into being.

"Just remember—"

"I know, Merlin can't hurt me, and I can't hurt him," I said, patting my dad's wedding ring, which dangled around my neck.

"And I'm going with Michael just in case there is more resistance than we accounted for," said Caspia. They wore similar robes to Adrian, when Adrian came to fay world, but today they were laden down with wine skins filled with water.

"Wait one minute, then go," said Olivier as she skulked off through the undergrowth. "Good luck everyone, and thank you for this."

"We're not doing it for you," said Caspia, their eyes focused on Olivier as she disappeared into the undergrowth.

"I'm sort of doing it for him; it'd be good to have a prince owe you a favour." Aechor's laugh was a low rumbling chuckle.

"See you on the other side." Ephyr and Rocco took each other by the hand and wind whipped up around them, lifting them clean off into the air. They floated past our hiding spot in the tree line. They moved almost like feathers caught on the breeze, only with a little more direction as they drifted over the entrance to Merlin's lair.

"Goblins and spiders coming this way, come quick," the twins called to the dryads stood either side of Merlin's door, beckoning them in the direction that Olivier had been travelling.

Once they were clear of the path we charged for Merlin's door. Aechor hunched forward, plunging his hands into the dirt, wrapping them round the nearest, biggest tree roots he could find. There was a low rumble and the ground started to shake, ever so imperceptibly.

"You're up, Prince Charming!" Aechor's voice rumbled, sweat beading on his brow as Caspia and I stepped through the threshold on Merlin's staircase. The further down the stairs we got, the more intense Aechor's tremors became.

"There is nobody here," Caspia said as we burst into the

main chamber where Merlin had first healed Adrian.

"Olivier said that Merlin has all sorts of rooms hidden down here." I said, looking around the room as bottles and jars tipped from high shelves, shattering across the cobbles, and bookshelves swayed menacingly.

"So, which path do we follow?" said Caspia, pulling open a door to what looked like a broom cupboard.

"Not that one. Perhaps—"

"Who goes there?" I span on the spot and there was Jamie, standing in a passageway that had formerly been a bookshelf. A grin curled across his lips, our eyes met, my muscles tensed, and electricity filled the air.

"Have you come for a rematch, prince?" Jamie snarled, a silvery axe appearing in his hand. My eyes narrowed as a calm came over me.

"It's not going to be much of a match, Jamie," I said, taking off towards him at a sprint. Jamie braced and brought his axe slicing down towards me. I tilted left, the axe cutting the air inches from my nose. As his arm sailed downwards, I grabbed his wrist and yanked him towards me, bringing him crashing into my knee with such force he was lifted clean off the ground. Jamie gasped as his body lifted into the air. I took my hammer with both hands, slamming it into Jamie's chest, sending him skidding across the room into a slumped heap on the ground.

"Remind me not to get on your bad side," Caspia said, poking their head through the entrance that had formerly been a bookshelf.

"Ha-ha, yeah, anyway, down we go," I said, doing my best to ignore the crunching sensation I'd felt as my hammer hit Jamie's chest. I'd always wanted to go through a secret concealed door behind a bookcase. This would have been fun if it wasn't for the evil wizardiness of it all.

Merlin squinted as he peered at the creaking walls of the chamber that had begun to shudder and quake. My eyes were glued to the entrance Jamie had been guarding, hoping in spite of myself that Michael would burst through at any second.

"This is a dryad's doing," Merlin muttered, approaching the cauldron and tipping me out onto the floor. I groaned, tumbling across the hard cobbles.

"What are you going to do?" I struggled to sit up as Merlin chanted over the cauldron. What flickering light there was in the room dimming.

"I'm going to kill all the roots in the area," he said, as casually as if he'd said he was going flower picking. I watched as a chilling cruelty emanated from the dark green mist coiling out of the cauldron. Then there was a crash and the cauldron span across the floor and a silver hammer clattered to the ground in front of Merlin.

"What the—" Merlin and I turned our heads to the entrance and there he was, Michael, standing at the bottom of the stairwell.

"Seize him!" Merlin bellowed as he made for his cauldron. The remaining guard jumped at Michael, who rolled onto his back and kicked the guard over his head sending them flying. I struggled to my feet as I heard Merlin chanting from behind me.

"Michael, look out!" I called as a great pillar of dark green mist poured over my head engulfing Michael and the guard.

"What are you doing? He's a prince remember, he's valuable," I pleaded with Merlin, my legs threatening to give way beneath me as I struggled to walk.

"If he's against me, he's got to go." I watched as Merlin's face twisted from a determined glare to a look of shock. "How is that... possible?" He breathed. I looked back over my shoulder as Michale strode out of the smoke towards me.

"That's not going to work on me, Merlin," said Michael, picking up his hammer as he approached me, taking my hand in his.

"If you don't stop now, I'll—" Merlin snarled taking a step towards us, his cauldron shifting to a glittering silver staff in his hand.

"You'll what?" Michael's voice was suddenly alien, radiating off Merlin's cobbled walls.

"That voice..." Merlin breathed. For the first time in my life, I watched fear flash through his silvery eyes.

"We're going now," Michael said, his hammer becoming a shield as he strapped it to his back and scooped me up in his arms.

"Michael, is this really happening?" I whispered.

"I promised I'd save you, didn't I?" Michael smiled down at me with tears in his eyes. I nodded and snuggling into his chest.

"Lord Adrian, you look awful!" Caspia's unmistakable voice echoed off the cobbles and I clutched Michael tighter.

K nock Knock

I booted the door twice as Adrian lay curled in my arms, resting into my chest. Every now and again, a little tremble would rock his body. I didn't know what had happened yet, but I could tell Merlin had done something awful to him. I'd seen it in his eyes. Caspia had tried to heal him, but it didn't seem to really take.

"Michael! You're home, thank God. I've been going round the twist with all this worrying." Mum went to hug me; I could see the turn in her face when she got a good look at Adrian, and she froze.

"Stick the kettle on, Mum," I said as she ushered us into the house, and I took Adrian into the living room and sat down in Mum's squashy chair as he curled into my lap. Peering down into his face, my stomach churned. He looked exhausted and there was something else, fear maybe? Etched into his features. Every now and then his body rocked with tiny tremors, and he would let out little panicked gasps.

"Adrian, tell me what happened, please," I whispered, and as I stroked his hair, his body tensed in my arms and his eyes flickered open. They looked glassy and distant.

"It's just normal, you know, used too much water and… Jamie was a bit rough and so were those vines and—"

"Adrian, this isn't normal. Please tell me what's wrong." I wrestled to keep the cracks out of my voice.

"Merlin might have… done something to me a couple of times." I could see fear flood into his eyes at the thought of it. Whatever *it* was.

"Tea is ready," said Mum barreling into the room with a tray, laden down with three large mugs of tea, a teapot, sugar, milk, and a mound of chocolate digestives.

"Thank you," Adrian whispered, struggling to sit up in my lap as Mum handed him his tea. I half expected he wouldn't even be able to hold the cup as he took it.

"So… Olivier's plan worked then?"

"You met Olivier?" Adrian asked in between deep gulps of tea.

"Oh yes, she came round and ruined the big cooking pot and my good sangria spoon," Mum chuckled.

"She did something to this… oh do you want this back Mum?" I asked, tapping dad's ring which was dangling round my neck.

"No lovely, you keep it. Wasn't doing me any good in the back of a drawer anyway." Mum smiled as Adrian inspected the ring, running his fingers over it.

"Olivier is a genius," he whispered.

"What did she do?" I asked.

"It's a really ancient spell, basically a legend, Merlin used the same one to get the best of a rival enchanter he had hundreds of years ago. Everyone in the fay world knows about it... but you'd never think to use it. It'd be like... calling on Father Santa in the still world." I chuckled as Adrian explained, trying the ring on; it was way too big for his fine fingers. I winced as I caught sight of the blood beneath his jagged, painfully cracked nails.

"You're adorable," I whispered, wrestling the sadness out of my voice as I ruffled his hair.

"More tea, Adrian hun?" Mum asked, pouring him another cup.

"Oh yes please," Adrian said, but as he took it, a tremor rocked his body. I steadied him, but not before half the contents of the mug had spilt onto the floor.

"Oh, I'm sorry." Embarrassment coloured Adrian's cheeks as he leant forward in my lap, trying to clean it, giving an involuntary groan as he did.

"Oh, don't worry dear, this carpet was past its best a decade ago," Mum said, chucking a tea towel on the spill and treading it down with her slipper before bustling out of the room. Adrian sagged and recoiled into me.

"Maybe I should get some sleep," he whispered.

"Shame Michael can't take you to the lake," Mum said as she returned armed with carpet cleaner. At the word lake Adrian's body locked up in my arms, his breathing becoming abrupt, ragged.

"Adrian, what's wrong?" I took Adrian's face in my hands and looked into his usually twinkling blue eyes. They were frantic, their sparkle dulled, and they were rapidly filling with tears.

"C-can't d-don't l-lake..." Tears spilled over as he struggled to speak.

"I think he's having a panic attack. Just breathe Adrian love, just breathe," said Mum, kneeling next to us.

"Don't worry, we're safe, Adrian," I whispered taking his hands in mine. He was squeezing my fingers as he clamped his eyes shut.

"Just breathe, love, just breathe." Slowly, Adrian's grip started to loosen up and his breathing came back under control.

"Let's get you to bed," I whispered as he flopped back against me.

"Okay," he mumbled, struggling to his feet, my hand still clutched in his.

"Come with me," he whispered.

"Of course." Mum gave me a worried look as we passed, and I followed Adrian as he slowly made his way up the stairs. Adrian was so exhausted he was asleep almost instantly. But as he slept he spoke, little heart-breaking pleas.

Please, not again or I can't do it anymore.

"What did Merlin do to you?" I murmured as I stroked his hair.

NINE

"Help!" I heard my voice echo off the walls, freezing as I found myself sitting bolt upright in the darkness.

"Adrian, you're okay. It was just a bad dream." Michael's hand wrapped around my arm as the golden glow of his lamp flickered into the darkness.

"I'm sorry..." Blinking the sleep out of my eyes, images of Merlin's cauldron flashed through my mind.

"You've got nothing to be sorry for Adrian. Look at me." I turned, meeting his eye in the half-light. I focused on the feeling of Michael's fingers running through my hair as I struggled to not let my breathing runaway with itself.

"Adrian, I should be apologising to you. I'm the one that left you, whatever happened to you in that room... with Merlin, it's my fault." Michael's eyes swam with tears. I shook my head swallowing around the lump in my throat.

"If you hadn't left me, we'd both of been trapped. I might be still there... in that cauldron right now if you hadn't gone." I shuddered, all my body's aches and pains reasserting themselves as the image of Merlin blowing black smoke into my face materialised in my mind. I sagged and Michael's hand wrapped around my waist, pulling me into his lap, his warmth.

"Adrian... I don't want to make things worse, but you know, whatever happened to you in that room, whatever Merlin did, you can tell me." I took a deep breath and steadied myself, turning to look into Michael's eyes. They looked like fire in the lamp glow. His voice was tender and warm but just around the edges of it was fear. I could hear it, feel it. He was scared to learn what had happened to me, imagining the worst things Merlin could do to a person, being done to me.

"He said he was going to... use me." Tears prickled my eyes as Merlin's mirthful voice echoed through my mind and for a second I thought I might be sick. Somewhere inside me I wanted to hide it, to never admit what happened, trying to wish it out of existence. But I couldn't.

"He was using my connection to Lake Nimueh, to look through me to see what the mirelings were doing there, he wanted to find Nimueh. It was like my mind was a looking glass, pointed at the Lake." My voice strangled in my throat as the tears tumbled down my cheeks.

"Take your time," Michael said, one hand stroking my back as he handed me some water. I took a sip and a deep, shaky breath.

"It hurt." I shuddered and gulped air as the memory rocked my body, strangling my voice. Michael's face hardened, as anger flashed through his eyes, just for a second, then it was gone.

"I couldn't get away... couldn't stop him." I choked on

my words, my body tight, shaking. "The longer he was in there, looking for her, the worse the pain... the more intense everything was. B-but I couldn't find her. He looked through me again and again... and again. She wasn't there... she wasn't." The world started to shrink around me as blackness encroached.

"Adrian, that's enough. It's okay, you don't have to think about it anymore. I understand." Michael was holding me in his arms. I suddenly realised I was shaking my head back and forth. The hairs on my neck were on end. I was soaked in cold sweat.

"I couldn't find her..." I whispered, unable to think of anything else.

"Adrian, I promise you, you're never ever going back to that man." Michael's voice was trembling but not like mine, I could hear it, the edge, it was rage. I lay in his arms all night listening to his breath, I didn't think I'd ever fall asleep, until I woke to wood pigeons cooing at Michael's window. A broken shaft of light peeking through the curtains. I sat up, yawned, stretched, and groaned as aches pulsed in my back and my legs and my head.

"Michael?" I blinked the sleep from my eyes, looking around the room, but Michael was nowhere to be seen. Reluctantly, I slid out of Michael's bed and threw on his biggest, softest hoodie. Then rooting though his cast offs, I settled for a pair of sweatpant shorts that were too loose and tied them to my waist with a stray dressing gown rope. As I padded down the stairs, Michael and Linda's voices carried from the kitchen.

"So, Merlin was doing spells on him?"

"Not just spells Mum, it was fucking torture."

I'd never heard Michael's voice like that, hard angry and hate-filled.

"Michael—"

"Merlin was fucking torturing Adrian. I can't stop thinking about it. It was going round and round in my head all night."

"That poor thing. Well, at least he's home with us now, we'll just have to keep an eye on him. Perhaps you two could celebrate your birthday today. Take his mind off it a bit."

"I don't know Mum, I feel like—"

"What's a birthday?" I asked, deciding now was the time to make my entrance.

"You don't know what a birthday is?" Linda asked, looking shocked.

"How much of that did you hear, Adrian?" Michael asked, ignoring his mother. He looked worried again; he'd looked worried a lot recently.

"I errm, I… not much… well enough." I couldn't bring myself to lie to Michael anymore. It made my stomach churn. Michael didn't say anything, but the look on his face was heartbreaking. I could feel it. I could feel his rage and his guilt and remorse and his arms wrapping around me, holding me close as his lips pressed to my forehead.

"Nothing like that is ever going to happen to you again."

"I've got just the thing for you two," said Linda's disembodied voice.

"What's that then?" I asked, peeking my head out over Michael's shoulder.

"Birthday cake!" she declared, laying down an unusually tall chocolate cake on the table.

"Oh yeah, I still don't know what birthdays are," I said as Michael let me go.

"You really don't have them in the fay world?" Michael asked, fixing his amber eyes on mine as he gently pushed my hair out of my face.

"Guess not," I breathed as my mouth went dry.

"Birthdays are a celebration of the anniversary of our birth. They're great, we get to bake cakes," Linda said, cutting an intimidatingly large slice of cake and dragging me back out of Michael's all-consuming eyes.

"Although they're not normally this big. When did you make this, Mum, and why is it so massive?" Michael chuckled, cutting a smaller slice for me.

"I had to do something to distract myself. Olivier's potion gave me the idea as it goes."

"Birthdays seem pretty fun to me," I said, taking a bite of cake.

"This isn't even the best part; when you have a birthday you can have a party, and people get you presents. Although Michael doesn't like birthday parties for some reason," said Linda, shooting Michael a look.

"Because my mother has a habit of turning them into enormous events," said Michael.

"Wild exaggerations and spurious rumours, hang on right there." Linda gave a wink as she bustled out of the kitchen.

"Here we go," Michael said and smiled, watching her go.

"What's happening now?"

"She's got a present for me, she just likes the theatrics of it all."

"Should I have got you a present?"

"'Course not. You didn't even know it was coming up…
or about the concept at all." Michael chuckled.

"I'm gonna get you a present, what d'ya want?"

"The idea is that they're usually a surprise Adrian," said
Linda, reemerging with her hands behind her back.

"Pick a hand, any hand."

"Left," Linda revealed the left hand opening it with a
flourish, there were two little slips of paper in it.

"Train tickets?" Michael asked, puzzling over them.

"And Adrian, you can reveal the other hand," Linda said,
beaming.

"Which should I choose? I suppose I'll go for right," I
giggled. She opened the other hand, revealing two more
slips of paper, these ones had a green woman in a conical
hat on them.

"Tickets for Wicked?" Michael asked.

"What kind of self-respecting musical lover would I be if
I let my youngest son turn eighteen without seeing the
greatest musical ever?" Linda chuckled, handing Michael all
the tickets.

"Thanks mum, this is great," he said, pulling her into a
hug. Michael towered over Linda's squat form so they
ended up making an odd sort of shape.

"I was going to come with you, that was the plan
anyway, but now you can take Adrian and it'll be romantic,"
she said in a sing-songy voice.

"Muuuuum," Michael groaned as his cheeks flushed.

"Oh, shush, I'm only messing, now give me those back
and I'll pop 'em in an envelope to go on the shelf, so you
don't lose 'em, the shows in a few weeks," she said immedi-

ately, taking them back off him and going to find an envelope.

"What're the chances she bought those tickets, cause she wanted to see that show and this was her excuse?" Michael asked.

"Pretty high… what's a musical?" I asked.

"You remember when we watched the Wizard of Oz?" I nodded.

"That's like a movie musical. This one will just be live on a stage, it's actually the story that came before the Wizard of Oz."

"Oh, sounds like, fun. Do people sing along?"

"Sometimes, you don't have them in the fay world? It's like a play, but most of the story is told in song. Do you have plays?" Michael asked.

"Sort of. We tell stories together, you know, legends and myths around a fire of a night, sometimes we even sing them. It'd be nice to hear something other than fay myths and fay music though."

"Do you sing?"

"Sometimes." Michael's face shifted, his eyes were wide, and excited.

"Sing for me, go on, I wanna hear you sing, come on."

"Maybe later if you're good," I said with a wink.

"You're such a tease," Michael said, his powerful arms wrapping around me, his probing fingers tickling me.

"You… you'll j-just have to…" I burst out laughing, struggling to speak as Michael tickled me into a corner.

"Resistance is futile," he cackled, grinning ear to ear.

"Wait-wait," I gasped, struggling out of his grasp.

"What, did I hurt you?"

"No, nothing like that, I just thought of the perfect present for you," I said, shooting off up the stairs. My old fay robes were shoved up the corner of Michael's room, covered in dirt, cuts, blood and stains from Merlin's smoke. They were ruined, but they still had pockets, so I rooted through them and there it was, a small, cool round stone. I grabbed it and hurtled back down the stairs.

"So, what have you got there?" Michael asked. I held out my hand, and in it was sat a sapphire, with a pin in the back of it.

"It's my stone of the Naiad, it symbolises my connection to the fay world and my people. I want you to have it, to symbolise my connection to you," I said, pressing it into Michael's hand.

"It's beautiful Adrian, but I can't take this, it's too precious." I shook my head.

"No, you're precious. This stone is supposed to symbolise a connection. At the moment, it's to a world that betrayed me and is at war with itself and... t-tortured me." The words sounded heavy in the air; Michael didn't speak, but his eyes swam. "Let's let it be a connection to something good now, something new, us." I smiled and left the stone in his hand as I kissed him again.

"A fresh start," Michael said with a smile.

CHAPTER

TEN

"Climb on," I said, kneeling in front of Adrian as we reached the treacherous hill that guarded our own personal Lake Adrian. Adrian's alabaster face took on a pinkish hue as he climbed aboard. His eyes were twinkling again, though there was still something delicate about him. More delicate than usual.

"Do you remember the first time you carried me?" Adrian's arms looped around my chest as he fiddled with the chunk of Excalibur and my dad's ring, which now dangled side by side around my neck.

"'Course I do. We were skipping school, cause you were so upset about… Cynthia." I gave him a peck on the cheek.

"You were my hero; you haven't stopped being my hero since I fell out of that tree the first day we met."

"Don't be daft. All I did was stand there like a chip when you fell out of that tree." I cringed at the memory.

"You helped me up, and you were exactly who I was looking for," Adrian said, giving me a kiss on the cheek in return as we crested the hill.

"I think you need to set your bar a little higher for what makes a hero."

"Okay, caught me when I collapsed, carried me up a slippery hill, fought a dryad assassin for me, got me help when I was poisoned and last but not least, rescued me from a centuries-old super wizard," Adrian said, counting off each deed in turn on his fingers.

"Well, when you put it that way, I am pretty great, aren't I?" I chuckled.

"That's what I've been saying," Adrian giggled.

"Well, whatcha gonna do to make it up to me?" I asked with a grin.

"You'll have to catch me and find out!" Adrian said as we reached the tunnel of trees. He hopped off my back and ran off down it, stripping down to his swim trunks as he went. I watched him go, letting him get a little head start, then followed, sprinting down after him. As I reached the water's edge he dived, and his slight, pale body sailed through the air so gracefully. I found myself, one leg in, one leg out of my shorts, staring at him as he entered the water. It was times like this I could really see what it meant to be a water nymph; it was as though in water he was at his fullest potential. Nothing as mundane as walking was holding him back. He was free.

"Are you coming in or are you just gonna stare at me?" Adrian called, grinning from the centre of the water.

"Can you blame me? I was watching the lord of all naiad swim, it's quite the sight." I winked, diving in after him.

"Ughhh, don't start calling me that, whatever you do," Adrian said as I popped up out of the water.

"Okie dokie," I said, grabbing him by the waist as he

swam circles round me. I pulled him into me, holding his little body against mine, I never wanted to let him go.

"What are you doing?" he whispered. I could feel his breath against my neck. I lifted him, raising him so that we were level with each other. Our eyes locked, and his twinkling blue orbs drew me in, my heart thundering in my chest. His fingers were wrapping around my arms.

"Adrian." I whispered, my breath drawing short.

"Michael." He nodded. I leaned forward, shutting my eyes. I pressed my lips against his, and he pushed back, his skin warm and soft against me. I wrapped my arms around his slender waist as tingles ran across my body, his fingers knotted in my hair, holding me close. We kissed and the world and time fell away, it was just me and him. My hands explored his delicate body as his fingers ran along my back tracing the grooves and striations. He wrapped his legs around my waist as we kissed, pulling us together. We couldn't be close enough, drawn to each other like magnets. We were lost in a haze. I carried him, still locked together, to the side of the lake, and we kissed against the bank. I don't know how long for until we broke apart, panting and trembling and entwined in one another.

"I love you," he whispered, resting his head against my chest as he struggled to catch his breath.

"I love you too," I said, holding him close. There was a rustling in the trees behind us as the world slowly came back into focus.

"What?" Adrian asked, looking at me, as I looked past him, over his shoulder to the source of the rustling, but it had already stopped. For a second, I thought I'd seen a flicker of something green. Must have been a bush rustling in the breeze.

"Errm, nothing. Don't worry about it," I said, planting a peck on his forehead as I did my best to ignore the hairs standing up on the back of my neck.

"Okay then," he said and smiled, still panting, his hands rested against my heaving chest. I found myself lost in his face as he gazed up at me.

"You're so beautiful," I whispered, his eyes twinkling like sapphires set into perfect marble. Every feature carved out to perfection and flushed pink.

"Your eyes are golden," he breathed, staring up at me, his mouth half open. I blinked as tears tumbled down my cheeks, and broke away, taking a couple steps back as laughter bubbled up out of me.

"I'm the luckiest man alive!" My shout echoed out through the forest, bouncing off the trees, sending birds flying up into the air as euphoria flooded through me. I watched as water swelled around me, then like little vines, it spiraled out of the lake. Tiny little dancing columns spinning around, catching the light, and twinkling like diamonds. I looked past them to Adrian, smiling back at me, his hands held just above the water, his fingers twitching ever so slightly, as if pulling strings.

"My magical boyfriend," I said to myself, passing my hands through the streams as they danced around me. Adrian was sitting on the bank now, his feet dangling in the water as his fingers twitched above it and then his voice rang out.

It was low at first, lower than I expected, reverberating through the forest, goosebumps ran along my arms. He didn't sing in words, it was like a melody, pure music pouring out of him. His voice swelled, climbing higher and lighter. I was drawn to him, like siren song. I walked through the spiraling water as shivers ran through me. I'd never heard anything like it. It wasn't a song; it was a primal sound, a feeling. I took his hands in mine, he smiled at me, and tilted his head up. He opened his mouth wide and one long note filled the air; it was as though the whole rest of the world fell silent to listen.

"What did you think?" he asked, suddenly shy as the last of his song echoed out through the trees. I swallowed around the lump in my throat, momentarily struck dumb.

"It was... you are amazing. What was that?" I asked, my mouth dry as tears tumbled down my cheeks.

"It was a fay song; we sing it when a new fay is born. It was the best thing I could think of for a birthday present," he said, wiping the tears from my eyes.

"What's it called?"

"Life of the Forest."

ELEVEN

Michael wiped his sweaty brow as we crossed the road to the park. Apparently, we were in an April heat wave, which was becoming a bit much. The fay forest didn't really get much in the way of changing weather conditions. Where it was sunny, it was sunny, where it was rainy, it was rainy, mostly it was shady.

"At least we're not in classes. This weather would be a nightmare in uniform,"

"Do I really have to go back to that next week?" I groaned, as memories of endless economics classes rose with the midday sun. Odd words like quantitative easing and inflation being bandied about re-asserted themselves; I still hadn't the foggiest what any of it meant.

"Wouldn't you miss me every day if you didn't come back?"

"You make a good point," I said, squinting as the sunlight blinded me.

"There!" Michael yelled and set off towards the ice-cream van.

"I'm finally gonna have one of those blue ice lollies," I grinned, following him. The last one had been rather dramatically interrupted by Minoty.

"You can have all the weird blue lollies you want," Michael chuckled, handing a note to the ice cream man.

"I am truly the luckiest naiad alive," I giggled as the ice cream man gave Michael a quizzical look and handed him the ice lollies.

"You're brave saying that out loud," he said, handing me a large blue ice lolly, as we plopped down on a bench under a tree.

"Well, there's a good chance he'd have no idea what a naiad is, and even if he does, what's he gonna do? Tell someone he met a naiad? They'd think he'd been out in the sun too long," I chuckled, licking my lolly.

"You're not wrong to be fair."

"Is my tongue blue yet?" I asked, sticking it out, and Michael smiled and then his face shifted. He looked past me; there was a searching look in his eyes.

"What is it?" I asked, looking over my shoulder.

"There's something rustling," he whispered.

"Maybe it's just a fox," I said, although I already had a sinking feeling in my stomach.

Michael slowly got to his feet, walking past me to the tree line.

"Stay behind me, Adrian." I followed, holding my breath as he drew back a leafy branch to reveal a forest clearing. At first there was nothing, then just out of the corner of my eye I saw something green dart behind a tree. Michael moved like a flash; he had my wrist, and we were walking away, back towards the street. We walked as fast as you could possibly walk before you have to admit you're jogging.

"It's a goblin," he said, his voice low.

"But what about everyone else?" I whispered, giving up on walking as I jogged to keep up.

"It's not up to you to protect them Adrian, you've been through enough and anyway..." His voice trailed off as we got to the edge of the park.

"Anyway, what?"

"I think it's after us specifically."

"Why?" I squeaked, my chest tightening.

"You remember at the lake the other day? I heard something rustling in the trees. For a second it felt as though we were being watched."

"Why didn't you say?" I said, my body starting to feel stiff as I stumbled across the road after Michael.

"I didn't want it to be true," Michael said, looking down the road, then back to me, his face softened.

"Adrian, I'm not going to let anyone hurt you, you're safe, I promise." He pulled me into his chest, stroking my hair. I breathed him in, trying to take deep breaths as I clutched his vest in my fists. I took one last deep steadying breath and pulled away.

"Something's wrong. If multiple goblins are coming through to the still world, something is going wrong," I said, scanning the horizon for the nearest big tree.

"Where are we going?" Michael asked as I started pulling him along.

"I've just got to see," I said, stopping in front of a conveniently wide oak.

"No way, Adrian, it's not safe."

"If there are mirelings in the still world, it's more dangerous not knowing."

"But—"

"And you'll be with me… right?"

"Of course, always," Michael said, giving my hand a squeeze.

"Here goes nothing," I said, stepping through the tree. The smell of ferns and general greenness swelled up to meet us as the world was bathed in dappled golden light. Then it hit me, that sound, my legs started to tremble, and my mouth went dry.

"Do you hear that?" Michael asked, as I stumbled back towards the grove, dragging him with me. I fell through the passage, my knees crunching against the gravelly ground of the still world as I gasped for air. The harsh sunlight of an April heatwave imposing itself upon me.

"Adrian, Adrian, what's wrong?" Michael asked. He was on his knees in front of me.

"That song," I whimpered, my voice catching as trembles wracked my body.

"It sounded kind of like your singing, only… angry. What does it mean?"

"It's our war song. The mirelings have invaded the forest."

PART FIVE
WAR & PEACE

CHAPTER
ONE

A drian got to his feet, his legs shaking as he stood, I held his hand, his face was busy with thought.

"We have to go back in," he said after an age.

"What? No way, Adrian, it's not your job to save everyone." The image of Adrian in Merlin's cauldron flashed through my mind as anger began to simmer in me. Spurred on by the heat of the sun, beating down on us.

"But what about Olivier, and the others and what's happening here, I've got to do something."

"What about you Adrian, what about your life, what if something happens, what if…" I locked eyes with him, trembling as I pulled his hand to my chest, choking on my words as images of disaster that I couldn't put into words shot through my mind. His twinkling blue orbs flitted from me to the trees all around us.

"I won't stay long, I've just got to know, to check on Olivier." He pulled away moving back towards the tree.

"No. Adrian please—" My voice caught in my throat as

he stepped towards the tree. Panic rushed through me like electricity.

"STOP," I barked, my voice bounced through the street. A flock of pigeons took to the air from the tree above us and Adrian froze stock still on the spot. "Adrian?" I whispered, as an awful realisation dawned on me. I stepped in front of him, looking into his glazed over eyes, but he wasn't moving, not a single flicker. Suddenly the world was cold and numb, the April heat wave washed away, and I was alone staring into his face. Time seemed to stretch into infinity, and then his eyes flickered.

"Michael?" He sounded confused, scared.

"Adrian... I'm so sorry." A cold sweat had taken me now, my hands were clammy, and my stomach lurched.

"What happened?" he asked, innocence pouring out of him as he looked at me searchingly.

"I didn't mean to," I whispered, wanting to grab him to hold him close, but somehow it felt wrong.

"What are you talking about? You didn't mean to what?" Adrian took my hands, pulling me towards him. His voice was full of kindness and understanding. It was as though I was drowning in guilt.

"I controlled you," I whispered, wincing looking down into Adrian's face, watching as the realisation dawned.

"With your voice?" he asked, not pulling away from me. I nodded, and my stomach lurched again.

"By accident?" I nodded again and he smiled and craned up, kissing me gently on the lips.

"That's okay, you didn't mean to."

"It felt so wrong, like I'd violated you. How did it feel?" I whispered, a bubbling disgust creeping up through me. Part of me wanted to drop to my knees, to beg him for forgiveness, but he didn't even seem to think there was anything to forgive.

"I dunno, it felt like I was just waking up, like I wasn't even there, but it didn't hurt or anything." Adrian gave me a tight squeeze and then let me go.

"Why aren't you angry with me?" I asked. It slipped out before I could think as a panic and self-loathing filled up my brain so much that it blocked out everything else.

"Why would I be angry at you, it was an accident, you didn't mean to," he said, reaching up, taking my face in his hands focusing his big beautiful blue eyes on me. I wanted it to make everything better, but I felt so guilty I thought I might be sick.

"I didn't mean to," I agreed. It was all I could muster as I looked down, staring at my stained white shoes. I couldn't meet his gaze anymore, it was too painful.

"Should we head back to yours?" he asked after a pause that lingered in the air too long to be comfortable. I nodded. I couldn't speak; he was doing what I wanted, what I'd made him do. I'd controlled him. I was disgusting.

That night we settled down with Mum to watch the telly, our giant mugs of tea in hand, but something was off. Adrian spent most of the evening staring off into the middle distance, worrying about Olivier I imagine.

"Are you two okay?" Mum asked, as Adrian disappeared off into the bathroom.

"Not really," I mumbled, letting my head drop.

"Did you have a fight?"

"Worse," I grumbled, slumping in my chair.

"Oh, come on Michael it can't be that bad, just tell me."

"I controlled him mum, I used this stupid power I've got, and I controlled him. It felt so wrong." I sagged further into the chair.

"Michael, why would you do that?"

"It was an accident," I groaned.

"Is he upset with you over it?"

"That's the worst part. He forgave me straight away, like it was nothing, but it's not nothing is it? It's me overpowering him; controlling him. It's disgusting."

"The worst part is that he forgave you?" Mum asked, looking puzzled.

"Well, if he was mad with me, I'd get what I deserve. This way I feel like I'm drowning in guilt. Like I've got to do something."

"How did it even happen, anyway, did you just say, 'pass the salt' and he did or something?" Mum asked frustratingly casually.

"No, he thinks something bad is happening in the fay world. He wanted to go and do something about it, but I wanted him to look out for himself just for once and I begged him not to go and suddenly... I stopped him." My stomach flipped again as images of his frozen glassy eyes filled my memories.

"Well Michael, I've got to say, it sounds like you didn't mean any harm by it. If Adrian doesn't think it's a problem perhaps you should let yourself off a bit." Mum said, reaching over to give my hand a squeeze.

"Did I miss anything good?" asked Adrian as he returned, nestling into my lap. I wrapped an arm around his shoulder and tried to quiet the guilt.

"Nothing much," said Mum, reaching for the remote to

turn up the telly.

"Do you know her, Michael, she looks about your age?" Mum asked, pointing a finger at the telly. I glanced up, there was a picture of a girl my age on the screen, with shoulder-length dark hair, olive tone skin and brown eyes. The story was that a Starkton girl named Wendy hadn't been seen by friends or family since yesterday morning. A shiver ran down my back as I listened to the details, *last seen taking a short cut through the woods on the way to her friend's house.* I glanced down at Adrian, his eyes fixed on the story.

"Well, it's just awful isn't it, her poor mother, my goodness, I wonder if they'll organise a search party. I think they should, I'd certainly go help search." Mum was talking to herself as much as us now and set off into the kitchen midway through a sentence.

"You don't think… it could be related to the goblin we saw, do you?" I whispered.

"I don't think so," Adrian said, but he didn't even sound convinced himself.

"What would mireling creatures want with a random teenager, anyway?"

"I've never really known what they wanted," Adrian said, looking puzzled.

"What who wants, dear?" Mum asked re-appearing with a glass of wine in hand.

"Doesn't matter Mum. I'm gonna have a shower before bed anyway, was boiling today," I said, making an excuse to disappear upstairs. Adrian was already in my room when I got out of the shower, fiddling nervously with a drawstring that had made its way out of some of my old shorts.

"Are you okay?" I asked. He didn't reply, he looked

distant, lost almost. "Adrian?" I said, sitting down next to him on the bed as I placed a hand gingerly on his shoulder.

"Olivier," he said to himself I think, as his eyes flickered back into focus.

"Are you okay?" I repeated.

"What? Sorry, I was a bit gone then, just tired I think."

"I understand you being worried about her, about everyone... I'm sorry I stopped you going in."

"Michael, it's okay, you were right, I don't know what I was thinking. What good would I have been to anyone? I'd just be a liability." His eyes dropped to his fiddling fingers; I shook my head.

"Adrian... that's not why I didn't want you go. Why would you say that?"

"It's not, it's silly, its nothing," he said, is voice cracking as he spoke, and my heart ached.

"It's not nothing if it's upsetting you," I said, shifting on the bed so we were face to face, eye to eye.

"It's just true isn't it, I am a liability. I put you at risk, your mum at risk, Olivier at risk, maybe the damn whole town at risk." Tears started to spill out onto the bed, as he looked down into his hands. Every unkind word stung and stabbed at me.

"Adrian, none of this is your fault, I'm fine, Mum's fine, and you said the mirelings have been at war with the fay for centuries, millennia even. It's not your fault there's a connection between Starkton forest and the fay forest. Why are you blaming yourself for any of that?".

"I don't know, I just have this... this awful nagging feeling in me, eating away at me," he sobbed, pulling his knees up to his chest. I wanted to reach out, grab him, hold him, but since I'd used my power on him it somehow didn't feel right to just control him.

"Adrian, when did you start to feel like this?" I whispered, wrestling with my voice to keep it from cracking.

"I don't know, I guess I've always had little doubts, but it's been worse since Merlin... had me." As he spoke, he buried his head in his hands, like he wanted to disappear. I couldn't resist anymore; I pulled him into my chest and lay with him in my arms.

"I understand," I whispered stroking his hair, as his little sobs rocked my body

"I'm sorry for always crying," he whispered.

"Cry as much as you need to." I kissed his forehead and lay there with him at my chest. I don't know how long for but eventually he fell asleep. Stunned glassy-eyed images of Adrian frozen at my command were seared into my mind. Keeping me awake. I was only pulled away from it by Adrian, talking in his sleep.

"Olivier, I'll find-I coming, Olivier, I'm coming," he mumbled in broken sentences, but I knew what it meant. I watched him struggle to find peace, even in his sleep, until I couldn't bear it any longer. I slipped out of bed and stalked downstairs, grabbing a pen and paper.

TWO

"**M**ICHAEL!" Linda's voice carried through the house. I sat up, rubbing the sleep from my eyes as I blinked them into focus.

"Adrian! Have you seen Michael?" Linda burst through the door, holding a sheet of paper in hand, and looking wild-eyed. I looked around the room confused and still half asleep; he wasn't here, and there was no sign of him. My eyes fell on the corner of the room where his fay armour had been piled up. It was gone.

"What's going on, his armour's missing?" My stomach lurched as a terrible realisation began to dawn on me.

"Read this," Linda said, sitting down on the bed as she thrust the sheet of paper into my hand. It was a letter, in Michael's handwriting. I recognised it immediately, it read:

Adrian, I'm going to find you some peace of mind. I'm sorry I left in the night, it's better this way, safer for you. I couldn't watch everything eat away at you and just do nothing. With any luck I'll be back before you're even awake and you won't even have to read this. And Mum, please don't worry, I know what I'm doing, I'll be back before you know it and good as new.

I read it over and over again, bitter questions running through my head. Why hadn't I woken up or just shut up about Olivier? We could have gone today, together, I'd have been with him, I'd know he was okay. Anything could be happening in there with the mirelings invading, ogres, goblins, dire spiders, and Michael was in there alone because of me.

"What is he talking about Adrian, why does he need to put your mind at ease? This can't all be to do with his controlling you can it?" Linda asked, dragging me out of my own self-loathing mire.

"You know about that?" I asked, shocked.

"He told me about it last night. It was eating him up." I sighed and sagged a little.

"I think he is getting upset because he feels like he's controlling me like Merlin did, but it's nothing like that. He didn't mean to, and he was looking out for me."

"So do you think that is what this is about?"

"Maybe part of it, but not completely."

"So, what's the rest?"

"The other day Michael heard rustling behind us in the woods and then again at the park yesterday. So, we followed it and we saw a goblin. It's not normal for a goblin to be here, they'd need to have access to the home grove, so I knew something was wrong. We went into the fay world to investigate, and the song of war was in voice. Which means

292

that the fay forest is at war, which means a mireling invasion. Then that kidnapping in the woods popped up on the news and it sort of felt like it might have been related. Then again, I don't know why mirelings would be taking human teens. Anyway, it was on both our minds and clearly, I was stressing him out so much with all my nonsense. He felt like he had to do something." Linda looked at me a little puzzlingly at first and a silence fell over us.

"Sorry… that's a lot to take in, dear," she said eventually.

"Should I start again?" I asked, fidgeting as a feeling of urgency started to take root.

"No, I think I got it. You saw a goblin, realised the fay were at war. Michael controlled you, you were worried the kidnapping was related… is that the headlines?" she asked, counting off the points of concern on her fingers as she went.

"Yes, that's about the sum of it," I said, climbing out of bed and picking up my fay robes. They were a bit tatty and torn… and stained and bloody, but they'd have to do.

"What are you doing?" she asked as I pulled them on.

"I've got to go in after him. He's all alone." Linda looked a little conflicted and I wasn't about to wait around for her to make up her mind in case she didn't think I should go. I was halfway to the door when I heard her thundering down the stairs behind me.

"I'm coming too!"

"Fine," I said, having neither the time nor energy to argue.

"Will I need a coat?" asked Linda, pulling on a large pair of ugly knee-high plastic-looking boots.

"Errm, I don't know," I said, struggling to process the

question as I opened the door and set my sights on the conveniently large tree in the Michael's neighbour's front yard.

"We're going through—" My mouth fell open as I watched a goblin charge through the tree wielding a rusty cleaver, followed by Michael bedecked in his fay armour, launching his silvery hammer through the air. It impacted the goblin with a stomach-churning crunching sound.

"Found him," I said too quietly for anyone but me to hear, watching bemused as Olivier emerged from the tree following Michael.

"What are we waiting f… Oh, he's there," said Linda, appearing behind me in the doorway. I watched as Olivier all too nonchalantly picked up the limp goblin and shoved it back through the tree. Depositing it in the grove of the fay forest.

"What is going on?" asked Linda. I shrugged my shoulders wordlessly as Michael and Olivier crossed the road towards us, looking surprisingly cheerful.

"I didn't think I'd be back here so soon," came Olivier's voice as she pulled down the hood of her cloak, revealing a shock of blonde hair.

"You're okay," I said, as confusion gave way to relief.

"Of course," she said, patting me on the back.

"Oh Michael, that letter of yours scared us both half to death!" said Linda.

"Sorry about that, I just felt like I had to do something. I couldn't sleep."

"Next time you can't sleep have a cup of warm milk. I don't think my nerves could take this again," Linda chuckled. "Tea everyone?" Linda asked as Olivier released me from the hug, and we headed back into the house.

"So, is there any news?" I asked Olivier as we filed into the living room.

"I take it you already know the mirelings have launched a full-scale invasion, well it's gotten dangerous. They seem to be focusing most of their efforts on The Hut, but they've also been launching attacks on the grove. Dispatching some of their number to the still world."

"Yes, we saw one in the forest."

"Michael said as much, and I'm afraid I can confirm a fear of yours. We think they've been kidnapping people, bringing them back with them."

"But why?"

"Our best guess is they're trying to use them to activate shards of Excalibur. They're looking for champions essentially."

"But the chances of just finding one by fluke are infinitesimally small."

"Presumably they're operating on the principal that a slight chance is better than no chance."

"Have you made any progress in getting any of them back?" I asked hopefully. A sombre expression took over Olivier's face.

"Some of the fay lords don't see it as a priority." A dull silence overtook us all as the words lingered in the air.

"I'll help." My voice was small, but it banished the silence.

"When we do save them, how will we explain a load of kidnapped kids turning up all talking about goblins?" asked Michael, forcing a smile.

"We'll cross that bridge when we come to it," said Olivier.

"In the meantime, we should probably stop them taking any more," said Linda, hovering in the doorway with a tray of teas.

"There is that problem to contend with as well. We've been trying to keep the mirelings away from the grove to minimise the issue, but it's been tricky. They seem to have intricate knowledge of our defences," said Olivier.

"Well, at least school will be starting up again soon. So we'll know where all the kids are, be much harder to kidnap them when they're in class," said Linda, popping down tea in front of us all. Olivier flinched at the mention of school.

"Well… that's not such good news as you might think. How many kids walk to or from Starkton High every day?" Olivier asked.

"Most of them," said Michael.

"And how many of them take short cuts through the forest?"

"Most of them," I said, as a dreadful feeling dawned on me.

"As I feared, Starkton High opening back up could be a disaster," explained Olivier.

"Well, there isn't much we can do to stop that happening, dear," said Linda as half of her biscuit plopped into her tea.

"I have an idea on that front actually, but Adrian, only you could do it," said Michael.

"Me? What could I do?"

"Flood the school."

"Michael, there's no way I could do that. I'm not powerful enough … not since Merlin. I would probably collapse after one room," I said, trying to ignore the feeling of shame bubbling up in the pit of my stomach.

"You are Adrian, you could do it, because the water is already there, in the pipes. Remember Mum? One year they closed school in the middle of winter cause the water froze in the pipes and they burst and flooded the school?"

"Now that you mention it. I do remember that it was an absolute nightmare, finding people to cover my shifts," said Linda.

"You could do that easy, Adrian. I've seen what you can do when you put your mind to it, and you could burst all the pipes in every room, on every floor. The whole place would be flooded. It would take them ages to fix it." Michael beamed at me, his face full of pride and faith. I swallowed the lump in my throat.

"I suppose... I could do that," I said, trying not to get choked up.

"That settles it then, the night before school opens, Adrian and Michael are going to sneak in and flood it," said Olivier, getting up from her chair after having barely touched her tea.

"Are you going?" I asked. I already knew the answer, but I didn't like it all the same.

"Have to, busy, busy, there is a war on after all, but hey, take this," she said, handing me a small black stone.

"A whispering stone?"

"And don't smash this one," she said with a chuckle, pulling me in for one last hug before making her way out of the house and across the street to the neighbour's conveniently large tree.

"Feel better now?" asked Michael, his hands appearing

on my shoulders as he planted a kiss on the back of my head.

"I can't believe you went into the forest without me," I said, spinning around on the spot.

"I had to do something, to get that smile back on your face." Michael grinned, poking at my lips as my cheeks flush.

"But it was so dangerous, anything could have happened," I said, resting my hands on his chest.

"What, for me?" he asked, flexing a bicep as he winked at me. I rolled my eyes and battled with the smile forcing its way across my face.

"Yes, for you, I don't want you putting yourself in danger over me," I said, craning up to plant a kiss on his cheek.

"Well, tough," said Michael, sticking his tongue out.

THREE

Adrian and I pulled on our long, black hooded cloaks as night drew in. I don't know why Halloween costumes are for sale all year round, but I'm glad they are.

"I'm still not convinced this is a good idea, boys," said Mum. She'd been nervously flitting about all day.

"Mum, even if we get caught in the school, it's going to look like there was some random plumbing malfunction. There's no way they could prove Adrian magically flooded the school. It's fool-proof."

"And you really think you're up to it Adrian?" she said, looking worried.

"Well, we'll soon see won't we," said Adrian, doubt dripped from his voice, it stung.

"Of course you can, you're the lord of all naiad," I said, giving his shoulder a squeeze.

"Ughhh don't remind me," he said, then gave a half-hearted chuckle as he pulled on his boots.

"Well don't say I didn't warn you," said Mum, waving us off as we stepped out into the night.

"Adrian, are you okay?" I asked, taking his hand as we made our way down the street, our cloaks billowing behind us like we were witches off to a coven meeting.

"I'm fine… I'm just worried I might let you down, that's all," he said, his voice soft and small.

"Adrian, you know in the time I've known you, you've never once let me down."

"You're just saying that."

"No, I'm really not Adrian, think about it, you saved me from Minoty, you tripped up that thug who was bullying Alex and Jack, you were the one that broke me out of fay prison. You always say I'm your hero, but really Adrian, I think you're the heroic one." Adrian sniffled and dabbed at his face; I couldn't see him under his hood, but I knew he was crying again. He'd been crying a lot recently.

"I don't know what's wrong with me, I just keep having these… doubts."

"Since Merlin, right?" I asked, giving his hand a little squeeze.

"Mostly, yeah, I think so." He nodded under his hood, and I took a deep breath, squashing the rage back down.

"Well, anytime you're ever feeling doubts, or worries, or anything bad, just tell me, and I can tell you the amazing stories of Adrian the Brave." He giggled, and my chest fluttered; it was a magic sound.

"Adrian the Brave, there are worse epithets," he said, wrapping his little arm round my waist pulling me into him as we turned down the path towards school.

"What would be mine d'ya reckon?"

"Michael the ermm... Magnificent?" Adrian chuckled.

"That sounds like I pull a rabbit out of a hat at a kid's parties," I said and grinned, giving his shoulder a squeeze.

"What about, Michael the Handsome?"

"It's an improvement, that's for sure, lot of pressure though. Imagine I turn up somewhere and they're expecting like... Ryan Reynolds or something and they get me."

"I think people would be happy at the upgrade."

"You're gonna give me a big head." Adrian and I were laughing when we rounded the corner and the school came into view. Suddenly everything seemed more serious.

"Do you think we should ermm... jump the wall here, rather than going through the front gate?" Adrian asked, stopping alongside the wall.

I nodded, weaving my fingers together, making a basket for him to step into. Adrian climbed on and I boosted him up so he could get his hands over the wall and balance himself before I shoved him up the rest of the way. He was so light, I almost felt like I could have just shunted him over.

Wordlessly Adrian offered me a hand, but I didn't take it. I was worried I'd pull him back down. I took a deep breath and performed a muscle up, heaving myself over the wall, enjoying the pink that flushed Adrian's cheeks as he watched me. I gave him a quick wink before letting myself drop down on the other side of the wall and held out my arms to catch Adrian.

Adrian looked down nervously. It was as if I could read his thoughts, worrying about hurting me as he jumped into my arms.

"I'll be fine, jump," I whispered. He nodded and slid off

the wall, falling into my arms. I planted a kiss on his nose before putting him down.

We stalked towards the school, stooped, sticking to the shadows and not uttering a word. It should have been empty by now, but there was something about sneaking in that made silence seem necessary. We got to one of the side doors and I tried the code, but it didn't open. I frowned and tried it again, but still nothing.

"What now?" I hissed, trying to ignore the sweats I could feel breaking out across my body. Adrian didn't reply, but offered a smile before raising a hand to the door. I watched, fascinated, as his hand was sheathed with water. I still never really understood where it came from. Was he drawing it out of the air, or himself maybe? Regardless, he placed his now water-sheathed hand on the door, and it slithered off into the cracks. Adrian's brows creased and a grin cracked across my face as his tongue poked out in concentration.

Seconds ticked on and I was about to reach for my shard, resorting to smashing the door down when the door shifted ever so slightly. I held my breath, gave the door another try and it glided open.

In one swift motion Adrian flung his hand out, pulling the water into himself, and stepped into the school, and I found myself hypnotised, staring at the coolest person I'd ever met. When I finally managed to stop admiring him, I stepped inside and noticed a little fuse box smoking slightly above the door.

Adrian took a deep breath as he crossed to a radiator and laid his hand on a pipe. I jumped as a gurgling, creaking sound echoed through the silent corridors. Concentration built on his face, his knuckles turned white as he gripped the pipe, veins beginning to pop out along his neck. I placed a hand on his shoulder, willing him to be okay, to do it, to know for himself that he could.

I looked around for the first signs of leaks, jumping again as Adrian's gasp caught me off guard. I looked back just in time to catch him as he stumbled away from the pipes, panting.

"Are you okay?" I asked, my heart suddenly racing as I looked down into his pale face.

"I'm too weak." He looked so ashamed, his big blue eyes swimming as he looked up at me, his face full of apology. I pulled him into my chest, kissing his forehead as he struggled to catch his breath in my arms and wished I could help him.

"I've got an idea," I said, taking Adrian's hand as I led him towards the loos, remembering Mum explaining why the pipes had burst once in winter. When water freezes it expands, the pipes burst because there wasn't room for it anymore. I could help Adrian, I just needed to introduce more water.

"All you've got to do is stop it coming out," I explained as I turned on every tap in the big boys' loos on the first floor. Adrian looked at me puzzled for a second before understanding dawned. He placed his hand on the main pipe connected to the sinks. There was a gurgling sound and suddenly the water stopped pouring out of the taps. I watched the veins pop up along Adrian's forearm and neck as his knuckles turned white, gripping the pipe again.

I held my breath watching him, willing him on, bracing him as he rocked back for a second, taking a shaky breath, but he didn't loosen his grip. All at once, creaking sounds struck out so loudly it must have filled the school. I crossed my fingers behind my back as I watched him. His eyes were shut tight, his jaw clenched.

You can do it. I mouthed the words silently to the back of his head, willing him on when suddenly a roaring, snapping sound shot out from the corridor. Adrian let go and slumped against me, panting, as a little sweat beaded on his forehead.

"You, okay?" I asked, dipping to deliver a quick kiss as hissing sounds started to issue all around us.

"Just a bit out of breath. It's kind of like flexing a muscle really hard," he explained between pants.

"I think you did it," I whispered into his ear, watching a puddle form at my feet. Back in the hall, water was spraying out of the pipes all the way down the corridor. I sighed with relief watching the corridor floor swell with water, only to be caught off guard as Adrian swept down the corridor, his footsteps splashing as he went.

"Where are you off to?" I asked. He turned to me, sweat beading his brow, his sapphire eyes twinkling, and a broad smile split across his face.

"I'm gonna do the second floor," he said, heading for the stairs, letting water circle around his wrists as we walked down the corridor. It trailed behind him in snaking patterns like crystal ribbons, his cloak billow behind him as water wreathed his hands.

Butterflies fluttered in my stomach and a shiver ran down my spine as I watched him disappear down the corridor and whispered, "You're my hero."

"So, what do we do with a totally unexpected, unpredictable, additional week off from school?" Michael asked, as he played with my fringe. My head rested across his chest as we lazed in bed on what would have been the first Monday morning back at school.

"Would it be wrong of us not to try and help with the, you know... the whole goblin kidnapping thing going, on?" I asked, trying to quiet the voice in my head that told me I should be out looking for goblins stalking the woods as we lay here.

"That isn't your job Adrian, you literally flooded the school last night. You're allowed a day off," Michael said, planting a kiss on my forehead as he pulled me into him tighter.

"I guess one day off wouldn't hurt," I whispered, nuzzling into him, closing my eyes, breathing him.

"Exactly, and what do you want to do with your one day off?"

"I think I'd just like to feel normal today. What do

normal seventeen and eighteen-year-olds do on unexpected days off?"

"Well… I guess, maybe, hang out with their friends. We could go see if Jack and Alex are free."

"That sounds perfect. I bet Alex will have all sorts of ideas for what to do and we could at least keep an eye out for any suspicious goings on around the edge of the forest, just when we're out and about," I said, trying to quiet the guilt already welling up again.

"If that'll make you feel better, of course we can," said Michael, slipping out from beneath me and shuffling off into the bathroom. I smiled as I watched him go, breathing in the morning, the sun's warmth bathing my face through the window.

I lingered a little before climbing out of bed and throwing on one of Michael's sweaters. Linda must have already left because there was no sign of her. Which was a bit odd, she'd usually barge in and wake us up in the morning before she set off for work. Perhaps she'd decided to take mercy on us since we'd had a long night of industrial sabotage. I liked her décor, it was full of whimsy; gnomes in the garden, little porcelain toad stools on the windowsill. Odd colourful knitted tea cozies and loud flowery paintings on the walls at odd angles.

I suppose it was ugly in a way, but to me it always felt like the house was smiling at me. I made myself and Michael tea in her mismatched chipped mugs and took mine outside to on the David bench. They never talked about David really, but I'd picked up bits and pieces. He'd died a couple of years ago in a car crash, before Michael's brother Dan left for uni. We fay don't really have relationships with our parents like I think Michael did. If we lost them, it would be sad, but only as sad as any other loss. David's loss had left a wound, especially for Linda.

"Sunbathing, are we?" asked Michael, who was now dressed for the day, in shorts, a t-shirt and dripping wet hair.

"Just thinking about your mum's excellent taste in interior décor," I said with a smile, scooting along the bench.

"You know, if she heard you say that it would make her day. Her week actually," Michael chuckled, plopping down next to me.

"Well, I'll have to remember to mention it then," I said, heading for the door.

"Where are you scurrying off to then?"

"I've gotta get changed. We can't go see Alex with me wearing one of your hoodies, he pays too much attention to clothes. Also, it's boiling." I chuckled, disappearing into the house. I'd changed into some grey blue jeans and a flowy baby blue shirt thing that Linda insisted on calling a blouse.

"How do I look?" I asked, presenting myself to Michael.

"Adorable," he said, planting a kiss on my cheek as we set off down the street.

"I'll just call him, so he knows we're heading over," said Michael, putting his phone to his ear. I didn't really like phones. We didn't have them in the fay world and they seemed sort of like distraction machines to me, but it was handy to always be within shouting distance of friends. And sort of a nightmare. Michael took his phone from his ear, frowning.

"He didn't answer. Alex always answers his phone. He's glued to it," Michael said, shoving his phone back into his pocket as I scanned every bush and tree along the roadside for suspicious rustling. So far I'd only spotted signs of wind.

"Maybe he's showering." I shrugged as we turned down the street.

"Yeah, for sure. Hope we don't catch him with a towel around his waist," Michael chuckled.

"Jack would have words with us."

"Oh, I could call Jack, let him know we're heading to Alex's."

"I say we just turn up by surprise, impress upon their hospitality, and expect them to entertain us."

"What else are friends for?" asked Michael with a chuckle.

"Exactly!" I agreed as we turned off the street down the road Alex lived on. It was an odd road, Michael said it was private. Which in practice meant it was unpaved, had cobbled pavements, massive trees along the edges, and Alex was walking down it as we turned up it. Although I don't think every private road came with an Alex.

"Hey Alex, we were just coming to see you!" Michael called, waving to Alex. He didn't react at first, as if he was on a delay.

"Oh, Michael… Adrian. Hi," he said, only seeming to notice us once we were right in front of him.

"Are you okay Alex?" I asked. He didn't respond at first, as he craned his neck, looking past us.

"Errm, sorry, bit distracted."

"What's wrong?" I asked, placing a hand on his shoulder.

"I can't get hold of Jack… I haven't been able to get hold of him since he left mine yesterday afternoon."

"Maybe he's just not been on his phone," Michael suggested, but Alex shook his head.

"He's never not on his phone for this long and he doesn't ignore telephone calls and I can't stop catastrophising. So I'm going to his house to shut my stupid panicking brain up."

"We'll come with you, if you'd like the company?" I offered.

"Yes, I could use the distraction," he said, setting off again down his street.

"Did you hear the school flooded?" Michael asked, giving me a little wink over Alex's shoulder.

"Yeah, that's another problem. If the stupid pipes hadn't burst, we'd be at school right now and I'd be with Jack, and I wouldn't be having this particular meltdown. I'd probably be having some other meltdown, but I'll take that one over this one in a heartbeat."

"Sorry about that," I said, freezing as I resisted the urge to physically bite my tongue.

"Why are you apologising? It isn't your fault," said Alex, looking at me like I was mad.

"Errm, I mean, just generally. Sorry you're having a... bad day."

"Adrian's very empathetic," said Michael.

"Sounds like a nightmare." Alex turned down a garden path as he spoke and marched up to the attached house's door. Banging its knocker like it had insulted him personally. There was a pause, and then the door swung open.

"Jack?" said a quite stressed-looking woman in the door.

"Is he not here?" asked Alex.

"We were hoping he was with you."

"Nope, I've been calling and texting him all night but nothing." My stomach flipped as the realisation struck me. I looked to Michael, he looked back at me, and we knew what had happened.

"Sorry Michael, Adrian, perhaps we can hang out some other time… I'm kind of… I can't hang out right now," said Alex as he disappeared into what I assumed what Jack's parent's house.

FIVE

"So, do you wanna go rescue Jack before tea or should we wait for your mum to get back from work first?" Adrian joked, although deep down, I knew part of him at least, wasn't joking.

"I always say it doesn't do anyone any favours to be a hero on an empty stomach." I joined in half-heartedly, but there was no joy in it.

"So, what's the plan? We sneak in, we scout around, try and work out where the mirelings are staging from?"

"I mean I'd say it sounds like a terrible idea, but I've not got a better one," I said, as Adrian flicked the kettle on for his fourth cup of tea. I was already desperate for the loo.

"That would be due to the fact that the idea is largely a terrible one," said Adrian, fiddling with a tea bag so feverishly it split over the counter, although he didn't seem to notice.

"Shouldn't your mum be home by now?" he asked. My eyes flicked to the clock and a terrible thought started to germinate inside me.

"Probably just stuck in traffic," I both said and hoped.

"Oh, that's weird, I'd have thought there would be less traffic with school being closed." Adrian shrugged, blissfully unaware of the dread washing through me.

"There would be," I said, as much to myself as anyone, denial slipping away.

"So, she should be home then?" Adrian said, now looking at me with concern. I paused, crossed the room and picked up the landline.

"What are you doing?" Adrian asked.

"I'm calling her office," I said, my hand trembling as I grabbed the office number off the wall. I stabbed the numbers with my shaking fingers and waited as the dial tone rang in my ear for what felt like an age.

"Hey, I'm Michael Tombs, Linda Tomb's son. I was just calling to check in to see if she'd left the office yet."

"Oh, hello Michael, sorry, but she never came in today. We assumed she was sick and forgot to call in. Is everything al—" The phone slipped out of my fingers and clattered across the floor.

"What's wrong?" said Adrian as he approached, taking my shaking hands in his.

"She never turned up to work today," I said, as the horrible thought entered full bloom.

"We'll get her back," said Adrian, giving my hand a squeeze, as he apparently caught up to my thought train.

"I don't understand. They took everyone else from the woods, and they were teens. Why would she be taken?" My chest became tight as panic set it.

"I can only think of one reason," said Adrian, his face twisted into angst, as though he didn't want to say it.

"Why?" I snapped, and he flinched as I winced. I didn't mean to, but suddenly everything was tense.

"Because if I knew… If I knew I was liable to come up against a prince, I would want something I could leverage against them." His voice was low, just above a whisper.

"How could they know that though?" I struggled not to snap again as the words tumbled out of me.

"Well… remember what Oliver said?"

"No!" I barked.

"She said they seemed to have intricate knowledge of fay defences, maybe they've got someone on the inside."

"Telling them about me?" I asked, releasing Adrian's hand, which I now realised I'd been crushing.

"Well, Merlin did give a big show of his new secret weapon," said Adrian, my fists clenching at the mention of his name.

"Okay, so we sneak in and we… attack… something and… what do we do?" I struggled around the lump forming in my throat. Mum had been all alone, scared, in danger, all this time and we'd just been drinking tea.

"I have one idea," said Adrian, as something shifted in him, like a wall had gone up. His twinkling blue eyes had gone steelie.

"What is it? It can't be worse than this."

"We could look for your mother for weeks, but could still not find her. There is only one person who could."

"You don't mean—"

"Merlin." Adrian's voice was heavy.

"No way. Not a chance. We can go to Olivier, and she'll find her, like the others." I struggled not to shout, wrestling to keep the anger out of my voice as my nails dug into the palms of my hands.

"Michael, think about it, this isn't like the other kidnappings, they were teens taken in the woods. Your mum isn't a teen, and she was gone before we woke up. They took her from this house, that means they took her for a reason, we need to get her back now."

"No but..." My voice trailed off as some of that bubbling resentment gave way to fear.

"We'll get her back," said Adrian, wrapping his little arms around me as he began to stroke my back. My legs began to tremble and suddenly I was on my knees. Adrian cradled my face against his stomach, stroking my hair as tears tumbled out of me.

"I'm scared," I sobbed.

"We'll get her back," Adrian repeated.

SIX

I held Michael's hand as we slipped into the fay forest. He was back in his leather-strapped armour. My now raggedy naiad robes whipped around me as we strode through the murky green. His eyes were locked, looking dead ahead, stalwart and stoic. He'd gone quiet as we'd prepared to enter the forest. The war song reverberated through the trees like a never-ending dirge, a reminder that you couldn't be safe. The spider-webbed yellow paths of the forest were damaged, with cracked scorched cobbles, some sporting murky brownish red stains I didn't care to think about.

I froze. Two dryad guards with their backs to us came into view, posted at the edge of the grove. Presumably ready and waiting for the next goblin attack.

"What do we do about them?" I hissed. Michael didn't reply. He barely even hesitated, and suddenly he was leading me, almost dragging me along.

"Halt!" called one of the guards as they rounded on us on

our approach, brandishing wooden staves similar to the one Minoty had twisted out of the earth.

"Piss off!" Michael barked, I shivered, something electric ran down my spine, and the guards froze for a second as their eyes glazed over and they disappeared into the undergrowth.

"W-well that works," I said, struggling to find my voice as Michael's rocked the forest.

"No time to waste," he said, stepping onto one of the winding yellow paths.

"Do you think he'll be at The Hut or his own little hole in the ground?" I asked, trying to ignore the butterflies flapping up a storm in my stomach.

"I'm betting he's in that creepy little room he... had you in." Michael faltered for a moment and glanced back at me, all that bullish confidence giving way to doubt. His face softened as his amber eyes glinted in the dappled light of the forest.

"Adrian... you don't have to do this. We can find another way. I promised you he'd never have control of you again." He turned to face me, taking my hands in his; his hands were bigger than mine, coarse and strong and gentle. I let my fingers snake into the gap between his, indulging the urge to hide behind Michael to bury myself in him, just a little bit.

"He won't, you'll be there the whole time," I said, trying to convince myself as much as Michael. I swallowed the fear; I couldn't let him down now.

"Okay, right, to Merlin's," said Michael, but we didn't move. We just stood there dreading what was about to happen until a bush rustled and we both jumped before setting off again. It was just the wind.

As we wound our way through the forest, two gnomes joined the path headed towards us both wielding little shovels.

"Should I?" Michael asked, taking a deep breath.

"Just keep walking." I hissed. The gnomes bustled past us, not even bothering to look up and catch a glance at our faces.

"So much for that prince champion, aye," said one as they passed.

"I heard he was kidnapped, along with Lord Adrian, by some rebels from the court."

"I heard the courts had been working with mirelings."

"Well, what a load of old—" The gnome's voice tailed off as he disappeared into the distance.

Michael gave my hand a squeeze as we stopped behind a large growth of trees and bushes.

"We're here aren't we?"

"Yep," my stomach dropped. I peered over the brush and there it was, Merlin's little circular door cut into the hill. Suddenly I felt as though I was zooming towards it, being dragged out of myself. Each breath harder than the last, shorter, my chest tighter. I was on the ground, Michael kneeling in front of me.

"Adrian, breathe Adrian, focus on me." His voice sounded distant, darkness was encroaching at the edges of my vision. Then there was a flash of gold in Michael's eyes, and everything went still. I was breathing again, taking long deep breaths and I couldn't move for a second, or speak or do anything except breathe. Like I was trapped in some sort of fog, breathing.

"Adrian, I'm so sorry. I did it again. I didn't mean to." I found myself pressed into Michael's chest as his smell filled me up. He smelled safe. My shoulders relaxed and my chest loosened.

"I'm fine," I whispered as I found my voice had returned.

"I didn't mean to do it, you just, you weren't breathing, I just wanted you to be okay." Michael's voice was trembling now. I pulled away and looked into Michael's eyes, gold flecks twinkling in the amber. Were they always there?

"Michael, please listen to me, this is the least of our worries," I said, keeping all my attention on him, desperate not look or see or think about what was behind him.

"I feel like I'm controlling you, like I'm not letting you feel anything," Michael said, letting me go, breaking from the hug as if he didn't have permission to touch me. All I wanted was his touch, to be buried in it.

"Michael, all you were doing was begging me to breathe and I did," I said, leaning up, looping my hands behind his neck as I pressed my lips into his. Pressure pushed into the small of my back as Michael held me in his powerful arms. His warm breath prickling the hairs along my neck, I melted into him, letting myself be pulled forward as he lay back in the grass with me laying on top of him. His knee moved up, splitting my legs, pushing me forward, so our faces were level. I let my hands run along his shoulders, his arms, his back, until he was all there was, and the rest of the world disappeared. I don't know how long we lay there, entwined in one another, before we finally broke to breathe, panting next to each other in the undergrowth.

"Well, there're definitely no guards on watch or we'd be stuffed," Michael chuckled.

"It doesn't seem like anyone's home," I whispered into his ear, my hands resting on his heaving chest.

"Good," Michael said, sitting up with me in his lap, turning to see the entrance.

"What now?"

"I guess we go in," he said, as we got to our feet and hesitantly made our way towards the entrance.

"So why're we doing this if he's not here?" I said, pushing down the dread as we crept into Merlin's hovel.

"Because he could have Mum here even if he isn't. You were right, someone could have taken Mum to get to me, but maybe that someone was Merlin! Not the mirelings, he knows where we live after all," said Michael, taking my hand in his as we snuck down the stairs into the main hall of Merlin's sanctum.

"You do make a good point," I admitted, as I attached myself to his arm for security. If Linda was here and Merlin wasn't home, things couldn't really go any smoother.

"I won't let anything happen to you," Michael whispered, my face burning as he gave me a peck on the cheek before glancing around the room. Books and scrolls carpeted the floor, vials lay empty, discarded, or smashed across tables, and the lights flickered grimly.

"Well, this is a mess," I whispered.

"Yes, I have rather let things get on top of me, haven't I?" My breath caught in my chest as his voice echoed through the room and my body went cold.

"Yes, I have rather let things get on top of me, haven't I?" Adrian's body stiffened against me and the hairs on my neck stood on end as instinct took over. I shunted Adrian behind me, back onto the stairs. Peering out into the eerie half-light of the chamber, Dad's ring clacked against the Excalibur shard around my neck. My vision fell on a hunched silhouette, which extricated itself from a shadowy bench in the far corner of the room the moment I set eyes on it.

"Stay where you are," I said, snatching the shard of Excalibur from around my neck. It burst into the glittering silver hammer, and I thrust it in Merlin's direction.

"You've no reason to fear me," said Merlin, holding his hands up as if he was surrendering whilst stepping out of the shadows into the light. He looked tired, older than I'd seen him look before, stooped with greyed hair.

"W-we've n-no r-reason to t-trust you," Adrian stuttered from behind me. His voice was small, trembling and heart breaking. I slipped my free hand behind my back for him to take hold of. His shaking hands took mine in his and squeezed, and I squeezed back.

"So then, why have you come here?" Merlin's mouth curled into a smile as he peered past me to Adrian.

"Someone took my mum, was it you?" I barked. I wished there was a way I could project myself outwards, to become like a wall between Merlin and Adrian. I wanted to stop him laying eyes on Adrian, and it was like he knew the effect he'd have on him. The way he'd scare him, and he liked it.

"Oh no, I've been quite busy enough trying to track down Nimueh and keep the monsters from our door. I wish I was speaking proverbially, but alas not."

"Why are you looking for her still?" Adrian squeaked. I could feel him cowering behind me, his little hands clinging to mine. Part of me just wanted to turn tail and run, to get Adrian as far away from this man as possible.

"Well, the mirelings seem to be operating on fairly sophisticated intelligence. They have to be getting it from somewhere. My current theory is they'll be torturing it out of her." My fist clenched at the mention of that word, my grip on the hammer was so tight my muscles trembled. He said it so casually, you'd think he was dictating a shopping list the way he spoke.

"Of course, we'd know by now if Adrian had been able to find her." Merlin's silvery eyes flashed as he fixed them on Adrian, and my blood boiled.

"You mean when you tortured him for hours, when you ripped into his mind and dominated him?" I growled.

"How ironic, a prince chastising me for dominating someone. Haven't you ever controlled poor sweet Adrian?"

My stomach flipped as a pang of shame washed over me.

"Of course, your being a prince is probably exactly why they took Linda. Can't risk you mucking up their plans, so they've got to keep security. Doubtless it was Nimueh who told them about you too." Merlin's voice dripped smugness as he went back to his desk and pored over a scroll.

"Shut up!" I barked, finding my voice again, but he'd already stopped talking, and he just smirked. I took a step forward, itching to swing for him, forgetting for a second I had Adrian's hand in mine, almost dragging him back into the room proper.

"Is there anything else I can help you boys with? Only I am quite busy, and must press on."

"Help me find my mother."

"And why would I do that?" Merlin asked. This time his voice was cutting for the first time since he'd emerged from his corner. He levelled his steely grey eyes against me. They flashed from within the darkness.

"I... because... if you don't, I'll—"

"You'll what?" Merlin grinned, enjoying watching me flounder.

"If you help find Linda... you can use me to find Nimueh." My stomach flipped as Adrian's voice shot out from behind me.

"No Adrian, you don't have to—"

"Now that's an enticing offer," Merlin crooned.

"Adrian, you don't have to do this." I looked over my shoulder. He looked so small, so afraid in his raggedy ripped robes as he stepped out from behind me into the chamber.

"I'm choosing to," he whispered. He was trembling all

over and his body was as stiff as a board. I reached out placing a gentle hand on his shoulder.

"Adrian, are you sure about this?" He nodded; I could see little tears forming in the corners of his eyes as he turned to face Merlin.

"First you find Linda, then I'll help you," he said, speaking as loudly as he could in his trembling voice.

"My, my, Adrian, so assertive," Merlin mocked. Sweat beaded on my brow as my heart raced, thundering so hard in my chest I thought I might burst. Everything in me wanting to scoop Adrian up, turn tail and run, but I couldn't, I could only watch.

"Can we get on with this?" Adrian asked. He almost sounded like he was begging.

"Very well, follow me, and grab a knife off the desk; there should be a few lying around," said Merlin, as he made for the staircase that had once been concealed by a book-shelf. I scanned around and snatched up the least malicious looking knife as we followed him. I watched Adrian descend the staircase. Each step was small, hesitant, as though every single one took a massive effort. I wanted to run for the hills with him in my arms, but I didn't, and now we were walking into Merlin's inner sanctum.

"Hurry along now, no time to dawdle," said Merlin, as we stepped into the square chamber. Torches flickering in the four corners and Merlin's cauldron glinting ominously in the centre. Adrian had frozen in the entrance; his breathing was short and ragged.

"Adrian…" I whispered his name, but I didn't know what to say, what to do.

"Sorry," he said, his voice tiny as he snapped out of whatever frozen trance he was in and stepped into the room proper.

"First things first, Michael, if you would be so good as to prick your finger."

"Why?"

"A drop of blood, to find your mother, not too high a price I hope?" Merlin crooned.

"Fine," I snarled, approaching the cauldron as I pricked my finger. Wincing as it stung, visions of nurses visiting school to deliver jabs popping into my head. *Short sharp scratch.*

"Just drop it into the cauldron my boy," Merlin instructed as he placed his hands on either side of the vessel. I dropped the blood in, and it began to smoke. First white, then darker, reddish hues billowing out of the vessel into Merlin's eyes and mouth, until his face was engulfed completely, and a silence took over the room. My chest was tight, my fist clenched around the handle of my hammer, and I realised I was holding my breath. I unclenched, or tried to at least, as the smoke dissipated.

"Well, isn't that a coincidence? She's at Lake Nimueh," he said, his cruel grey eyes looking past me to Adrian. I stepped into his line of sight, wanting to hide Adrian.

"Why should we believe you?" I barked.

"Why would I lie?" Merlin asked, his cruel grin plastered to his cruel face.

"W-why would y-you?" Adrian stuttered.

"I only lie when I need to Adrian. I'd hope you'd have realised that by now, after all, you yourself have been a prolific little liar these past months haven't you." Adrian's eyes dropped to the floor as he shrank back even further.

"Don't listen to him Adrian, that's not the same, you didn't have a choice," I said, pulling him into a tight hug.

"We always have choices Michael, for instance, now I am choosing to tell the truth, and do you know why?"

"Why?" I grunted, again putting myself between Adrian and Merlin as I broke the hug.

"Because your mother doesn't matter, not one iota. She could live forever or die tomorrow for all I care. Why would I trouble myself to lie about such an irrelevance?" Every muscle in my body tensed fighting the urge to cave his skull in, as I watched the smile on his face grow ever broader. He was getting to me, and he liked it.

"Ready Adrian?" Merlin asked, leaning around me to speak to Adrian.

"If it's that simple, can't you do that to find Nimueh? You don't need to do… whatever it was you did to Adrian the last time," I said, getting enough control of myself to stand between them again.

"Would that it was that simple. Unfortunately for poor sweet Adrian, I don't need just to find Nimueh. I need to see what they're doing at the lake and what they're doing to her and for that, I need more… invasive magic." A smile flickered across his face as he spoke and my stomach flipped, I turned on the spot.

"Come on Adrian let's—" I froze. He was there, already climbing into the cauldron.

"Adrian, what are you doing? We got what we need, let's just go," I said, grabbing him by the arm, ready to lift him clean out of the cauldron.

"I'm afraid not," said Merlin, stamping his foot. The thud echoed through the chamber and the door swung closed.

"If you don't let us go, I'll—"

"You'll do nothing, and you can put your hammer away Michael. I'll admit it was a clever trick and I fell for it. Not many people would ever think to use a mutual protection charm, but it worked. Unfortunately for you, however, I won't be falling for it again. You can no more hurt me than I can hurt you, and a deal is a deal. Adrian owes me this favour."

"Adrian owes you nothing! You're a vindictive possessive old man and—"

"That's as may be, and Michael, the truth is, you can leave if you want to. I can't stop you, but Adrian won't make it out of here alive if you do."

"What are you saying?" Adrian squeaked, cowering in the cauldron.

"I'm saying if your dashing prince tries to take you out of here before you help me, I will kill you." A shiver ran down my spine as his pleasant tone boiled my blood. I snapped and span around on the spot, bringing my hammer crashing down on Merlin's skull. I braced for the crunching, crushing sound, but it didn't come. In fact, my arm stopped dead in its track, trembling in the air. My eyes grew wide. The tip of the hammer was just resting harmlessly against his brow.

"As I said, you can no more hurt me, than I can you. Now, have you got all that out of your system?" Merlin grinned. I panted, my chest heaving, my body trembling not with fear but rage.

"Michael, it's okay, let's just get this over with." Adrian's voice was barely a whisper, as he reached out, placing his hand on mine. I turned and to look at him and the rage ran out of me like water, in its place was cold terrible guilt. There he was again in this evil bastard's cauldron, trembling, and I was helpless again. He blinked the tears out of his heart-breaking blue eyes and set them on Merlin.

"Do it," he whispered.

I watched as Merlin raised his arms above the cauldron. Blue smoke began to bubble up around Adrian, washing out of the cauldron. The room grew darker as black smoke billowed from the torches that lit the corners of the room. I watched as Adrian's eyes went glassy and he began to sway back and forth. Merlin breathed in the black smoke, his eyes turning pure black. As he approached Adrian, my fists clenched as he began wrapping his hands around Adrian's neck and blew the blackness into him. His little body began to shake and convulse in the cauldron. I wanted to look away, but I couldn't. Tears pricked my eyes as he went still then his face scrunched up in agony.

"I see the lake," said Adrian through gritted teeth.

"Find your mother." I turned to look at Merlin as he muttered commands and my stomach turned. They were there, Adrian's glittering blue eyes. Merlin had them. It was like he was wearing Adrian contacts and it made me sick. Adrian winced as Merlin spoke, cowering away from him.

"I can't see her," he said, his breathing becoming more ragged by the second as tears began to stream from his tightly clenched eyes.

"Stop this!" I barked, but neither of them seemed to hear me.

"Towards the centre," Merlin muttered. His eyes, Adrian's eyes, flitting back and forth in his head as Adrian squirmed and pulled his knees up to his chest, veins now bulging along his neck.

"I see her," Adrian whispered, struggling against some invisible force wracking his body.

"There!" Merlin spat, his eyes suddenly focused, his face contorted into a snarl.

"I can't hold it," Adrian whimpered between sobs. I grabbed him, holding him still as he started to convulse, slamming himself against the walls of the cauldron.

"This is over," I said, lifting him out of the cauldron, cradling him in my arms as the smoke fell away from his body.

"That traitor!" Merlin yelled, as he began pacing back and forth across the length of the chamber, seemingly no longer interested in our presence. I took one more look back as he stalked through the room. There was something in him of a captive animal, like a tiger prowling its cage.

"We're leaving," I spoke only to Adrian as I made for the entrance, kicking the door open and dashing out of the chamber. Adrian's face was pale, not his usual sweet pinkish alabaster but greyish white, angry bulging veins only now subsiding in his neck. Bruises already forming along his arms where he'd slammed himself against the cauldron.

"Adrian speak to me please," I whispered, as we escaped into the open air of the forest. My heart thundered in my chest as a lump formed in my throat.

"Adrian please," I begged.

"I saw her," he breathed, his trembling muscles relaxing as he curled into me.

"I know Merlin didn't seem happy at whatever Nimueh is doing," I gave a weak laugh, kissing his forehead.

"Not Nimueh, I saw Linda, she's okay." A tiny smile crept across his face as his twinkling blue eyes opened just a crack. I was drawn in, the forest dropped away and my whole world was his face, his smiling, perfect face, with its twinkling seams of sapphire. My legs trembled and gave way as I sank into relief, and I began to sob.

EIGHT

My arms looped over Michael's shoulder as he piggybacked me through the viridian undergrowth of the fay forest. As tightly as I could, I clutched the straps of the armour that bound his chest, although I couldn't seem to muster any strength in my fingers. I breathed in his smell, a pleasant warm musk, and tried to immerse myself in his heat. Losing myself in Michael, escaping my body. The wracking ache of Merlin's poison rocking through my head, my chest, my stomach, and into my bones.

"Adrian, I think I should take you home, then come back for Mum." I shook my head and coughed, clearing my throat.

"No, you can't do this alone."

"You're in no fit state to go anywhere but into a bath right now. You can't go fighting goblins."

"Just wait a moment," I said, reaching down into my pocket to withdraw a small round stone which I pressed into Michael's hand.

"What's this?" he asked, holding it up to his eye like an appraiser.

"It's a whispering stone, Olivier gave it to me, which means she has one linked to it. You can speak to her through it."

"Adrian, you're a genius!" Michael said, twisting to plant a kiss on my cheek. A smile cracked across my face as a little flicker ignited in me.

"Just whisper into it, keep it short, things get a bit echoey through those things."

"Okay, gotcha," he said and lifted the stone to his lips.

"Olivier, Adrian is hurt, where can we meet?" he whispered, before taking the stone from his lips.

"I'll be fine,"

"You're not fine now though," Michael said, placing his large strong hands-on top of mine and giving them a squeeze. I took a deep breath and for a second the world span around me and I slumped against his shoulder.

"Adrian... are you—"

"Put the stone to your ear," I mumbled, cutting him off as a hissing started to emanate from his hand. *Toad's cave, toad's cave, cave, cave, cave* the message echoed and slowly the words began to overlap.

"Toad's cave, you know where that is?" Michael asked, shoving the stone into his pocket.

"You'll have to let me down so I can lead us."

Michael knelt, and I slid off his back. As my feet hit the floor my knees trembled. I lurched towards the ground as it rushed up to me, just as Michael's strong arms snaked around my waist, pulling me into his side, and holding me up.

"We'll go slow," he whispered, kissing my cheek. I took a shaky breath and tried not to feel like an incredible burden.

"Just hold me close, just for a second," I whispered as tears prickled my eyes.

"Of course," he said, as his arms wrapped around me, enveloping me. I gave up supporting myself and let him hold me to his chest, my arms dangling by my side. I could have stayed there forever, disappearing into a cocoon of Michael.

"I'm just tired," I mumbled, muffled by his chest.

"That's okay, we can take as long as you need." He ran his fingers through my hair, gently rubbing my scalp.

"Three to six months then," I mumbled, and Michael chuckled. I giggled, and the world lurched again, but this time it wasn't just me. Michael was on his back, holding me to his chest as chuckles rocked his body.

"Are you okay?"

"I just love you," he said and a rush of heat burned across my cheeks as the flicker inside me burst into a true warm heat.

"I love you too," I said, snuggling into his chest as my arms

---

snaked around him, holding him as tightly as I could.

I tapped my foot impatiently, passing the whispering stone through my fingers as I watched the cave entrance. I'd have polished this thing to a perfect button by now if it weren't already a perfect button. Michael had said Adrian was hurt. Why Adrian seemed to be constantly getting hurt I couldn't say but it was doing nothing for my nerves, and they weren't great at the best of times. I got up off my stump to pace pointlessly around the cave and kicked over my tea in the process. What I wouldn't give for Linda to brew me a cup of tea in her screaming silver jug thing right now.

"Olivier? You there?" Michael's voice echoed through the cave. I spun on the spot, looking to the entrance as the boys staggered into view. Adrian looked awful, greyish, his eyes, usually a brilliant blue, looked almost bloodshot. Although the veins were not blood red but black. An image of him as a little boy, playing in a puddle shot through my head, and I almost wanted to cry.

"What on earth happened to him?" I asked, helping Michael get him seated on my stump.

"Merlin did some sort of spell on him."

"How on earth did Merlin get hold of him?"

"I made a deal with him." Adrian sounded exhausted, his voice strung out, cracking.

"A deal for what?"

"To find Linda."

"What?"

"They took my mum, Olivier... we didn't know what to do. Adrian thought Merlin could help find her but then, he insisted on this."

"And you let Adrian go through with this?" I snapped, bristling. Michael recoiled a little and I felt like I'd kicked a pixie.

"It was my choice," Adrian croaked.

"Olivier, do you have any water? He's really struggling," said Michael, kneeling in front of Adrian now, Adrian's hands in his. They seemed scarcely able to take their eyes off each other.

"Of course," I said, flicking my wrist and guiding a stream from the trickle that ran down the cave wall towards Adrian. He lifted a trembling arm and let the coil wrap around his hand, snaking down his arm to his mouth where he drank it in.

"What is this place?" Michael asked, seemingly only now noticing his surroundings. Every wall sported its own unique mushroom carvings, lit by phosphorescent fungus.

"It's a place sacred to gnomes, it's a great place to come and think when you don't want be around dryads, naiads and sylphs." I explained, plopping down on a particularly bushy patch of moss.

"It's beautiful," Adrian chirped, offering a weak smile. I'd taken him here as a boy when his mother was being particularly grand and distant. Which was a lot of the time. As I cast my eye to the broken boy before me, the memory of him playing in the phosphorescence almost got me misty eyed again.

"Was it worth it, this spell? Did Merlin find Linda?" I asked, snapping myself out of it.

"They're keeping her at Lake Nimueh, but that's not all we found out," Michael explained.

"I saw Nimueh, Olivier. I didn't see much, but she didn't look like a prisoner, I think she's joined forces with the mirelings." My jaw clenched. I couldn't say I was surprised, Nimueh never had been the type to let loyalty or morality stand in the way of her own interests.

335

"That would explain how they've known all our key strategic locations," I thought aloud, my mind racing, plans and questions circling, just out of reach. Half-formed ideas flickered, but I couldn't grasp them. Something in what Adrian said didn't sit right, it was tripping me up.

"What do you mean, you saw them?" I asked, as a small pit began to form at my core.

"It's the spell Merlin insisted on, as the trade for finding Linda," Michael said, the look in his eye only amplifying my worry.

"What exactly did this spell do?"

"He said he was using me, or my connection to the lake, to look through me to the lake, it's a bit like I'm there as a ghost, but with him in my head." Adrian shuddered as he spoke. I took a step away, drawing more water from the cave stream into guiding it to Adrian as my hands trembled, my body clenching at the thought of Merlin had done. Visions of drowning the man or perhaps watching some potent poison strangle the life out of him flickered through my mind.

"You know what he did don't you?" Michael asked, watching me, and I nodded pushing as much water Adrian's way as I could muster.

"What Adrian was doing is called astral projection, and it's very dangerous and it's very advanced. But what Merlin was doing is disgusting," I snarled and ended up losing control of the stream as it splattered like a jet against the wall. Michael pulled Adrian into his arms, stroking his hair and cradling him as Adrian rested against Michael's chest. He didn't speak for a little while and when he did, his voice was trembling with barely concealed rage. It was good to know we were on the same page.

"Explain," was all he could seem to push through his clenched jaw. I wasn't sure if he should hear it or not, but I continued anyway.

"Astral projection is the act of sending your essence, or soul if you like, somewhere else. You can normally only do it to somewhere, or someone you're connected to. What Merlin was doing was piggybacking on Adrian's essence, forcing himself into Adrian's being. What's worse, Lake Nimueh is warded against all sorts of interference. Adrian would have been allowed, but those wards would not allow Merlin to project himself there easily. By riding Adrian's essence like that, he would have let Adrian's essence take the brunt of those defences. He wasn't just riding Adrian's projection; he was using him as a shield."

"It did feel pretty shitty," Adrian grumbled.

"Is this what he was doing the last time?" Adrian nodded.

"If the mirelings don't kill him, I think I might just have to myself."

"You'll have to join the queue," Michael said as he tended to Adrian, pushing his floppy blond hair out of his face as he wiped away ash and tear marks.

"At least we can get Linda back now," Adrian whispered.

"Hang on, why would they have Linda anyway? They've been taking kids up until now," I said, only just registering the fact they'd taken Michael's mother hostage.

"Nimueh knew about Michael's powers and his name. I think she meant to use Linda as some kind of insurance against his powers. If we set off now, we can sneak in when they're sleeping, as night falls." Adrian's voice was little more than a whisper, as he struggled to his feet, using Michael to steady himself.

"Adrian, we don't have a plan, and even if we did you can't come. You're too weak right now," I said, resisting the urge to forcibly sit him back down on his stump.

"I've got a plan and I've got to come; can't you feel it? Nimueh has sealed off the lake to fay. If I'm not with you, you're not getting in." I paused. He might have been right, the truth is I couldn't feel it. Being half gnome, I'd never been quite as connected to the lake as other water nymphs, let alone Adrian.

"Okay, so say you do come, what's the plan?"

"Nimueh has sealed off the lake, so short of Merlin unlocking it most fay can't get in. So they're probably not on high alert, and they've got to sleep. We sneak in when most of the camp is asleep and snatch Linda and Jack and go."

"So, your plan is literally just sneak in when they're sleeping and hope for the best?" I asked, doing my best not to roll my eyes.

"Do you have a better one?" asked Adrian.

"Not exactly, but give me a day or two to plan and gather people."

"We're talking about leaving Michael's mum and friends languishing there as prisoners, we haven't got days," Adrian snapped, rocking back on his feet momentarily. Michael sprang into action, steadying him.

"And what happens when we wake up the guard and they catch you, and then you're their prisoner, Adrian? What then?" I snapped back. Echoes of adolescent squabbles over whether or not he had to attend certain important fay functions flashing through my mind.

"No-one's laying a hand on Adrian again," said Michael, wrapping his arm around Adrian's shoulder.

"That's a lovely sentiment but—"

"It's not sentiment." Michael cut me off and as he spoke his eyes flashed gold. Goosebumps raised across my whole body and a shiver ran down my spine. I gulped; I'd never experienced the power of a prince before now. It flowed out of him like heat off a fire, wrapping around the two of them, and suddenly they seemed untouchable.

NINE

"So, we wait for nightfall, Adrian gets us in. We sneak along the tree line until Adrian sees something he recognises from his vision. Adrian keeps watch, we find my mum, get her out and then try to find the other captives. Is that the plan?" I asked.

"It feels a little bit thin on the ground doesn't it?" Olivier said, flicking a mushroom cap absentmindedly.

"It feels like a lot of wishful thinking," I admitted, flopping onto my back. We'd been going on like this for hours and we were getting nowhere fast.

"And we can't use the royal courts again?" I asked for what must have been the fourth or fifth time.

"No, the moment they realise Nimueh has decided to turn against Merlin they'd be liable to join her side."

"So, we're stuck with plan wishful thinking then." I sighed.

"I might have an idea on that front," said Adrian, pushing his still dripping wet hair out of his face as he emerged from the chamber at the back of the cave. He'd been recuperating in a little pool whilst we planned. He was wearing the clothes Olivier had given him to replace his old naiad robes. A string woven white vest covered by a patchwork blue cardigan with wide bell sleeves and baggy shorts. Technically, they were trousers, but for a gnome, all in all, he looked adorable. His eyes twinkled blue with flecks of green in the phosphorescence of the cave.

I didn't speak, as I heaved myself off the cave floor and pulled him into my chest, holding him as tight as I could without squashing him.

"I should dress gnomish more often," Adrian chuckled, his voice muffled by my chest. I just stroked his hair, breathed him in, held him tight and tried to forget the image of him in that cauldron.

"So, what's this idea then?" asked Olivier, prompting me to finally let Adrian go. I'd sort of forgotten she was there.

"I think we've been thinking about this all wrong," said Adrian, perching on Olivier's stump as he spoke; he was hiding it well, but he still seemed drained.

"How so?" Olivier asked.

"Well, Nimueh has been able to get the mirelings to work with her, which means they want something she can get them. Or at least, something they believe she can get them. And they're probably offering her something as well. I don't think they want to take over the whole fay forest, otherwise if they did, she wouldn't help them. She must think she can come out of the situation better than if Merlin wins and her position as Lady of the Naiad's is maintained." I couldn't make out exactly what Adrian was going on about, but from the look on Olivier's face, it must have been genius. I could feel a smile creeping across mine.

"Sorry I'm not following," I said, trying desperately to listen to Adrian rather than just staring at his beautiful face.

"Adrian is saying Nimueh wouldn't help the mirelings unless they've offered her a better position than she would have if Merlin won."

"But she's already one of the most important fays in the whole forest," I said.

"Exactly, the only way her position can be improved is to be made the leader, to take Merlin's spot basically," said Adrian.

"Which means they must not want control of the fay forest," said Olivier, giving the impression she was thinking aloud as the pieces slotted into place.

"And that means there is something else they want. If Nimueh can give it to them, maybe we can too, maybe whatever it is they want, we can give it to them in exchange for Linda and the kidnapped kids," said Adrian, his eyes shining. Warm feelings were creeping into me now, as he was almost radiating hope.

"But what if we get there and what they're asking for, we can't give them? What if they want to take you hostage too?" said Olivier.

"That's where Michael comes in."

"No one is taking Adrian again," I said, almost without thinking.

"Okay so do we still need to wait for nightfall?" Olivier asked.

"I think so. We're trying to cut Nimueh out of whatever deal she's made, so ideally, we don't want her to be there, which means it's best to do it at night. We just need to find whoever speaks for the mirelings in the camp," said Adrian.

"So how do we find that?" Olivier asked.

"I bet Mum would know." Mum always paid attention to that sort of thing. She said it was always good to know who was in charge in case you needed a favour and to know who to get on the good side of. Of course, she was normally talking about office politics or at big parties. But I'm sure she'd have thought the principle applied to invading forces as well.

"So that settles it then, we go at nightfall," said Olivier.

That night we set off along the winding spider path of the forest. Adrian's hand in mine, with Olivier walking a little ahead, with enough confidence in her stride you'd think she could split an ocean.

"How are you feeling?" I asked as we walked.

"I've definitely felt worse," Adrian said, offering me a half-smile. I squeezed his hand tight and swallowed the confusing cocktail of rage and guilt that had just bubbled up.

"But you could be better, right?" He nodded. I sighed and leant down, kissing his cheek.

"When all this is over, I'm going to make it all up to you."

"You don't have to make anything up to me," said Adrian, leaning up, wrapping his arms around my neck as he kissed me. My hands snaked around his waist, lifting him up, pressing him against me.

"We're here," Olivier said, rather loudly. I planted Adrian on the ground and looked down from the top of the hill we'd been trudging up.

"Where is it?" I asked, looking down onto the lake, or rather, what should have been the lake. Now our vision was met with a line of trees.

"She's barred entry," Adrian explained as he knelt, placing both hands on the ground.

"She can do that?" I asked.

"Well, effectively, this place is bound to the naiads, and she is a royal naiad, so she has dominion over it," said Adrian.

"A sufficiently powerful enchanter like Merlin could get in but otherwise it's pretty tricky," Olivier added.

"So why didn't you guys just stop people accessing the grove, so the mirelings couldn't reach the still world?"

"If we'd done that only the highest rank of dryad could enter the still world as well, we'd be locked out. Not to mention it takes a lot of time to—"

"If you wouldn't mind, a little quiet would be great," said Adrian.

"Oops sorry," I said, watching as he began taking slow, deep breaths. At first nothing happened but little by little, flecks of light began to shine through the tree line before us. Little shafts of grey blue moonlight poking through as if the trees weren't solid. The shafts steadily grew wider. At first peeking through the leaves, then almost passing through whole tree trunks. I watched as the veneer of the tree line peeled back, revealing the moonlight reflected against Lake Nimueh. It was almost like watching old camera film burn up when left on a projector for too long. But where there had once been a beautiful shoreline of grass and wildflowers, there was now a camp. Littered with crudely constructed huts built of twisted thorny wood, speckled with sickly yellow half-light, the only source of light in the camp.

Adrian sighed as the lake revealed itself, and I offered him a hand as he struggled back to his feet.

"You okay? That was amazing," I whispered into his ear as we started down the hill, sticking to the edge of the path, bent low behind the undergrowth.

"Just a little out of breath, but it's amazing she ever managed to put it up," Adrian replied, ducking behind a tree as the path began to level off.

"Okay, so stay low, and let's look for anything familiar," I whispered, putting myself between Adrian and the camp as we crept along the tree line. Adrian's gamble had paid off, as a chorus of snores hummed out of the camp.

"There!" he hissed, pointing to the largest structure we'd passed so far. Constructed of many thorny twisted branches, bathing the surrounding area in pale yellow light. Two goblins were situated outside the structure.

"It sort of looks like a miniature of The Hut," I whispered.

"Don't remind me," Adrian and Olivier said in unison.

"Well, here goes nothing," I said as I stepped forward, only for Adrian to grab my hand and pull me back.

"Wait a second," he whispered. "Watch." He pointed to Olivier, who'd planted her fingertips into the dirt.

"Three, two, one and..." Olivier whispered as mushrooms bloomed before the goblin guards. They peered down at them inquisitively just as the mushrooms began releasing puffs of mustard spores into their faces. The goblins gasped, wheezed, and slumped forward with a small dull thud. Which sounded like the loudest thing I'd ever heard in my life as we crept through the night towards the entrance.

I held my breath as we tiptoed between the now sleeping goblins and poked our heads into the darkness of the mini hut. I blinked as my eyes adjusted to the half-light glow. I couldn't make much out as I crept in a little further and froze as I watched something small begin to grow out of the ground in front of me. I turned back just in time to find Olivier become bathed in a phosphorus glow, kneeling with her hands in the dirt again.

"Michael?" I span on the spot and my vision fell on Mum huddled in a corner with her hands bound and looped over one of the beams of the structure.

"Mum!" I whispered and bolted for her. Even cast in only sickly yellow half-light I could see the purple stain of bruised cheeks and red raw skin around her bound wrists. Part of me, the part that could hardly bear to look at her cuts and bruises, wanted to smash in the head of every goblin within a five-mile radius, but I didn't. I knelt and cradled her in my arms and suddenly I didn't ever want to let go.

"Michael, we're not alone," she breathed, barely daring to speak the words at all. I froze, my heart was suddenly thundering so loudly I was sure it would give us away.

"Here," Olivier hissed, sliding a knife into my hand, which I immediately began to cut into Mum's bindings with. The knife cut agonisingly slowly, each slide of the blade I winced, barely daring to breathe. I watched unblinkingly as little by little the rope broke apart. It frayed away from itself, until I froze. A slight rustle from behind, which sounded as loud as thunder against the silence. I held my breath, counted to five and took another slice.

"Linda, you don't happen to know who is in charge

around here, do you?" Adrian whispered, kneeling next to her as I sliced through her binds. Mum nodded and opened her mouth to speak, just as all the air was sucked out of the hut.

"That would be me," came a cracked, dry old voice from behind us. I froze, dropping the knife and wheeled around in the dirt, only to find two large yellow globes staring at me out of the darkness.

TEN

There were two echoing taps, and the space was bathed in a sickly yellow light, which glowed from little seams in the gnarled wood, like embers. I flinched as the echo filled the camp and crossed my fingers that the horde didn't wake and find us. The light carved out the silhouette of a stooped older woman, leaning on a cane. Michael leapt to his feet, placing himself between Linda and I and the stooped figure.

"What do you intend to do now, young man?" asked the old, cracked voice.

"I errm—"

"We've come to make a deal," I jumped in. I could feel Michael struggling for words. As I spoke, I stepped out from behind him, my hands raised.

"You appear to be stealing my prisoner," came the cracked voice, curling through the air.

"You kidnapped her!" Michael snapped, his shield glinting in the dim light.

"We can give your something in return," I said, taking another step forward.

"Oh yes, what exactly can you give me, little naiad boy?"

"Nimueh must have offered you something for you to be working with her. What did she offer?" I asked, fighting the nerves.

"Nimueh offered to give us Grandfather when we conquer the grey witch and to ensure we never have any more trouble from the likes of him." She took a step forward, thrusting her cane towards Michael. Now she was in the light I could finally make her out. She was like a goblin, but about twice the size and with softer features, her skin a murky greenish brown. The lines of age ran across her face like a map. My mouth went dry as I took her in. I'd always thought they were myths; she was a hag.

"She's lying, she could never give you Grandfather Tree, the fay would never stand for it. Even if you did get rid of Merlin," said Olivier. I could hear a quaver in her voice I'd never heard before.

"Not your Grandfather Tree, our Grandfather," the hag snarled, drool dripping from her distended lips and as she spoke, the hairs on the back of my neck stood on end. Instincts within me to freeze and to run were competing for attention.

"What is your Grandfather?" Michael asked, confused.

"The likes of you took it!" she spat, again thrusting her cane towards Michael, so that it was inches from his shield. It glinted in the yellow half-light and a realisation dawned on me.

"You mean The Hut, don't you?" I breathed, thinking

aloud as images of the gnarled iron wood roots riddled with a yellow glow flashed through my mind.

"That is what the grey witch calls it, took it with conquerors help he did." She spat on the ground as she said the words as if they were bitter to her.

"A conqueror?" Michael asked.

"You! You are a conqueror!" she barked.

"I think she means a prince," I whispered. She snorted.

"You call it a prince, but it took our Grandfather, it conquered, it is a conqueror." Barely contained fury vibrated off her as she spoke. I took a deep breath, placing a hand on Michael's stomach, and pushed him back as I stepped between him and the hag.

"Trust me," I whispered, and he resisted for a moment before taking a step back.

"So, what can you offer me little naiad boy?" she snarled, I gulped and Michael gave my hand a squeeze.

"We can give you everything Nimueh is offering… and I think we can end the war, no more fighting," I lied, or I suppose, I hoped I wasn't lying, I was gambling on myself.

"How can you promise this, little naiad boy?" She smirked, flashing her jutting fang-like teeth as she took another step towards me. I could feel Michael bristling behind me.

"He can't," cut a familiar cool, cruel voice through the air and my chest tightened. Nimueh strode into the room, her diaphanous gown and white-blonde hair billowing behind her.

"Nimueh, you know this child?" the hag asked, a cruel smile curling her lips.

"I am his mother—"

"Some mother." I jumped as Linda snorted from behind us, pulling herself up and taking a step out into the glow.

"Something you'd like to add, Mrs Tombs?" Nimueh's voice cut like a knife, but Linda paid her no mind, directing her attention at the hag.

"You would trust the word of a woman who abandoned her own child to die for her own ends? Someone who'd choose status over the lives of her people?" her voice boomed.

My nose prickled as tears swam in my eyes. Linda might have been tiny and in rags and with cut ropes dangling at her wrists, but she radiated ferocity. Motherly instincts like nothing I'd ever seen in the fay. The hag had paused, seemingly stunned into silence by Linda's outburst.

"Regardless, Adrian has no authority to make such an offer," Nimueh added, a hint of nervousness sneaking into her voice.

"Actually, he does, sister," added Olivier, taking a step forward, so that I was flanked on all sides by Olivier, Michael and Linda.

"Nonsense," Nimueh spat.

"I'm afraid not. Merlin declared Adrian the Lord of the Naiad after your home fell to the mireling invasion. Adrian is one of the high lords of the fay," said Olivier, sweet smugness wafting off her.

"That is my position!" Nimueh snarled, darkness taking over her features as her hands curled into claws. The grass beneath us cracked and turned brown as water was drawn out of it towards her. I crossed my arms as she lunged forward, two jets of water crashing against me. I pushed into them with all my might, but couldn't hold the crushing pressure back. It was like a stone slamming against me.

"KNEEL!" The voice that I'd come to learn was Michael's, even if it was not the one I recognised, thundered through the camp and the pressure stopped. I lowered my arms and Nimueh was kneeling before me, ice cold hatred pouring out of her. I slumped against Michael as his arm wrapped around my shoulder. Silence fell in the camp in the wake of Nimueh's rage. Panic set in as I realised, I didn't know what to say next. I looked around the stunned faces of the group avoiding Nimueh's eye. A second stretched on into what felt like eternity until finally one of us spoke.

"Pathetic excuse for a mother." Linda's voice, trembling with rage, finally broke the silence as she took a step forward and punched Nimueh square on the chin. My mouth dropped wide open as Nimueh hit the ground with a thud and Olivier gave a distinct gasp.

"Linda, that was ama—" I froze as the sound of footsteps filled the air, lots of chattering little footsteps. Michael pulled me back behind him, raising his shield as a bristling array of spears appeared at the mouth of the shelter.

"We don't want to fight you!" I called, wrestling with the fear that strangled my voice.

"That is because you'll lose," said the hag.

"Maybe, but with Adrian you can win this whole thing," Olivier shouted over the chittering snarls of the amassing goblin horde. The hag raised a hand as the spears were slowly lowered.

"Tell me again, little fay lord, what is your promise?" asked the hag. Her venomous green eyes flashing in the flickering flame light of the torches the goblin horde were wielding. I took a deep breath, Linda placed a hand on my shoulder and gave it a squeeze as I stepped out from behind Michael.

"I can end the fighting, give you your Grandfather, hand over Merlin. In return you must give us every prisoner you've taken and leave Lake Nimueh." Half-baked plans thundered through my head and my palms grew sweaty as I spoke.

"Big promises little lord, big promises," said the hag, exposing her pointed browning teeth and blackened gums as a smile curled her thin lips.

"Give me two days, and if I fail, you can have me in exchange for the prisoners." I could barely hear the words over my heart thundering in my ears.

"Adrian! No!" Michael, Olivier and Linda all barked in unison.

"It'll work," I said in a strangled voice as the hag offered her hand to shake, tears tumbled down my cheeks as I took it, wincing as her grip crunched my hand. Her talon like nails grazing across my wrist.

"Take this Linda and go, I'll see you soon little lord," said the hag, glee dripping from her voice.

"Take this. It'll speak to you when the time is right," said Olivier, tossing a whispering stone to the hag as we made our exit.

CHAPTER

ELEVEN

Olivier shut the door on her little cottage behind us and we all breathed a collective sigh of relief. In fact, I was so relieved that I was almost able to forget I'd been wearing this same nighty since those little bastards had kidnapped me yesterday morning. Almost. It was a nice little cottage. Shelves covered virtually every wall, each laden with books and scrolls and what looked like several potted mushrooms. I'd never seen anyone pot mushrooms before.

"Okay, so what now?" asked Michael, as he peeped out of Olivier's window to make sure we weren't followed before drawing the curtain.

"Can we go home? I need to change out of this nighty," I said, rubbing my wrists anxiously. They weren't really that sore. It's just what everyone does in the movies when they escape whatever nonsense situation they've ended up in and I always thought it looked so glamorous.

"Of course we can Mum. Are you okay?" said Michael,

pulling me into a big hug. I sighed and hugged him back, letting some of the stress drop out of my shoulders.

"Here," said Olivier, handing me a flowy yellow cardiganish thing, a bit like the blue one Adrian was wearing.

"Are your wrists okay?" he asked, obviously having noticed me rubbing them.

"Oh, they're fine dear." I smiled, but it didn't stop him placing his hands on them. He was ever so gentle, with his light little fingers. I watched as droplets of water beaded at his fingertips, soaking into my wrists and within seconds what little pain there was had vanished.

"Better?" he asked, his eyes now heavily lidded.

"Much…" I breathed, finding the rest of my words had abandoned me.

"Adrian, why don't you sit for a second," said Michael, pulling up a chair for the little love which he slumped into.

"I hope you didn't mind me punching your mother." The words escaped me, before I could think, and they sounded rather odd in my voice. I'd never expected to say something like that.

"That was amazing," he said, offering a weak smile, although his voice was a little hollow sounding.

"Actually, that was probably the best thing I've seen in weeks." Olivier chuckled; it was infectious, and I couldn't fight the grin spreading across my face, which matched the one spreading across Michael's as he gave me a cheeky wink.

"I'm glad you thought so," I said.

"Almost good enough to make me forgot about the promises you made to that woman," Michael said, kneeling in front of Adrian.

"I've got a plan for that," Adrian said, rubbing his eyes as Olivier handed him a cup of water to sip.

"So, what's this plan then? Because there is no way I'm letting you hand yourself over," Michael said, taking Adrian's free hand in his and squeezing it.

"Well, I figure we can just give everyone what they want, right Olivier?"

"You make it sound a little simpler than it will be, but you might be right."

"How's that then?" I asked.

"Well, the fay don't want the fighting to carry on, and most of the fay lords don't like Merlin. So, two birds with one stone. We give up Merlin and the fighting ends. We just have to set it up right," said Adrian.

"What about The Hut?" Michael asked, sounding anxious.

"Well, nobody really likes The Hut, its Merlin's base of operations for the Excalibur system, no more Merlin, and maybe no more hut will be fine."

"And no more Excalibur system," added Olivier.

"Isn't that system the reason you and Michael met in the first place?" I asked.

"It is," Michael said, and Adrian nodded.

"But maybe we can come up with something better, something that means charges can still come here, but they won't be used like weapons anymore." Adrian smiled, his eyes fixed on Michael. It was like some sort of magnetism existed between the two of them. They couldn't seem to tear their eyes away from each other.

"So how do we pull this off then?" Michael said.

"Well, you've got to blindside this Merlin chap, haven't

you?" I said, seemingly catching them by surprise, because they only just managed to tear themselves away from each other to look at me.

"How do you mean?" Adrian asked.

"Oh, you know, classic ambush tactics. You make sure everyone in the meeting knows ahead of time what it's about except the one person you want to ambush. And then you catch 'em flat footed. Office politics at its worst, it's sort of like the evil version of a surprise party," I said, flashing back to the meeting that poor James from accounting got fired in. All he'd done was steal a couple of rolls of the office loo roll.

"You know, that might actually work," said Olivier.

"To surprise Merlin, the best way would be at a meeting at Grandfather Tree. He'd never expect it there, it's a position of power for him. So, if we set up a meeting there, but Olivier explained everything to the fay lords before we summoned Merlin, maybe—"

"No, it would have to be you Adrian, you have to be the one to tell them. I work for Merlin, they'd never trust me, but you're one of them. You're a high lord of the fay, if this is going to work, we need them to trust the plan. We need them to trust you." The poor little love gave such a gulp you'd think he was a cartoon character.

TWELVE

I held Adrian's hand in mine as we made our way along the path of leaning trees that formed an arched emerald tunnel. The impossibly thick trunk of Grandfather Tree looming in the distance. The way its roots bulged from the ground was surreal, like the veins of the forest started here, like this was its heart. Everything was so huge and ancient here and Adrian seemed smaller than ever. I kept catching myself glancing at him nervously out of the corner of my eye, he looked so tired, like he might run out of steam at any moment.

We took our places, Adrian standing in the centre before Grandfather Tree, where Merlin had stood the last time we were here. I stood just a step behind, he had hold of my hand and wouldn't let go. I didn't want him to anyway. We watched as the fay leaders that Olivier had summoned filed in, Adrian mumbling who they were under his breath. I wasn't sure if it was for my benefit or just nerves.

"Mu-terra, lord of all dryad, Wynda, matriarch of the sylphs, Yonda and Dazzle, partnered leaders of the gnomes

…" With each heavy name his grip on my hand grew a little tighter. Mu-Terra led the procession in such a way that I got the impression he'd been leading his entire life. He was tall, six feet six at least, if I had to guess, and broad. With dark brown, almost black skin and long braided green hair twisted into complex knots, which reached to the small of his back. Wynda followed, taller still, taller than any person I'd ever seen and far too thin. With long spindly arms that hung down unnaturally far, her hands resting by her knees. Her hair was shorn and silvery grey, against her ghostly pale skin, but not like Adrian's. Adrian's skin was immaculate, like fine porcelain, while hers was faintly lilac and looked stretched thin over the bone. Her eyes were the most striking of all: wide, deep purple globes set deep into her face.

Following these two giants, Yonda and Dazzle didn't strike anything like the same impression. Yonda, the taller of the two with about a foot on Dazzle was perhaps four feet six. They both had warm olive skin, pudgy rounded faces and striking shocks of golden hair. Dazzle's hair stood on end as though he'd rubbed it against a balloon. Yonda's was braided into long, tight plaits, like the ropes people use to tie their curtains back in old-fashioned houses. The most striking thing about them both was their mouths. So wide that were they to smile, it would truly be from ear to ear.

Adrian turned to me, just for a moment and nodded. His face was soft and kind, as ever but his eyes carried boundless emotion, exhaustion and fear and determination.

"Merlin has some nerve, having his Lieutenant summon us here and then being late himself." Mu-terra was the first to speak, his voice was heavy and low and vibrated through the earth. When he spoke, everyone else fell silent.

"Merlin didn't have Olivier summon you here, I did." Adrian's voice was strangled at first and then too loud, like he was fighting to make a sound at all.

"Why, Lord Adrian, last I heard you were living under Merlin's protection," said Yonda, the female leader of the gnomes, her voice softer, inquisitive and kind. Wynda snorted.

"Hah, Lord Adrian absconded with his champion before the first invasion of the grove," said Wynda, lazily flicking her wrist in my direction.

"Merlin never told us," Dazzle, the male gnome leader protested.

"Merlin didn't tell us a lot of things, I'm here today to tell you everything I've learned!" Adrian interjected.

"Go on," Mu-terra's voice boomed, and the clearing fell quiet again.

"As you all know, Nimueh, and Lake Nimueh fell to the mirelings. Merlin told you he was taking me under his protection at that time. That was a lie." Adrian had found his voice now, and as he spoke the leader's eyes narrowed to slits. Sweat beaded across my brow as the intensity of their gaze impressed itself upon us.

"Merlin was not protecting me. He was using me, forcing me to astral project into the lake, spying on the mirelings."

"You must be mistaken Adrian, that kind of magic is extremely dangerous, for Merlin to use you like that would be tantamount to... to—"

"Torture." I heard the word echo through the grove and

suddenly all eyes were on me, I flinched, it'd just slipped out.

"Yes, quite. There is no way Merlin would ever do that to a person of the fay, let alone a lord," said Yonda.

"I'm afraid he did, and he'd do it to any one of us if it served his ends," said Adrian.

"Have you any proof of this," boomed Mu-terra.

"I errm, I don't." Adrian shrank a little as doubt spread across the faces of the fay lords, my body clenched as I watched them doubting him, choosing Merlin over him.

"I was there, I witnessed it," I barked.

"What did you witness? Describe it," said Wynda, her voice sharp, sceptical. I closed my eyes and I was back in Merlin's chamber, every horrific image playing out again in my head.

"He had Adrian in his cauldron, blue smoke surrounding him. He conjured black smoke out of the flames and took them into himself before blowing the smoke into Adrian. Adrian's eyes went glassy and..." I gulped as a lump rose in my throat. "And he said he was there, at the lake. Merlin gave him commands, instructions on who to find, what to look for, but the whole time he was hurting Adrian. I could see it, veins building along his neck and face. He was squirming in the bottom of the cauldron. It was like something massive was inside his head, pushing, trying to burst out and rip him apart." I opened my eyes as a tear rolled down my cheek as Adrian gave my hand a squeeze. The lords glanced across the grove to each other, doubt colouring their features.

"There is no way... he wouldn't—"

"Are you really so naive Yonda," spat Wynda.

"You believe this?" Mu-Terra asked, turning on Wynda.

"Don't you? Deep down? We are the latest in a long line of our predecessors, the lords of the fay, but Merlin has ruled over us all for a millennia. Nobody could hold onto that power, for that long, without some degree of ruthlessness. We've all heard the rumours." Silence fell in the grove as the unpleasant truth started to set in.

"What did you see, in your projection?" asked Dazzle eventually. Adrian took a deep breath, steeling himself before answering."

"A large mireling encampment occupying the lake, which we already knew about." The leaders nodded.

"And also, Nimueh, but she wasn't a prisoner, she was working with them."

"She would never," boomed Mu-terra.

"She's far too proud," said Dazzle.

"Her pride is exactly why she's working with them. In exchange for helping them get what they want, they've offered to let her rule all of the fay, to take her position now and Merlin's."

"And what is it that they want?" asked Wynda.

"They want to take back control of The Hut. They say it is their Grandfather, like ours here," said Adrian, glancing back to Grandfather Tree behind him.

"How could you possibly know all this?" asked Mu-Terra.

"We went there, they took Michael's mother, to hold her hostage as insurance against Michael's powers. We went to get her back and we spoke with their leader. The Hut wasn't all she wanted, she wanted Merlin. Nimueh had promised to help her take control of the forest and to get to Merlin, and in exchange they would leave her to rule over all the fay."

"To rule over us?" Wynda sneered.

"The realm wouldn't stand for it," Mu-Terra growled.

"They might, if it meant the fighting would end," said Adrian.

"Well, we can't allow this, we must inform Merlin immediately." Mu-terra got to his feet turning to march out of the grove.

"There is another option," Adrian called, Mu-Terra halted in the arch of the trees.

"I spoke to their leader too. She accepted an offer from me, but we only have a short time to deliver it."

"What offer?" asked Wynda.

"We give back The Hut, in exchange for Lake Nimueh, and they leave the fay forest in piece—"

"Merlin would never give up The Hut," interjected Dazzle.

"Well… we would also, be giving up Merlin." The grove fell silent. I watched as each of the fay lords in turn exchanged nervous glances. Adrian turned to me, and looking up into my face, his eyes were searching, for comfort I think, for security.

"That… would be treason." Yonda's voice was small now, nervous, as if she was scared someone was listening in.

"It's only treason if we fail," said Wynda.

"How would we do it?" asked Mu-Terra. For the first time his voice had softened, he was almost whispering.

"Olivier is already evacuating The Hut, under the guise of orders from Merlin. I've given the mirelings a whispering stone, if we agree we send them a signal to come and we summon Merlin to meet us here, where we spring our trap."

"You gave them a whispering stone?" Mu-Terra asked, disapproval colouring the edges of his voice.

"They've already taken Lake Nimueh, Excalibur and they've managed to access the grove. You think they couldn't get hold of a couple of whispering stones of their own accord if they didn't want to?" Wynda sneered and Mu-Terra puffed out his chest in return.

"And what's to stop Merlin turning his power on us, when he realizes what we've done?" asked Dazzle as they others continued to bristle at each other.

"Michael, he and Merlin are bound together, Merlin can't hurt him. With Michael by our side and all of us fighting, here, in Grandfather's grove, I think we can win." I winced as again their eyes fell on me. I stepped forward and nodded.

"I promise you, if you go through with Adrian's plan, I won't let any harm come to you," I said, trying to sound how I imagined a proper champion of the fay would sound.

"And what's to stop the mirelings turning on us all once they arrive?" asked Yonda, fear shaking her voice.

"Adrian faced the mireling leader in their camp, on their terms, surely you the leaders of the fay can face them here, in the centre of your power? Besides, I will be here, my powers work on mirelings just like they do fay," I said, surprising myself as the argument spilled out of me.

"And how do we know we can trust you to protect us?" Wynda asked, her eyes narrowed to searching, sceptical, slits.

"If they turn on you, they will have betrayed Adrian, they

will have turned on Adrian. You can trust me not to allow that."

"Loyalty to your lord is one thing but—"

"It's not loyalty, it's love," I interrupted Wynda as I wrapped my arm around Adrian's waist and pulled him towards me. He resisted, for a split second and then gave in and relaxed into my body and for the first time since we reached Grandfather Tree, I took a full, deep breath.

For a moment I fought him, protocol and decorum and years of fearing these people trained my body to be rigid, no sign of weakness, give nothing away. Michael melted those instincts away in an instant, my heavy eyes closed, and my body slumped into his, supporting me as every ache and the weight of tiredness was lifted off me, just for a second. There was a long silence before anyone spoke again.

"Who rules once Merlin's... removed?" asked Wynda, a smile playing at her lips. Mu-Terra's chest inflated with self-importance as he cleared his throat.

"No-one does, not like before, not like Merlin. We all rule as a council," I interjected before anyone could make this more complicated than it already was. All the eyes in the room moved to Mu-Terra, silently awaiting his response. Michael's arm flexed around me bracing for resistance.

"Send the signal, summon Merlin and the mirelings," he said at last.

"Very well," I nodded, slipping a trembling hand into my

pocket and withdrawing a whispering stone. Now connected to not only Olivier but also the hag.

"The trap is set, bring on the change," I whispered, and my words echoed back at me through the stone. I slipped it back into my pocket and turned to face Michael.

"Are you okay?" he asked, placing his large hands on my shoulders, bracing me.

"My heart's beating so hard I'm surprised you can't hear it," I whispered, anxious that the fay lords didn't hear me.

"You're shaking, maybe we should sit, so you can catch your breath."

"Follow me," I said, leading Michael behind Grandfather Tree, where we could hide and not have other eyes on us for a moment. It wasn't until we got back there that I realised I'd never actually seen what it was like back there.

"Oh, and Adrian, congratulations," said Wynda, catching me with her flashing lilac eyes just before we disappeared behind Grandfather Tree.

"What for?"

"Being the first person from your family to have an original thought since the first Nimueh a millennia ago," she said, as she turned her back on us and took her position.

"This way Adrian," said Michael as he tugged at my wrist leading me carefully through the overgrown mossy roots that had burst the earth until we were entirely obscured behind Grandfather Tree. I don't know what I was expecting but from behind it was remarkably like any other tree. Brown, a little damp to the touch, just much, much wider. I sank to the ground and leant against it, Michael sat next to me, with my hand in his and for the first time in a while we were alone.

"I'm so proud of you," Michael whispered, as the sounds of other fay filling into the grove began to vibrate through the air.

"What for?" I asked, fighting the smile that was already tugging at my lips.

"Are you kidding?" he asked giving me a quizzical look. I shook my head looking back and watched as a smile broke out across Michael's face followed by tears tumbling down his cheeks.

"Are you okay?" I whispered, reaching towards him.

"You're so ridiculous," he half chuckled, half sobbed, pulling me to his chest and squashing me into him as his fingers laced into my hair, massaging my head. I melted as shivers of pleasure ran through me and for a second, I forgot where I was. The whole world could have been contained within his arms. Eventually we separated and Michael looked down at me with his full, warm, amber eyes, still glistening with tears as he gently pushed my hair out of my face.

"Why are you crying?" I whispered.

"Because of you, because you're the most amazing person I've ever met in the whole world. Heck, worlds, bar absolutely no-one and it's not even close and you don't have any idea how brilliant you are." I shook my head, swallowing around a lump as my nose prickled.

"You're just saying that," I whispered, part of me wishing he really meant it, whilst another part refused to believe him.

"I'm not, Adrian, I'm not. You don't even realise what you're doing as you do it. Adrian, in the space of two days you've stood up to your torturer, rescued my mum, negotiated a peace treaty with two warring factions and you're about to ambush and capture a dictator. You're so strong it's insane."

"I'm not strong." The words slipped out of me before I could stop them as tears tumbled down my face.

"You're the strongest person I've ever met, Adrian, you held worlds apart for me." Part of me searched for a chink, an indication that he was joking or flattering or lying but there was nothing. Nothing but love shining out of Michael.

"You really think so?" I whispered, my voice strangled.

"I do and I'm gonna make you believe it." His breath brushed against my lips as he leant forward. Our eyes locked, my breathing faltered, and I was drawn in closer until there was barely an inch between us. I shivered as the hairs on my neck stood on end. His arms wrapped around me, and our lips met. He was warm and gentle and soft and strong, and I was helpless to resist him. My hands exploring his body as my fingers slipped beneath the armoured straps bound to his heaving chest. My heart thundered as he lifted me into his lap and I pressed myself against him.

"Why have I been summoned here," a familiar voice wrung out through the clearing. All sound dropped away, and Michael and I froze in each other's arms. There was a pause and then whispering broke out, thundering through the crowd. Michael and I crawled to the edge of the tree and peaked out. Merlin had his back to us, addressing the thronging fay, Mu-Terra, Dazzle, Yonda and Wynda stood before him.

"Speak, one of you, where is Olivier?" My stomach squirmed as he spoke. Wynda met my gaze and nodded almost imperceptibly, my heart jumped into my throat.

"I'll be right here with you. He won't touch you." Michael whispered, planting a kiss on my cheek. I stood, my legs trembling, a cold sweat blanketing me as my mouth went dry and I stepped out from behind Grandfather Tree. Michael was just behind me, with a hand on my shoulder.

"Olivier isn't here," I said, though really it was more like I squawked, my voice cracking embarrassingly halfway through. Merlin whirled around on the spot and his cool grey eyes met mine. For a split second his sadistic smile flashed across his lips, and then the mask slid on.

"Lord Adrian, what could possibly warrant all this?"

"I have good news. I wanted all of the fay here, to hear it." As I spoke my voice sailed through the air reverberating around the crowd. My eyes flicked to Wynda who offered a tiny wink, her fingers twisting and curling at her side as she manipulated the wind, carrying my voice with it.

"Well don't keep us in suspense. Share your glad tidings child," said Merlin, his voice as I had once known it, almost akin to that of a doting grandfather, and it made my skin crawl.

"I have found a way to end the fighting with the mirelings, to bring us a lasting peace. The other fay lords have already been informed and they agree."

"Oh, they have? Have they?" Merlin shot a look at the four of them, and Mu-terra met his gaze.

"We have," he boomed.

"So, what is this miraculous discovery?" Merlin asked, not quite managing to keep the tone of mockery out of his voice.

"I went to Lake Nimueh, I met with Nimueh, and the

leader of the mirelings, a hag." I paused as thunderous whispers, and an air of fear, took the crowd.

"A very dangerous thing to do I must say, Lord Adrian," said Merlin.

"Michael ensured my safety, I was never in any danger." I smiled as for the first time a chink of frustration broke through Merlin's mask as his eyes flicked to Michael.

"I spoke with their leader, and we agreed, they would return Lake Nimueh, and leave the fay forest in peace."

"Incredible, I must—"

"In exchange, we shall return something to them, something that was ripped from them a long time ago. The Hut." As I expected, yet more whispers filled the air throughout the grove, looks of shock and fear in their dozens, but Merlin was all I cared about. Just the tiniest spark of recognition flickered across his face.

"To give up The Hut, is to give up our greatest defence." He said, quieting the whispers.

"To give up The Hut is to give up the need for our defences. The Hut is to the mirelings as Grandfather Tree is to us," I said, laying a hand on Grandfather Tree behind me, running my fingers along the ancient bark.

"And their many, many captives?"

"They have already returned one captive, as a gesture of trust, the rest will be returned in exchange for... you." My voice sounded distant, like it wasn't my own as it echoed through the grove. Deafening silence surged through the crowd as fury flickered across Merlin's face. I couldn't feel my body, I was numb, a spectator, Merlin span around on the spot to face the crowd and the lords.

"What is the meaning of this?" His voice was hard and

harsh, but it reached me as little more than a distant whisper.

"You've ruled for far too long, Merlin!" Mu-terra's voice barely reached me, like an echo in the wind.

"It's time we cut the poison out," said Wynda, as Yonda and Dazzle nodded their assent.

"Take back the fay forest for the fay." Caspia's voice was barely recognisable, barely audible from within the bowels of the crowd.

"Enough of this," Merlin snarled as his glittering cauldron erupted into being. The lords leapt clear as coils of blackness whipped out of the cauldron, rotting the ground it touched, pooling in formless masses of black. Wind whipped my hair as a silver shield streaked past my head from behind, crashing into the cauldron, sending it skittering into the crowd. Mu-Terra seized the opportunity, plunging his hands into the ground. The roots of Grandfather Tree groaned as one coiled around the cauldron, pushing it down below the ground and another swung towards Merlin. He darted to the left as it slammed into the grove, shaking the ground. I stumbled falling to my knees blinking as the world moved in slow motion around me. Merlin charged, fear and rage and animal ferocity in his eyes. His arms outstretched, his hands like claws grasping for me as Michael planted himself bodily between us. The enchantment did its work, Merlin was stopped in his tracks, as if stuck on pause.

"It's over Merlin, you lose." I blinked as Michael's voice rang in my ears and the world zoomed back towards me. My chest was tight, I was panting, I could barely breathe, barely stand.

"Michael," I called, or at least, I tried to call, but it came out as a whisper. The crowd was parting from the back, gasps and screams filling up my ears and then she appeared. From the throng emerged the hag. She strode through the crowd as it parted in her wake. Even the lords gave way to her, until she reached Merlin, their eyes met, and she smiled a broad, sadistic smile.

"You're coming with me, witch." She spat the words, through her jutting, fanged teeth as a retinue of goblins descended on Merlin, grabbing at his wrists and ankles, dragging him kicking and spitting and screaming through the crowd.

"You'll regret this! I'll make you regret this! I'll be back! You need me! You've always needed me!" His voice shrank as he disappeared into the crowd. I watched him go until all I could see was the tops of goblin spears bobbing overhead.

THIRTEEN

I watched Merlin as he was dragged back through the crowd. My palms were sweaty, and my legs were trembling, but I couldn't fight the grin that had plastered itself across my face. When he finally disappeared into the sea of bodies, I at last turned away, my eyes falling on Adrian, on his knees, with what I guessed must have been an elf next to him.

"Adrian, are you okay?" I asked, rushing to his side. My stomach flipped, he was drenched in sweat and panting heavily, he didn't speak, he just nodded.

"I think he's a little overwhelmed, my cottage is nearby. Would you like to come hide out for a little while?" The elf was only about 4-foot tall, with long pointed features, a shock of bright red hair and large spikey eyebrows. Adrian nodded again and struggled to stand. I slipped an arm under his shoulder supporting him and lifted him back to his feet. He was as light as ever as he slumped against me.

I was supporting him, leading him away from the throng of fay that had closed around Merlin's goblin entourage when I saw something large peek through the crowd, entering the clearing. It was hard to make out from what little I could see, but it almost looked like a giant bird cage, with a footprint the size of a four-by-four truck. A word, shot through the crowd at a whisper, following its arrival.

"Humans."

"Just wait here a moment. I'll be back," I said, guiding Adrian to a mossy stump and setting him down, planting a kiss on his forehead before I pushed into the crowd. Wynda had somehow managed to find her way to the front of the mass of fay and was clearing an area around the cage. It was suspended on a series of rolling planks, which the mirelings seemed to have abandoned once they'd reached their destination, already disappearing down the arched tunnel that led to Grandfather Tree. I closed in, and my heart leapt as my eyes immediately found Jack's face. He was sleeping suspiciously soundly among the bodies of four more teenagers, including the girl Mum had pointed out to me on the telly just the other day. All were bound in a cage of twisted black vine and root.

"They've been given something to make them sleep," said Wynda, her eerily long fingers reaching into through bars of the cake to flick Jack's eyelash. He gave no response, not even a flinch.

"How are we going to explain this?" I asked, looking from the captive teens to the magical forest they'd been kept prisoner in these past days, imagining the hundreds of questions they'd have when they woke.

"Gnomes have a knack for brewing some marvellous mushroom teas," Wynda remarked casually.

"And?" I asked, in a pricklier tone than I intended.

"They play havoc with one's memory," she said, offering me a wry smile.

"Oh," I said, looking from Jack to Wynda, then anxiously over to Adrian slumped on his stump, then back to Jack in his cage.

"Leave this with me Michael, they'll be back in Starkton forest with no idea how they got there before the day is out, and by the looks of things, you're needed elsewhere," she said, her eye almost imperceptibly flitting in Adrian's direction; a moment later she was orchestrating fay folk to start pushing the cage out of the clearing and seemed to be done talking to me. I watched the cage trundle off, squashed a pang of guilt, and hurried back to Adrian.

"To my cottage!" declared the elf rather chipperly, who set off as soon as I'd helped Adrian back to his feet.

"Is Jack, okay?" Adrian asked in a small voice, as the elf led us through the grove pushing past the tree line, to a little hut that sat just a couple of hundred feet away.

"He's fine, sleeping. Wynda said she'd take care of it, so don't worry okay?" I said, planting a kiss on his cheek.

"Welcome!" said the elf cheerily as he flung open the door to the small, thatched cottage. I had to duck my head not to bump it on the ceiling as we slipped inside. I felt a bit like Gandalf visiting Bilbo. I perched Adrian on a low stool and knelt next to him, rubbing his back gently.

"Lord Adrian is terribly brave," the elf chirped.

"You know, I've been telling him that for weeks now," I chuckled, and gave Adrian's shoulder a little squeeze.

"Are you feeling better?" I asked.

"I think so," he whispered, turning his heart-breaking blue eyes on me, still just as dazzling as ever but my stomach lurched as I noticed the big dark circles under them. They were new. Before I realised what I was doing I was holding his face in my hands. His cheeks were flushed, and I was struggling to work out what to do next. I just had an overwhelming urge to hold on to him.

"You'll sleep for a week after all this, I bet," I said eventually, after a pause that took far too long. He laughed and I laughed, and I think part of me wanted to cry.

"Amber?" asked the elf, setting down two little brown cups in front of us.

"Oh, thank you," I said, taking a sip; it was thick and warm, and very sweet, almost like drinking honey.

"Sorry, what's your name?" Adrian asked, as he licked the amber off his top lip.

"Cherry, 'cause of the hair," said the elf, smiling as he pointed to his hair, and Adrian smiled in turn.

"Thank you for offering me your home to hide in," he said.

"Oh, it's an honour. I've never hosted a lord before, let alone a high lord! Let alone a high lord of the elemental fay." I grinned as Adrian struggled to hide his embarrassment.

"I'm really nothing special, honestly," he said, shrinking a little.

"Oh, but you are Lord Adrian—"

"Please, just Adrian is fine," Adrian pleaded. Cherry looked at him wide eyed and nodded.

"Even if you don't think much of all those fancy titles, you're still special. You've saved us from all this fighting." Cherry smiled and topped up Adrian's amber.

"Told ya so," I said, grinning.

"And you! Wow, you must be one in a million, or even

rarer. To think I'd have Lor... Adrian and his prince champion in my home on the same day, wowee, I'll be telling people about this one for years." Cherry grinned from ear to ear, literally, his mouth was very wide.

"You tell him Cherry," Adrian giggled, obviously enjoying the attention being off him for a moment. I couldn't help but smile, it was so good to see him relax a little.

"Well you know the funny thing is, if I remember the story rightly. Correct me if I'm wrong Lo... Adrian, but it was Nimueh who first found Merlin about a millennia ago. Two of them, along with the prince champion Arthur that first took over The Hut for our people. Funny to think her descendant and another prince champion would be the ones to give it back and get rid of Merlin all these years later." Adrian and I shared a look as a little shiver ran down my back.

"Ooo look at that, it's given me goosebumps just thinking about it," said Cherry, pointing to his arm.

"You don't think it's something like destiny?" I asked, suddenly wondering if there was some ancient fay prophecy me and Adrian had just accidentally fulfilled. That would be a very us thing to do at this point. Adrian and Cherry just shrugged in unison.

"Maybe, maybe not. I don't know why people get hung up on prophecies anyway. If it's destiny it's destiny, it's gonna happen whether someone wrote it down or not," said Cherry.

"If destiny is even really real," added Adrian.

"You don't think it's destiny that we met?" I asked in a

mock horrified voice. Adrian grinned as a little pink hue coloured his cheeks.

"I think we met 'cause I've got terrible balance and I'm easily startled," he giggled.

"Hmm, both of these things are true," I said, grinning, and gave him a peck on the cheek.

"Now that sounds like a story worth writing down," said Cherry.

"I don't think anyone would believe us," Adrian chuckled.

"I would! It'd be a good distraction from the inevitable chaos to come," said Cherry swilling his amber.

"You mean now Merlin's gone?" I asked.

"Oh yes, I'm sure there will be more than a few people who fancy themselves for the top job."

"Cherry, who do you think would be best to lead us?" asked Adrian, leaning forward a little in his seat.

"Well now that's the ten thousand orchard question. I reckon whoever they pick will be the wrong one. Look at Merlin, I'm sure he meant well in the beginning... but by the end he did seem to have lost sight of things."

"Well, I don't think no-one is an option." Adrian sighed.

"Well why not everyone? Or at least, a good few people, you know, a group of you lords maybe." Adrian's brow furrowed as Cherry spoke.

"What about some people like you. Cherry?" he asked.

"What would I know about being in charge of anything though?" asked Cherry looking a little taken aback.

"You'd know what it's like for someone to be in charge of you, that might be better," said Adrian. Cherry opened his mouth to speak then closed it again and fell silent.

"I think it sounds like a great idea, makes more sense than a one-thousand-year-old wizard running everything anyway," I said, giving Adrian a wink.

"Well, I can't argue with that," chuckled Cherry.

"Cherry, do you have anything I could write a letter with?" Adrian asked.

"Course I do, hang on," Cherry said, skittering off into a corner.

"What are you scheming?" I asked, taking Adrian's hand in mine and giving it a squeeze.

"Oh, you know, just trying to save the world again," he giggled. I chuckled and then felt the overwhelming urge to wrap my arms around him and squeeze him. So, I did.

"You're crushing me," he wheezed, hugging me back feebly with his trapped arms.

"Sorry, it was just a very urgent hug," I said, grinning sheepishly as I let him go.

"I didn't say stop." Adrian laughed and all of a sudden, my cheeks were burning. I'm sure they'd gone an embarrassing shade of red.

"Here ya go," said Cherry, planting a quill, ink pot and long roll of parchment on the table.

"Well, here goes nothing," said Adrian, as he started writing.

"What's it like?" Cherry asked after a minute or two, breaking the silence formally only populated by the scratching of Adrian's quill.

"What's what like?"

"The still world."

"I errm, I don't really know," I said, wondering how to explain to someone what a whole world is like.

"I've never been, is it scary?" Cherry asked.

"Errm, it can be, but then sometimes it's peaceful, and sometimes well I don't know. I suppose the big difference is we don't all know each other like you guys do. You know, we all live in our own little families. In our own little world."

"Do you like it?" Cherry asked, with a look of wonder in his eyes.

"I suppose so, I like it a lot more since meeting Adrian. He, sort of, brought it to life."

"With water?"

"Not quite," I chuckled, and Cherry looked a little confused.

"How then?"

"Well then, a couple of years ago, my dad...it doesn't matter." I sighed a shaky breath. Not sure what had come over me or why I was telling all this to Cherry.

"Go on," he coaxed and looking into his big globelike pinkish eyes. I felt suddenly like it was all welling up inside me, like if I didn't talk, I might drown in it all.

"Well, my dad, died a few years ago and it totally destroyed Mum. People say those sorts of things are when people should come together but it drove a sort of a wedge between us. For me and my brother anyway, and he left shortly after, for uni. And then it was just me and Mum and I felt like I had to make sure nothing else bad happened because I wasn't sure Mum would cope with it. So I didn't tell her when bad stuff would happen. People treat you differently when you experience a tragedy." Cherry nodded.

"They don't want to make things worse. So they don't

know how to act, and then in acting different they remind you of what happened," said Cherry.

"Exactly, Cherry," I said, letting out a breath as if something heavy had just lifted off my chest.

"And then because of all that you end up feeling distant from everyone, or at least, I did, and suddenly I had Mum and I had my friends, but everyone seemed so far away. I was on my own somehow."

"That makes sense." Cherry nodded.

"And then Adrian came along, and he wasn't like that, he wasn't like anyone. I got to remember what it was like to want to be close to someone. It was like all that distance just melted away." I said, with a sniff as my nose prickled and I blinked my stinging eyes.

"I think I'm finished!" said Adrian, looking up from his parchment.

"Oh, that was quick," I said, rubbing my eyes as Cherry gave me a little wink.

"Yes, it all sort of spilled out of me, didn't miss anything important, did I?"

"Nope, can I read it?" I said, giving cherry a wink back as Adrian passed me the parchment.

"Sure, see what you think." I took it, looking it over.

To Mu-Terra, Wynda, Dazzle, Yonda and the rest of the fay courts.

I hope this letter finds you well. By the time you receive this, I shall be back in the still world. If you need me, I'm here, but I'm begging you, please don't need me.

I think I should start by saying I shall be stepping down from the position of Lord of the Naiads. Of course, you don't have to listen to me concerning the subject of my replacement, but if you want my advice, here it is. Take Olivier, you'd be mad not to, she's a genius, she understands the positions of leaders and normal fay and she understood Merlin's whole system. She'll be an asset to you in all things. Oh, and put her in charge of the Excalibur system, as she's the only one who ever really knew the ins and outs of it, anyway.

Further, on the subject of my advice that you needn't heed. I'm sure by this point the subject of who shall take over leadership of the fay has crossed all your minds already. To me the answer is simple, you could go through some protracted power struggle in the shadows that threatens the peace we've just won. Until finally one of you or someone else comes out on top with half the forest already resenting them, or you could rule together. But please, for heaven's sake, if you do rule as a group, don't let it just be lords and ladies. For every noble fay in your council take two who have no claim to nobility at all. They are in the vast majority, and they should have a say in how their world works.

Take my friend Cherry here. They've given me more wise council in one day than Nimueh did in my whole life.

That's all I've got to say really, I hope you heed my advice, good luck with it all!

Yours, the former Lord of the Naiad, Adrian Lake.

P.S. I mean it, please don't need me.

"Adrian, are you sure?" I asked, as I handed back the note.

"Sure, about what?"

"Giving it all up?"

"The only thing I've ever been surer of is you, Michael,"

he said, as an enormous grin peeled across his face and my stomach fluttered.

"Cherry, could you give this to the lords for me? I've got to run, I'm afraid."

"'Course I could, do come visit sometime won't you, Lo... I mean, Adrian?"

"It would be my pleasure," Adrian said, leaning down to give Cherry a big hug, before standing again and making for the door.

"Right, let's dash."

"I'm right behind," I said, giving Cherry a little squeeze myself before heading for the door and hitting my head again on the way out.

"Right, climb aboard then," I said, kneeling in front of Adrian as we stepped out into the forest.

"What for, I can walk," Adrian said with a giggle as his fingers wrapped around my arms.

"I'm not taking any chances with his former lordship," I said, giving him a wink. Adrian rolled his eyes and then hopped on, and I set off through the forest.

"You just like showing off," he said as he rested his head on my shoulder.

"I thought you deserved a rest, that's all."

"I'm fine really," he said through a yawn.

"So, what will you do, if they don't do what you said in the letter?"

"You mean picking Olivier, or the council thing?" he asked, his little fingers tracing along my back as I carried him.

"Either, or both I suppose."

"Nothing," he said and shrugged.

"Nothing?"

"Yeah, can't go round forcing people to do what I want just 'cause I want them to."

"So that's it then?" I asked, a little spark of excitement forming in the pit of my stomach.

"That's it," he said, hugging me across my chest from behind.

"What's your next grand plan then?" I asked, kissing his hand as it looped under my chin.

"I want to go to the park and have a whole one of those blue ice lollies without some disaster befalling us."

"Ooo so you're a risk taker now?" I chuckled, he giggled, and I took a big breath as my chest loosened up.

"I guess I am," he said, again through a yawn.

"You, okay?" I said, as I felt his grip on my arms slip.

"Adrian?" I asked concerned, but when I turned to look, he was already asleep. I smiled and planted a kiss on his cheek, before turning back to the path and finding we were already at the grove somehow. I don't think I'll ever get used to that.

"Home time," I whispered, as I stepped through the tree.

THE EPILOGUE

"Because I knew you, I have been chaaanged for good," Adrian sang again, for what must have been the fifth time since we'd left the theatre. His voice was beautiful enough that I'd almost convinced myself I needed to buy a karaoke machine.

"So I take it that was your favourite song then?" I asked, grinning as we walked hand in hand down the London streets.

"That and the bit where she flies off and has the massive cloak billowing behind her."

"Defying Gravity, that's Mum's favourite song too, I think."

"Oh and Popular," he beamed.

"Yes, that's the funniest bit."

"And No Good Deed too," I chuckled and wrapped Adrian up in my arms pulling him into a hug. He was so light as his feet lifted clean off the floor.

"You're adorable." I grinned, kissing him on the nose and spinning him round before I put him back down again.

"You're not so bad yourself," he giggled, the light of streetlamps and passing cars illuminating the cute pink stain that had flooded his cheeks.

"I'm glad you think so," I said, doing my best to do a cool wink, although it might have looked more like I'd just got an itchy eye.

"Do you think we could see another musical?" Adrian asked, my stomach flipped as he looked up at me with his big sparkling eyes. I had the sudden urge to move to London and just take him to the theatre every night.

"Of course we can, we can see whatever you like," I said, giving his hand a squeeze.

"Which one should we see next?"

"Well, Mum always says Les Mis is the best, but I think it's supposed to make you cry a—" I paused as we passed a newspaper stand and the headline court my eye.

"Mysterious Re-appearance of the Starkton Six"

Just below there was a picture of Jack and the five other victims of the mireling kidnappings. It had been taken in the press conference that had shortly followed their re-appearance. Along with the promise of a tell-all interview on page five.

"What's caught your eye?" asked Adrian, tugging at my arm and drawing my eye back to his sweet face.

"You're sure they won't remember anything?" I asked,

for perhaps the hundredth time since we'd gotten them all back.

"I'm sure, Olivier saw to it as soon as the hag delivered them all back to us during the exchange. The tea she gave them was brewed from some very particular mushrooms." It's true none of them seemed to remember anything about their disappearance or knew how it was that they were found. Wandering aimlessly out of Starkton forest just days after they'd vanished.

"It's just when I see the newspapers still talking about it, it makes me nervous," I explained apologetically.

"It's okay, remember, the camera crews disappeared after a couple days when they couldn't get a good story. Just like your mum said, they'll get bored and within a week something else will be happening, that people can actually remember," Adrian said, giving my hand a consoling squeeze.

"You're right. How are you so calm about this whole thing anyway?"

"Because I'm too excited about what's about to happen," he said with a grin before he tugged at my arm gently, dragging me down a different street.

"Hey where are we going?" I asked as I let him lead me off course for the train station.

"I've got a little surprise for you. This was supposed to be your birthday present after all," he said, grinning back at me.

"You've got a surprise for me... set up in London?" I asked, more than a little shocked.

"Sure have."

"Adrian, I don't wanna ruin your plans, but we'll have to

be quick, or we'll miss our train otherwise," I said, glancing at the time on my phone.

"Don't worry about any of that," said Adrian as he came to a full stop in the middle of the pavement, and I almost walked straight into the back of him.

"Why are we stopping?" I asked, looking around. We were standing in front of one of those hotels that's so posh it makes you a bit nervous to go inside in case they charge you for looking.

"This is your surprise," he said, gesturing broadly to the hotel front.

"Adrian, what do you mean?" I asked as he started walking towards the hotel doors.

"I got us a room," he said, beckoning for me to follow, which I did, jogging to catch up as a man in a full uniform and black hat opened the door for Adrian to step in.

"Adrian, this must have cost a fortune," I hissed as we strode towards the check in desk.

"You can thank councillor Olivier for that," he giggled.

"Can I help you?" asked a very well put together lady behind a desk working from a laptop that probably cost more than Mum's car. I looked around the lobby anxiously, grand white columns were dotted throughout the lobby as if we were in some ancient Greek palace. Various staircases led off out of the lobby with plaques above them saying things like *Executive Lounge* and *Piano Bar*.

"Hello, we'd like to check in, the booking is under Adrian Lake," said Adrian, like it was nothing, as I swallowed through my rapidly drying mouth.

"Ah yes here you are. We have you in one of our river suites. There is already a card on file for your stay, so all that is left is the keys, would you like a personal tour of the room?"

"No that's okay, I think we'll be fine," said Adrian, reaching across the desk to take the key cards.

"Have a delightful stay," said the lady at the desk as we turned away.

"Adrian, what's a river suite?" I hissed as we walked across the lobby, our footsteps echoing off the high ceilings.

"I think it means it's a suite with a view of the river, also, why are we whispering?" he whispered back, looking at me mischievously.

"I don't know, I think I'm nervous," I whispered back, a smile spreading across my face as we reached the elevators.

"Why?" Adrian asked, leaning up to kiss me as the elevator doors opened.

"I've never been anywhere this fancy before." Adrian shrugged and stepped inside.

"They're lucky to have you, I bet they don't get many princes." He said, giving me a wink which was much smoother than I imagined mine was.

"Or lords."

"Former lords!"

"I bet they get even less of those," I chuckled.

"Probably true actually."

"Looks like we're here," I said as the lift stopped at our floor.

"Yep." Adrian smiled, taking a step towards the door before I darted forwards scooping Adrian up into my arms, carrying him bridal style out of the lift.

"What are you doing?" he asked, smiling cutely as his face flushed pink again.

"I wanna carry you across the threshold," I said, planting a kiss on his cheek as I carried him down the corridor.

"Do you like your surprise?" Adrian asked, running a finger down my chest as he gazed up at me.

"Love it," I breathed as a little shiver ran down my back. He reached out tapping the card to unlock the room, I gave the door a nudge and it swung open. The door led through into what looked like someone's super fancy living room. There was a glass table surrounded by furniture that looked too expensive to sit on, decorated with big glossy books. In the corner there was an already set up chess board and a huge TV built into the wall. Various glass jars of what looked like sweets and biscuits were dotted around the room.

"It's huge," I breathed, stepping into the room.

"Chocolate?" Adrian asked, reaching into one of the jars and offering me one.

"Sure," I said, taking a bite as I sat us both on the most lavish chair I'd ever sat in, in my life.

"Well, this is nice," said Adrian, swiveling so he was sitting in my lap, facing me as he popped a chocolate into his mouth.

"Hang on, where is the bed?"

"I think it's through those big doors. This is just the living room," said Adrian, pointing behind me.

"There is more?" I asked, craning over the chair to see the double doors behind me.

"I think so." I shivered, I could feel Adrian's breath on my neck as he spoke. I turned back to him, and our eyes met, his twinkling blue globes stole my breath as my hands moved to his waist without me telling them to.

"Thankyou… for doing this," I breathed, my voice trembling as my heart thundered in my chest.

"Happy birthday," he whispered, drawing a little closer. His hands snaking across my shoulders, his fingers pressing gently into the grooves of my back.

"You've spoilt me," I mumbled, my voice going low and husky as I drew closer still, until there was less than an inch between us. I could feel his breath against my lips, our eyes still locked. His fingers running through my hair as they ran along the back of my head. My own hands tentatively slipping under his shirt as I explored his delicate form, his skin was so soft.

"I love you," he whispered as I closed the final inch and our lips met, and as he pressed into me, I could feel his slight frame against my chest. His lips were soft but he kissed me hungrily. I panted as his fingers entwined and knotted in my hair, pulling me into him. My grip on his waist tightened, and I lifted him, holding him in my arms as I stood, and he wrapped his legs around my waist. I held him to me with one arm as the other slipped across his stomach and heaving chest. He gave cute gasps and whimpers as my hands explored his body. I broke the kiss for a second and gazed into his hungry, half-lidded eyes.

"Is this, okay?" I almost growled as passion rumbled through my voice. Adrian nodded as he unbuttoned my shirt, sending shivers down my spine as his hands ran across my torso. Our lips crashed together again, and I pulled him in closer, sharing our warmth as the cool air prickled my skin. I kicked open the bedroom door and carried him inside as it slammed behind us.

AUTHOR'S NOTE

I wrote this book in somewhat of a blur between May and October of 2022, or more accurately, I re- wrote it.

This story, or at least a very rough first draft of it, came to me when I was sixteen. I was gay and out of the closet, in my catholic sixth form, which made me a rarified breed. It also made me lonely. I couldn't have a love story back then; in fact, I couldn't even really find one to read about. Not one that looked how I wanted it to anyway, but I could imagine one. I'd been escaping into magical imaginings about Greek gods and Arthurian knights (and sometimes the X-men) for as long as I could remember. So naturally when I started my own love story, that had to be magical too.

It also had to be true, unadulterated, heart aching, lose yourself in their eyes, soul mate love. I didn't need back and forth, will they, won't they? Love triangle love. I needed the real thing. So that's what you get with Adrian and Michael, axis shifting, tooth aching, unadulterated love.

Adrian and Michael are for anyone who likes to escape into a world of romance, or magic, or both, and I hope they enjoy it. Though my dearest hope is that it reaches a lonely gay sixth former who's struggling to imagine a love story for themselves.

ACKNOWLEDGNMENTS

First, I have to thank my mentor, Emma, who turned me from a person with ideas to a writer, and my editor Steven, who made that writing intelligible.

Then I come to my parents, Jane and Simon, thank you for reading me bedtime stories about wizards and witches and goblins and gods. You lit my imagination on fire and never did anything but encourage me.

My brother Henry, thank you for loving fantasy along with me, so I always had someone to rewatch Lord of the Rings with and debate Legolas vs Gimli. You were right, Gimli totally wins.

Finally, to Jake, my fiancé, I wrote a love story, but you let me live one of my own and never gave up on me trying to become a writer. Even if it did take me a bit longer than we'd have liked.

SIGNUP PAGE

Hey there! It's me again, the author.

I just wanted to let you know that I have a website! If you liked this book and think you might enjoy reading some more, you should check it out.

You can even pre-order the second book in the series, Mothers, Witches and Queens on there today!

I have a mailing list and everything (very high tech I know) but don't worry I won't spam you. I will, however, send you the first chapter of any new books I write before I even release them, for free!

Also, I have all sorts of social media, so you can see little clips of me being silly/having an existential crisis/with bad hair. Best of all, they're also all on my website, with handy dandy clickable links that someone else set up for me because I'm useless with everything of that nature. If that sounds like something you're interested in, you can find me at this link:

https://www.albertjauthor.com/

COPYRIGHT

Printed in Great Britain
by Amazon